Rowing in frantic semicircles, I managed to reach the outboard, crashing into its side with a thud that echoed across the lake. It was the same boat I'd seen in the snapshots, its anchor chain disappearing into the water.

And it was the same woman, her body sprawled awkwardly on its back on the bottom of the boat. Her skin was pale white, so pale it seemed to glow with a blue tint. Several inches of water washed around her in the bottom of the boat, lifting her hair up and out from her head, then dropping it again, in time with the rocking of the boat. The water looked gray and murky in the moonlight. I knew it was actually rusted with blood.

★

FIXED
in his
FOLLY

David J. Walker

TORONTO • NEW YORK • LONDON
AMSTERDAM • PARIS • SYDNEY • HAMBURG
STOCKHOLM • ATHENS • TOKYO • MILAN
MADRID • WARSAW • BUDAPEST • AUCKLAND

To Ellen, wife and friend

FIXED IN HIS FOLLY

A Worldwide Mystery/July 1999

First published by St. Martin's Press, Incorporated.

ISBN 0-373-26315-5

Visit us at www.worldwidemystery.com

Printed in U.S.A.

The city of Chicago and its bordering towns of Evanston and Oak Park, as well as many of the other places found in this work of fiction, can be found also in "real life." But many of the locales—such as the Wilson Harbor Yacht Club and Bullhead Lake—and every last one of the people are fictitious. And that's a fact. I did once know an actual person named Malachy P. Foley, but he's long dead and his own eccentricities, though noteworthy, were far different eccentricities from those of the Malachy P. Foley that popped out of my imagination and led me to the Lady and the rest of the cast in this story.

Back on the "real life" front, I owe particular gratitude to Larry Raser, for information about firearms; to Michele Mellett, M.D., for her suggestions about what bullets might do inside a large human body; to Phebe Waterman and all her Herrings, Red and Green, for criticism and encouragement; and to Jack Chapman, for not taking "later" for an answer.

ONE

IT WAS MORE a wasteland than a neighborhood. Just south and east of the Loop. No one lived there, no one worked there, and no one in their right mind would have left a car there, even on that sunny afternoon in early May.

But that was before my meeting with Happy Mallory, and money was far too scarce to waste on parking—or another ticket. So I parked the Chevy Cavalier, the only car beside a block full of nothing but the scattered remains of demolished apartment buildings.

In the middle of the lot, a large black woman in a wide straw hat and a tentlike dress—red, with big white polka dots—overflowed a folding chair beside the tailgate of an ancient Ford pickup. Nearby, a tall rail of a man in faded jeans was sifting the rubble for unbroken bricks and carrying them, a few at a time, to the truck. There was nobody else in sight.

As I crossed the lot, the woman pointed back at the Cavalier. "If it was mine, mister," she said, "I'd lock it up—even *that* beat-up ol' car."

I grinned and shrugged my shoulders, then walked on downtown to meet Happy Mallory.

Two hours later I was back.

The pickers were still there, their truck sagging now under a growing load of bricks. The Cavalier was still there too. Unhappily, though, a couple of punks were with it, one sitting on its hood, one lounging against the passenger door—watching, waiting. And another car, a dark blue Bonneville sedan, sat across the street.

When I spotted them, looking past the Ford from across the vacant lot, there was plenty of time to turn around, and that was an idea that appealed to me. But if I'd been sticking to what appealed to me I wouldn't have been within ten miles of downtown, or had Happy Mallory's twenty percent advance in my pocket, in the first place. So, leaving the sidewalk, I cut across the lot—straight toward the two punks.

Puffs of ancient dust lifted and swirled in the breeze, and with them the stale, sickening odor of burned-out tenement. Stopping at the Ford, I pulled some of Happy's money from my wallet, put two fifties in my shirt pocket, and shoved a five at the fat woman on the folding chair.

"For two bricks," I said.

She stuffed the bill down the front of the polka-dot dress, nodding silently. With a brick in each hand, I marched on.

The punks and the Bonneville just didn't fit together. The Bonneville was clean and handsome, shiny new, with dark-tinted privacy glass all around. The thugs were scarred and misshapen, society's sediment, like so many clients I'd met in lockups around the city, back before my law license was lifted. Two black men without hope, lives pretty much over before they got started, menace multiplied because they lived on borrowed time—and knew it. Give me a break? Show a little mercy? Street-raised and ruthless, two like these could hack off my thumbs and leave me spraying blood in the gutter, then wander off to a bucket of chicken wings. Mercy was a luxury—as foreign to them as fine French wine or a father's advice. Part of another world.

I pitied them.

And they scared the hell out of me.

So I walked straight at them, hands hanging at my sides, each grasping a brick by its end. They both stood now beside the car, unmoving and silent.

Fifteen yards away. "Whaddaya say, fellas?" I called. "Car's yours for twenty-five hundred. Some rust. Runs great. As is." I was quoting the ad I ran from time to time in the *Tribune*. If they understood what I was talking about, they didn't let on.

I kept walking.

Five yards. They leaned just slightly forward and grinned—one showing yellow teeth, the other no teeth at all. Eyes as smooth and blank as the dark windows of the Bonneville.

I kept walking.

A yard short of the Cavalier's rear bumper I stopped, turned aside, then charged full speed across the empty street, straight at the Bonneville. Arms outstretched and stiff in front of me, I rammed the ends of both bricks, with all the force of my running weight, into the driver's window. The safety glass sagged first, then gave, and I broke through, driving bricks and bits of glass into the side of the driver's face. The Bonneville's engine roared to life and the car lurched forward, catching my arms and pulling me with it. I wrestled my hands free to avoid being dragged down the street, but momentum spun me like a top. When I regained my balance, the Bonneville was around the corner and gone.

Jagged pain shot up and down my arms, like they'd been wrenched from their sockets. Looking down, I saw the backs of both my hands running with blood, and saw that one of my bricks must have stayed in the car.

I wanted to sit on the curb then, to calm down and pick granules of glass from my hands. But Yellow Teeth and No Teeth were headed my way. Cradling my remaining brick in my left hand, I lifted my right palm toward them. "Let's be reasonable, fellas," I said. "You just lost your job. The man's gone."

"Fuck that shit," Yellow Teeth said. "You here, ain't you? The man was gonna pay, an' you was gonna be hurt. Now *you* gonna pay. Plus, you still gonna be hurt." He grinned. "Maybe you even be dead."

Two long blades snapped open, flashing in their hands. The appeal to reason wasn't working. I needed an edge. Maybe madness would do the trick.

"Well then, hey, let's go then," I began, my voice high-pitched but not loud, moving into a singsong cadence. "Let's go then, Mr. Brick." Kissing the brick in my hand, I bowed dramatically, wanting to convince them I was crazy. "Ah yes, Mr. Brick. Let's go." I giggled and did a little shuffling two-step, imagining Peter Lorre imitating Muhammad Ali.

They raised up on the balls of their feet and I danced in front of them, weaving my right hand and the brick in my left in frenzied circles. "Let's go, my pretties." Giggling again.

They just couldn't decide, face-to-face with a raving lunatic. Uncertain, they dropped down onto their heels.

That was all I needed—my chance to take them—and I stepped in. But the problem was...I wasn't really crazy enough. The coming crunch of brick against human skull flashed across my brain, and I hesitated. No more giggles came. And—just as they'd lost it an instant before—I lost the fleeting edge I'd gained.

They spread apart and came at me, knives slicing, carving the air between us, belly-high.

Picking the one on my right, No Teeth, I went for him. No hesitation. No pity. It had to be. It was my life or—

A harsh voice shattered the air. "All right, hol' it! All y'all...jus' hol' it!"

We all froze in our tracks, and three heads turned to where the breeze flapped white polka dots around the fat lady on the sidewalk. Her left hand clamped the straw hat to her head. Her right hand held a small, cheap revolver—steady as a rock. The thin man in faded denim stood beside her, leaning forward, peering through thick glasses. He pulled a wrinkled gray handkerchief from his pocket and blew his nose—loud and long.

"Now y'all put them knives away and run along, you two," the woman said, waggling the gun at them. "And you, man, bring that brick back here and go 'bout your business." She shook her head, for all the world like a discouraged schoolteacher. "Each one of y'all jus' as crazy as the other."

"Now mama," Yellow Teeth said, "you ain't gonna shoot nobody with that thing."

"That's right. Not 'less I have to." She didn't waver. "And lemme tell you, son, I was shootin' snakes along the bayou 'fore you was born. Now y'all run along like I said, lest you get a hole in your foot."

The standoff lasted maybe three seconds. They folded their blades, then swiveled and walked away, heads high as though leaving were their idea, hands at their sides—palms rearward.

I handed the remaining brick across to the thin man.

"This here woman never could tolerate violence," he said. "Now I s'pose you want a two-fifty refund." He grinned. "Then again, maybe we're even."

"No, not even." I took one of the fifties from my shirt pocket and handed it to the woman.

The fifty joined the five down the front of her dress. "Them poor boys," she said, shaking her head sadly, "they don't know no better."

"I know," I said.

"The hell they don't," the rail of a man said. He spat on the sidewalk. "That's bull shit."

They turned back to their truck and their bricks. I went to the Cavalier. Halfway down the block, I caught up and drove slowly beside the walking men.

"This for what you know about the two in the Bonneville," I said, waving the fifty.

They kept walking, but their faces turned my way. Fifty bucks is fifty bucks. "We don't know shit, man," Yellow Teeth said. "We only seen the driver. Tol' us to give you a message. Said tell you they don't want you bein' even close to happy."

"Close to happy?"

"That's what he said."

"Oh," I said, *"Happy."*

"I *tol'* you. That's what he said. Or some shit like that. Tall dude, brown coat. That's all we know. 'Cept I know we shoulda got the fuckin' bread up front."

"Yeah," I said. "Or at least twenty percent."

"Say what?"

"Here," I said, stretching a bloody hand out.

"Most white folks be crazy," he said. "But you even more'n most." He took the fifty and I drove away.

I'd gotten a glimpse of the two men in the Bonneville. I didn't know them. How did they know me?

And how did they know I was working for Happy Mallory?

TWO

An hour and a half earlier, I myself didn't know I'd be working for Happy Mallory.

We'd gotten off to a bad start when Jerry Wakefield called me a "cheap fucking private dick" and I declared the conversation over if he stayed in it. He turned toward the wall of windows, and I sat back down. The remark was typically Wakefield. I'd run into him years before, when he was a cop, and he'd been no good then, either.

It was the "cheap" part that bothered me, since I'd quoted the highest fee I could say with a straight face, figuring they could take it or leave it. In fact, their leaving it would have suited me just fine. Whoever they were looking for could stay hidden, or missing, or whatever. Or somebody else could look.

Now, with his broad, silk-shirted back to me and his hands on his slim hips, Jerry stood at the window, three hundred fifty feet above the Loop. Out past Meigs Field a jet-prop nervously circled above Lake Michigan's choppy waters, trying to figure out how to land in the face of a wind that just wouldn't stay put. Jerry, though, was staring down at the tiny cars that scooted along Lake Shore Drive, probably wondering, like King Arthur, what those simple folk in their little cars did with their little lives.

Jerry hadn't moved now for a minute and a half. I was keeping track. On the other hand, his wife, Harriet "Happy" Mallory, hadn't stopped moving since I'd entered her office. She paced. She sat down behind her huge walnut desk. She stood up. She smoothed her blond hair, twirled one of her silver bracelets, tugged at her ear, picked lint from her sleeve, patted her thigh.

If she was reassuring herself that her body was still there, I could have saved her the trouble. It was there all right, and she must have poured a lot of sweat and nonbillable hours into keeping it in the shape it was in. If you didn't look too close at her hands, you'd have thought she was younger than I was.

Happy Mallory was a partner in a blue-ribbon firm, and one of the few women who placed somewhere among the fifty highest-paid, most influential lawyers in Chicago. On top of that, she looked great. I knew I shouldn't even think it, but the old me kept wondering whether she'd have done a lot more for the planet as a jazz singer, or an aerobics instructor.

As a lawyer, she had the reputation of a pit bull, if you were an ally—or a viper if you weren't. Her bio said "Happy" was a nickname she'd carried since childhood. I decided to think of her as Harriet.

She sure could be charming, though, when she wanted to. She smiled. "That's substantial remuneration for a private investigator, Mr. Foley."

"That it is," I agreed.

"And particularly so, when we've scarcely discussed the nature of the proposed engagement." A perfectly manicured little finger smoothed a perfectly shaped eyebrow.

The ex-cop at the window was a lawyer now, too, with his own high-profile, high-profit divorce firm that had bought his way into the big-time world of the likes of Harriet Mallory. But I translated for him anyway. "She means I want too much money just to find someone, Wakefield, especially when she hasn't even said who it is, or why me." I must have forgotten I'd ordered him out of the conversation.

Jerry turned around. He was a perfect match for Harriet, thick, jet-black hair combed straight back from a broad, tanned forehead. He was so good-looking no one with any sense would trust him. But lots of clients did, maybe eighty percent of them female, all wealthy or married to wealth, too many of them willing to waste a good part of a fortune—and often enough their children's psyches—to beat their soon-to-be ex-spouses out of a buck.

He spoke to Harriet, not to me. "Like I said before, babe, I got investigators I use all the time. But you're doing the hiring. It's your call whether this...uh...gentleman is right for the job. The money part, though... forget it. Who cares?"

I couldn't believe the man actually said *babe,* even Jerry Wakefield.

Harriet didn't bother to answer him. "I'm sure that's higher than your usual fee, Mr. Foley. Perhaps we can work something out.'' She could afford five times the fee I quoted. But her lawyerly instincts said negotiate, and she was no better at fighting her instincts than I was.

"Yes, it's higher than usual," I said, "and no, we can't work something out."

"Oh?"

"Because first, I don't like your husband very much. Second, I need the money. And third, I don't like you very much either."

So much for marketing skills.

Jerry shook his head as though I were a pretty sorry specimen, and turned back to the little people and their toy cars on the Outer Drive.

Harriet stood up and circled behind her chair. "How about ten percent up front, nonrefundable, and ninety percent if you show him to us?"

I stood up too. "What I said was twenty percent now and eighty when I identify him, wherever he is, dead or alive."

"OK, OK," she said, smiling again. "Never hurts to try, does it?"

I sat back down.

"I gotta go, babe," Jerry said. "It's past four o'clock. The Bulls are on the tube tonight and I gotta get ready to go before Judge Prinkle with a child custody hearing tomorrow at ten."

Harriet snorted. Not a pleasant sound. "Sit down, Jerry, for chrissake. You've watched every road game at Slammer's for three years and you'll be two drinks early for this one, same as always. Besides, there's not a goddamn custody fight in the world you couldn't do in your sleep."

He sat down on a leather sofa off to my right and started pulling papers out of a huge briefcase. If he weren't such a big-time hot-shot lawyer, I'd have sworn the look on his face was a pout.

Harriet sat behind her desk and smoothed her hair back with both hands. "Now, Mr. Foley, as for why you," she said, "I was given your name by a friend. You did a job for...for that person. You acted with dispatch, and you were very...ah...discreet."

"She means I work fast and keep my mouth shut, Wakefield," I translated. I only did it because it probably irritated him.

"As for whom you are to find, it's...well, it's my son," she said. "He'll be thirty-one years old this month. I've never set eyes on him." She started drawing circles on a yellow legal pad. "He was adopted, and I don't know his name." When she saw me start to respond, she held her palm up toward me and kept going. "I don't want him, or anyone else, to know I'm looking for him. That's extremely important. That's why I'm willing to pay you so much. For that—and for fast results. I don't want him told about me. I don't want to meet him. I just want to know who he is, and that he's all right. And I don't want to waste any time."

"Two questions," I said. "Why now? And why *shouldn't* he be all right?"

She put her pen down. "My birthday's coming up, too. It's my...fiftieth."

I'd found that out before I kept the appointment, but I put a surprised look on my face. She liked that.

"Yes," she said. "Most people are surprised. Anyway, my...my baby was born on my nineteenth birthday. I'd gotten mixed up with a wild group of kids and... well, the baby's father died in a motorcycle accident. He never even knew...not that he'd have cared, I suppose." Her voice started to trail off a bit, but she caught herself. "There was a privately arranged adoption. I went back to school. I've scarcely thought about him all these years. He's not been a part of my life."

"Not to be repetitious, but why the parental interest now?"

From the corner of my eye I saw Jerry lift his eyes and peer over his reading glasses at his wife.

Harriet stood and walked across the office. "Now?" she said, facing out the windows. "Now I've lived half a century. I never had any other children. I married, but I was too busy building a career to bother with children. Then I was divorced. Then for a while I was a judge. And now...now I'm back in private practice, I'm married, and I'm successful. In fact, *quite* successful." She turned and looked at me. The hint of softness that had crept into her demeanor was gone. "I don't regret not keeping the child, Mr. Foley. But I want to know where he is."

"There are ways of doing that," I said, "organizations that—"

"I don't want him to know I'm looking for him. I don't want *anyone* to know. I told you that."

"So you did. Why do you think he might not be all right?"

"I didn't say that."

"You implied as much."

"I don't think I did. And if I did, I didn't intend to."

"Fair enough," I conceded. "So I'll just ask. Any reason to think he might not be all right?"

"Absolutely not, Mr. Foley. I'm a mother, with a natural curiosity about my child. It's as simple as that."

Of course it was. And shame on me for suspecting otherwise.

And shame on me for not changing my mind when I cashed her check and went back to my car—and just happened to run into some muscle who didn't want me "even *close* to Happy."

THREE

A WEEK LATER my hands were healing nicely, and I was driving up Route 14, about fifty miles northwest of the city. The Lady—that's Lady Helene Bower—had come along. It was her car.

I can't say I'd done nothing but look for Harriet's boy the whole time. I worked out at Dr. Sato's, bought groceries, paid bills, took out the garbage, and spent most of my nights at the piano in a place called Miz Becky's Tap, drinking complimentary beers and working on my repertoire. I bought a bottle of brandy for the Lady. It was expensive as hell but would probably last her a year. I called René Caroux and told him I'd come into some money and had him tune both pianos, the one in my coach house up the drive from the Lady's mansion in Evanston and the one at Miz Becky's. I even sent daffodils to Cass—my wife. She'd been gone six months this time and the daffodils brought no response.

In short, life went on. The only surprising thing was the lack of progress in my search for Harriet's boy. That's how I thought of him—as "Harriet's boy"—even though he was thirty-one years old.

Certainly I was hobbled by her requirement of secrecy. Not only wouldn't she use the ordinary procedures available to locate a child placed for adoption but she absolutely refused to participate in any way. She'd sign no releases, make no requests. She wanted no record of her search for her son. Even so, I'd expected more progress by then, "cheap fucking private dick" or not.

Harriet's parents had long ago gone to their respective graves, and she had no brothers or sisters, no cousins, no family at all. The physician who'd delivered the baby had been dead twenty years. A lawyer set up the adoption, but even if Harriet had known his name, he'd been elderly and, like every other possible lead, was surely dead by now.

Even Infant Jesus Hospital, where Harriet's boy had been born, had expired several years ago, no longer able to survive on the delayed, inadequate payments doled out for treating the chronic diseases and gunshot wounds of Chicago's West Side. The nuns had quietly folded their oxygen tents and stolen away to far-off Oakwood, a growing village in McHenry County, where they opened Holy Madonna Medical Center. That's where the Lady and I were headed.

I swung the Lady's five-year-old Lincoln Town Car off Route 14 and headed straight north. We had another ten miles or so to go. My own car, the Cavalier, was in the shop, hemorrhaging again.

"Look at this," I said. "Rolling hills, horse farms, private airstrips. Money, money, money."

The Lady's the widow of Lord Richard Bower. She'd come over with him from England on one of his lecture tours and, after he died, she'd never gone back. Everyone calls her "the Lady" when she's not around. In person, though, she prefers Helene. Nothing else will do, certainly not Lady Helene, which Cass tells me is the proper address.

I'm willing to call her anything she wants. She's my landlady, but she's more than that, too. She's like a big sister to me—maybe a mentor, I don't know. Certainly far more than just a friend.

"Looks to me," I continued, "like the good sisters cashed in their chips and ran about as far from urban blight as they could get."

"It's lovely countryside," she answered. She didn't respond to my sarcasm. She wouldn't. The Lady's not perfect, but she comes damn close—which can be pretty irritating to people. Thing is, she doesn't care much what people think. Which can also be irritating.

Anyway, those were our first words in over an hour, since I'd finished explaining my reason for going to Holy Madonna. I glanced across at her. She was enjoying herself, absorbing the sunlit world passing her open window. It showed in her face, a face that had seen maybe twenty more years than mine, maybe more, and had long ago learned the secret of enjoying every minute of every year. It wasn't just the smell of the fresh spring grass, or the tiny leaves lacing the trees against the clear blue sky. The Lady would have been happy riding through a cold, gray sleet. A person could learn a lot from her. A person like me, for instance.

"Sorry about that crack about the nuns," I said.

Moments passed before she spoke again. "I suppose most of them that are left are a bit elderly for running. You know, Malachy, we all do the best we're able. Even you, in fact." That last part was her idea of a joke. "Anyway, isn't it a coincidence that you've a job that takes you to Holy Madonna, when I want to go there also?"

"Coincidence? Maybe. But you knew I was working again, and couldn't resist hearing about the case."

"True. But it *is* a wonderful opportunity for me to make a proposal to the substance abuse people at Holy Madonna. So many of my women need drug rehab. And they'd all do well to get away from the city for a time." She paused, then added, "Oh, I *do* hope I can convince them to take a few. Don't you?" Her voice had that clipped, lilting accent she'd brought with her from London.

"I don't *hope,* Helene. I *know.* When's the last time you tried to convince someone and failed? You're...well...you're irresistible."

"It's kind of you to say that, Malachy. And you? Will the hospital give you the records you want?"

"I'll try to wheedle the records out of them, but they probably won't agree. If they do agree, they probably won't be able to find them. If they do find them and give them to me, who knows if the records will say anything about who adopted Harriet's boy?"

"I should think you'd do better with a more optimistic attitude about finding the young man."

"Oh, I'll find him. I don't doubt that. It's the individual steps I don't have much faith in."

I turned into Holy Madonna's sprawling, tree-lined parking lot and found an empty slot not far from the entrance. The Lady and I passed through silently sliding glass doors into the hushed lobby, and then went our separate ways. She'd go to the Substance Abuse Clinic and tell the simple truth about her shelters for battered, abused women. I'd find my way to the Medical Records Department and tell some elaborate lies.

THE CLERK had a great smile. She also had thick auburn hair, a lovely light tan, and deep, dark green eyes. She was young, and she had an understanding attitude. But...

"...but it's hospital policy, Mr. Franklin. You leave the subpoena here. We add it to our stack and, in about seven days, we'll
mail copies of the records to...uh...who's the attorney of record?"
She leaned over and ran her finger down the subpoena I had spread
on the low counter between us. "Ah, yes," she said, "Mr. Glickman."

I knew the name well. After all, I'd typed the subpoena myself,
with its made-up case name, its made-up court number, and its
made-up attorney, Mr. A. C. Glickman. She looked up from the
paper and, when her eyes met mine, her hand went instinctively
to her neckline.

"Yes, ma'am," I said, giving her my own version of a great
smile and an understanding attitude. "I'm very familiar with hospital policy. That's why Mr. Glickman said to come here in person
and not just mail the subpoena. You see, this is an emergency.
The hearing's tomorrow, and the judge won't continue it,
and...well...actually I was supposed to serve this subpoena last
week and...I forgot all about it. And so here I am. It's a very
important case. We're up against a big insurance company, you
know. They want to take this poor retarded man's benefits away."

"Well, I..." She stopped, but there was a spark of interest to
be fanned.

"Mr. Glickman's handling this on a pro bono basis. That means
for free. Anyway, he has to show that his client and this Mallory
baby are the same. Well, we didn't think they were going to contest *that* part of it. But now they are. And now we're really up
shit...oh, darn, I'm sorry, ma'am...but I mean we're up against it
if we don't have these records. You must have read about the case
in the papers. Although...I forgot, the case is in Cook County and
you might not have heard about it."

"No, I don't think I have. What's—"

"Well, I guess I should be straight with you. One of the big
things is...well...Mr. Glickman is a great guy, you know, and he's
representing this handicapped man for free and all. But he's real
mad at me, 'cause I told him, I *guaranteed* him, I'd get these
records in time. Now, if I don't, well, I'm just an investigator—a

one-man shop, you know? I mean my wife helps a little when the kids are in school. But really it's just me. And Mr. Glickman's my best client, and I'm afraid he's gonna cut me off, you know?"

"Gosh, Mr. Franklin," she said, "I'd really like to help. But my supervisor's not in all day and there's no one I can ask." She didn't know she'd said the nicest thing I'd heard all week. "And if they see that I let records out the same day the subpoena came in I might get in trouble. Plus, these are records from the old hospital and they'd be on microfilm."

"Well," I said, dropping my chin to my chest, "I guess that's it, then." I looked up at her. "Except...do you think...oh, I guess not."

"What?" she asked.

"Well, maybe I could just *look* at the records, and not take any copies. Then, if they say what we think they say, Mr. Glickman could put me on the stand and I could tell the judge what the records say. It wouldn't be good evidence, you know, but it might convince the judge to give Mr. Glickman a continuance long enough to get the actual records. Do you think that's possible?"

"Well, I don't know. Actually...we're not very busy to-day...and—"

"And no one would have to know. I wouldn't be *taking* any records. And it sure would be a big help."

"Well, why not? I can get the film and put you in one of the dictation cubicles. I don't think it'll hurt anything."

I folded the subpoena quickly and returned it to my pocket. "You're great," I said. I meant it, too.

She blushed a little, under the lovely light tan.

The dictation cubicle was a tiny roomette where doctors could sit and dictate reports with patients' charts in front of them. It didn't take long for the clerk to find the record of Harriet Mallory's hospital stay, insert the film in the machine, and get me started.

"How are you going to remember everything?" she asked.

"Oh, when I see what I'm looking for, I won't have to mem-orize a lot. But it might take me awhile. I'll have to read care-fully."

"Well, then, I'll just leave you here. You buzz me on the phone there, extension 3526, when you're finished. I...uh...I'd rather you didn't just come walking out when people are around, you know?'' She winked at me. We were coconspirators.

"Oh, sure," I said. "And...thanks a lot."

She closed the door behind her. I took the Minolta from my pocket and photographed every page from the screen, going through the chart twice, using different rolls of film and different settings on the camera.

When I tapped out extension 3526, she came and got me.

"I found what I was looking for," I said, as she led me back to the reception counter. "But, you know what? I don't think it's what Mr. Glickman thought it would be. In fact, I don't think you'll be hearing back from us at all."

"Oh, I'm sorry," she said. But she looked relieved.

"But not to worry. At least now we know. We'll leave the worrying to Mr. Glickman, right?"

"Right."

"And you know what? You're still great."

She blushed again. She felt good. I patted her arm. I felt good.

And, when the Lady met me in the lobby, I could see she was feeling good, too. Of course, she'd have felt good even if she *hadn't* convinced the substance abuse team to provide services to her beat-up, doped-out women. Which, naturally, she had.

FOUR

By NOON the following day, I was at my kitchen table in the coach house. I'd retrieved the Cavalier unrepaired. Adding oil with each fill-up was more affordable than major surgery. I'd read a copy of Harriet's chart and found no entry like: "Baby discharged to Mr. and Mrs. X, the adoptive parents." Or anything close.

Now I was waiting for a call from Carol Billingsley. She was a nurse who'd "retired" to take care of four kids. She supplemented the family income by reviewing medical records for lawyers. I hadn't told her what to look for in Harriet's chart, other than whatever struck her as unusual.

While I waited, I stared out the kitchen windows toward the east. Another warm spring day, but overcast, misty. It wouldn't be long before the leaves, first the maples, then the oaks—the only two varieties I really knew—would fill in most of the space between my high, second-floor windows and Lake Michigan. In the meantime, the lake was visible out there, still and quiet and gray.

As I stood to carry the breakfast and lunch dishes to the sink, the phone rang. It was Carol Billingsley.

"I didn't find much unusual," she said. "Patient a nineteen-year-old college student. Accompanied by her parents on admission. Fairly long labor. But...normal delivery, mother's fine, baby's fine. Baby's adopted. But I'm sure you saw that."

"Yes."

"You know, I hate to say it. But if you've got a mother looking for her child—and that's my guess—there's some important medical records missing."

"Missing?" Going back for more records would make two crimes.

"Sure. The *baby's* chart."

"I...uh...hadn't thought of that."

"Of course, I doubt you'd find the names of the adoptive parents there, either. Probably just that the baby was given to someone—a social worker or something—to be given to the adoptive parents.'' She paused. ''Anyway, there *is* one thing here, this note by the attending physician: 'Dr. Celia Cunningham to review chart.' Then later, a nurse writes: 'Dr. Cunningham here. Reviewed chart.''''

''I read that. Is that unusual?''

''Well, there's no explanation for why a consultation. No report by Dr. Cunningham. Doesn't even say the doctor saw the patient. Just says 'reviewed chart.' A little strange, that's all. I wonder... This is what...thirty, thirty-one years ago? That's probably about right.''

''About right for what?'' I asked.

''About right for the only Dr. Celia Cunningham I know of. She'd be over sixty years old by now.''

''You *know* her?''

''Well, I've heard of her. Celia Cunningham's kind of famous. She was a well-known ophthalmologist in Chicago for years.''

''And now? Is she still practicing medicine?''

''No. I doubt they'd let her practice.''

''I don't understand.''

''Last I heard, Celia Cunningham was in jail somewhere.''

THERE WAS NOTHING in the chart as to why an eye doctor was involved. Harriet Mallory might know, and I wanted to ask her in person. I parked illegally near the building that housed her firm, Brothers and Cruickshank.

The receptionist's desk had a plaque that identified her as J. BIRNBAUM. She called back, and Harriet's secretary came out to talk to me. I remembered her from my first visit. Her desk had a similar plaque that said R. PENNINGTON, and was just outside the office with the plaque that said H. MALLORY, fixed to the wall beside the door. The firm seemed big on first initials. Egalitarian, nonsexist, and probably saved money on plaques.

Anyway, R. Pennington looked more like an account executive than a secretary to me—and not a happy account executive. She had the clothes and personality of an I. Magnin mannequin. Maybe thirty-five years old, she was as smooth and polished as the marble and wood of the reception area, and not a whole lot warmer.

She remembered me, too. "I'm sure it's extremely important, Mr. Foley," she said, heavy on the sarcasm, "but Miss Mallory will be in federal court before Judge Klapp all afternoon."

"Fine. I'll catch her there."

R. Pennington didn't say anything, unless you counted her face, which said she didn't care much what I did.

Back on the street, there was a ticket on the Cavalier. It went into my glove compartment. I hate paying huge sums to park in a lot for half an hour. So, in the end, I have to pay parking tickets. Things don't always make sense.

THE HAROLD WASHINGTON LIBRARY is just a few blocks from the federal courthouse. Chicago's first elected black mayor hadn't outlived his term of office, but he has a hell of an impressive building to carry on his name. Since Harriet would be busy awhile, I went inside to read up on Celia Cunningham, M.D.

She was in jail, all right, the Federal Correctional Institute, Lexington, Kentucky. In her younger days, she'd juggled a private medical practice with an interest in research, publishing scholarly articles about what makes the eye able to tell one color from another. Along with that, she'd had a longtime interest in the civil rights and peace movements. Ten years ago, long divorced and with both her children grown, Celia Cunningham reduced her private practice to concentrate on research and teaching, and on antiwar activities.

Eventually she pulled three years for conspiring to destroy government property and interfere with the lawful activities of the United States Marine Corps. Armed with sledgehammers, crowbars, and a few jars of fresh blood, Celia Cunningham and four coconspirators had entered a marine recruiting center about four o'clock one morning in Ames, Iowa, and created what havoc they could. Then they sat on the floor in a circle to pray and hold hands until the marines arrived. Now the coconspirators were scattered across the country in five different federal jails—maybe to keep them from praying together.

There are close to two million books in the Harold Washington Library. But I hate to fill out forms, so I don't have a library card.

I learned what I could about Celia Cunningham, then left empty-handed and walked to the courthouse.

TWIN GLASS-AND-STEEL-BUILDINGS—with all the architectural flair of a couple of big cornflakes boxes painted a dull, dark brown—tower up from either side of South Dearborn Street in the 200 block. They're called the Thaddeus P. Kluczynski Building and the Everett R. Dirksen Building, and I never try to remember which is which. The one on the west side of Dearborn is full of government offices, including the one where I go for the periodic audits that usually show the IRS owes me something. My onetime law partner, Barney Green, says I'm paranoid and overpay my taxes. I say I've done jail time and, at the cost of a few dollars, I'd rather try to keep the Feds happy.

The building on the east is the courthouse. I went through the revolving door, past the metal detector that showed I wasn't carrying, up the elevator to the twenty-third floor, and into the courtroom of the Honorable Asa W. Klapp, Judge of the United States District Court for the Northern District of Illinois, Eastern Division.

The courtrooms were designed to impress the public with the majesty and power of the law. The ceilings are two stories high, the walls paneled in dark wood, the floors carpeted. Judges look down from massive benches on the lawyers below and say wise and intelligent things—a few of them frequently, most of them just now and then. The lawyers look up at the judges and act pretty much the same. The public sits in wooden pews like believers, shivering in July and sweating in February, wondering why the majesty and power of the law can't manage to get the temperature right.

Judge Klapp had his hands full. His courtroom was jammed with spectators, and marshals were scattered around to manage the crowd. Attorneys lined both counsel tables in the area between the spectators and the judge's bench. You'd have thought it was the trial of a serial killer or a mafia don. But it wasn't a trial at all. The lawyers were arguing motions. I stood just inside the door from the corridor.

A marshal in a blue blazer leaned close to my ear. "Standing is not permitted, sir."

I squeezed in at the end of the last bench, making a whole row of people unhappy.

"What's going on?" I whispered to the gray-haired woman to my right.

"No talking!" the marshal said.

Heads turned our way. I shut up.

My seatmate nudged me and pointed to the newspaper that lay in her lap, folded to show a headline: LAWYERS CLASH IN *BOULEVARD CENTER VS. KRACKAUER.*

I sat and listened for a while, as the lawyers rose and made their arguments. Harriet Mallory's clients were Boulevard Center and its coplaintiffs, a group of abortion clinics. They were trying to get an injunction against Constance Krackauer and her codefendants, who, for their part, were determined to shut the clinics down. Harriet was strident, sarcastic, mean-spirited, and brilliant. She addressed Judge Klapp with all the proper formalities, but as though they were equals, and he responded in kind. She had, after all, once been a judge herself, even if not a federal judge. Lead counsel for the Krackauer group, a Mr. Brimly, was lower-key, but equally sarcastic and mean-spirited. He addressed Judge Klapp as his superior, and the judge's tone to him was impatient and condescending.

Although the points at issue were legal and constitutional technicalities, phrases like "bomb throwers" and "anarchistic terrorists" kept breaking through and clashing with "innocent blood" and "murder by suction." I sensed that only the marshals kept the audience from applauding as each side made its points.

The lawyers looked as though they could keep it up for hours, and intended to. I had other things to do.

Harriet was sitting at her table, furiously scribbling on a yellow pad amidst her team of lawyers, and Mr. Brimly was standing before Judge Klapp, quietly ranting, when I stood and walked up the aisle, through the swinging gate, and into the attorneys' area. I leaned over Harriet's shoulder.

"I need to talk to you," I said, in a phony hushed tone that could be heard by everyone in the room.

She jumped. "What are you—"

"Oh, sorry," I interrupted, this time my voice at full volume. "What I said was I need to talk to you. It's important."

Mr. Brimly turned his back to the judge and stared at us. The teams of lawyers began to whisper among themselves. Then it spread to the spectators and a murmur arose from the benches on both sides of the aisle. A female marshal put her fingers to her lips and hushed at the crowd to no avail. A male marshal hitched back his blue blazer and his hand hovered over the pistol on his hip. Amazing.

Judge Klapp was banging his gavel. "Counsel, what is going on here?"

Harriet rose to her feet. "Your Honor," she said, "apparently there's been an emergency. May it please the court, I would like a short recess."

"Ten minutes, Miss Mallory. But no more. I intend to finish these motions today."

"Certainly. Thank you, Your Honor." She turned to me. "Come with me."

She stalked through a door labeled JURY. I followed her into a room that was empty except for a long table and lots of chairs—probably twelve, although I didn't count. A very young, very earnest-looking woman who'd been sitting next to Harriet scooped up a legal pad and came in behind us. She wore a dark blue suit and a tailored white blouse, and the eyes behind her glasses were wide with anticipation.

Harriet's glare stopped her in her tracks. "Corinne, did I ask you to come in here?"

The anticipation in the young woman's eyes turned to terror. "No, Miss Mallory. I...I just thought..."

"No, Corinne, you didn't *think* at all. As a lawyer, you're *paid* to think. But you don't *think*. If you did, you'd be on the phone having a clerk get a copy of *Reynolds versus Heckler*. How do you suppose I'm going to respond to that bastard Brimly when I don't even have the case in front of me?"

"I'm sorry, Miss Mallory. I...I'll get it." She fled the room, closing the door behind her.

"And as for you, Foley, what is *wrong* with you? Are you crazy?" She twirled her watch around her wrist.

I sat in one of the chairs and tilted it back on its hind legs like my mother always told me not to do. "What's that girl's name?" I said.

"She's not a *girl*. She's a *woman*."

"Sure. And I suppose you're her *mentor*."

"Very funny. Her name's Macklin. What's the difference?"

"I want to send her the name of a good career consultant—before it's too late."

Harriet paced up and down the room, the length of the table. "Just tell me why you're here, will you?"

"I'm here because you hired me, remember? You wanted a job done—quick and quiet. I've been quiet up to now. This is the *quick* part. But forget it. I'll talk to the Ice Lady—your secretary—and try to get an appointment." I stood up and turned toward the door.

"Sit down, Mr. Foley," she said.

With one hand on the door handle, I twisted to face her. "Look, I don't sit down when I'm told. I don't stand up when I'm told. And—" I paused for breath and only then realized I was being as obnoxious and petty as she was, maybe more. After all, I'd been the one who broke into her concentration, not the other way around.

I sat down. "All right," I said, "I apologize. But I've been getting nowhere. Now I've got what could be a lead. And I have a question."

She sat down. "What is it?"

"When you were in the hospital, after the baby was born, were you examined by an eye doctor?"

She stood up again. "No, of course not. There's never been anything wrong with my eyes. Why?"

"It's... just an idea I have. Maybe it's nothing." I stood up.

"Wait a minute," she said. "What—"

"I want to check something. It might be nothing. Anyway, I've kept you too long. I'll be back in touch."

Before she could object, I went out the door, through the buzzing courtroom, and into the corridor. As I headed for the elevators, I met Corinne Macklin turning away from a row of pay phones.

"You know," I said, "you should really kiss that... uh... woman good-bye."

She knew exactly what I meant. "I know, but... I can't. This job is the chance of a lifetime."

"'The chance of a lifetime,'" I repeated. "What? A chance to make money? A chance to be like Harriet?"

"A chance...to be successful. I don't know."

I looked at her. "Repeat these words," I said, *"I can walk away any time I want, and I choose to stay for now."*

She stared at me, suddenly remembering I was a stranger. "What are you talking about?" she said. "I don't even know you."

"Just say the words, Corinne, would you?"

"Well..."

"Humor me, please. It can't hurt."

She gave in. "I can... walk away any time I want, but—"

"Wait," I said. "Say *and,* not *but.*"

"I can walk away any time I want, *and* I choose to stay for now."

"Say it every day," I said, "often. You might be surprised. It gives you another chance."

Someone called from down the hall. "Hurry up, Corinne. The judge is ready."

She turned and hurried toward the courtroom.

Three of us rode the elevator down. Two guys with bulges under their coats and bored looks on their faces—F.B.I. agents. And me—a cheap fucking private career consultant.

FIVE

THE TAXI RIDE to Midway Airport, on the southwest side, didn't take as long as the evening flight to Lexington's Blue Grass Field. It only seemed that way, through rush hour. I'd shaken the tail that fell in behind me on my way home from the courthouse, then circled back and parked in a lot near downtown. I was being watched, and wanted to move before they could pick me up again.

Lexington was too cold for spring in Kentucky and the rain came sideways as I drove a rented Ford Tempo to the nearest Motel 6 and asked myself questions I had no answers for. Who knew I was looking for Harriet's boy? Why should anyone care? And why did their sending goons to scare me off only make me more determined?

The next morning I ran five miles in a drizzle, showered, and ate bacon and eggs—over easy, no salt, lots of pepper—at a place called Skip's, a tavern-diner in a not-so-tony neighborhood. A hand-printed sign in the window read: OPEN 24 HOURS. BRAEKFAST AND BEER ALL DAY EVER DAY. The food was better than the spelling.

It was eight o'clock Chicago time when I called the Lady from my motel room. "Lexington," she said, "the Women's Detention Center. Does it have something to do with Harriet's boy?"

"Yes. I may have found something. There's a Dr. Celia Cunningham in jail here."

"Celia Cunningham. That's where she'd likely be. Most of the women in the federal prison system are there. Possibly all of them. She's a remarkable woman."

"You *know* her, Helene?"

"Certainly. Well, I mean, I've met her. She wouldn't remember me. Will you see her today?"

"I don't know. I...uh...came down here last night without an appointment. This morning that seems kind of foolish. And, well, that's the reason I called. I wondered if you knew someone, or..."

It wasn't such a strange request. The Lady knows an awful lot of people. And she's very persuasive.

I spent most of that drab, sunless day in my motel room, watching the phone and checking on the progress of a small orange-brown spider that scrambled, apparently haphazardly, though the empty space between my first-floor window and a nearby bush. I knew it must be building a web, but any pattern to its work was as invisible to me as the strands it spun. Finally it stopped, hanging motionless in midair. By leaning at just the right angle, I saw the web for the first time, hundreds of tiny rectangles made of space and sticky filament.

The spider waited. I waited.

I went out for coffee, then for newspapers, then for lunch, then for a map of Lexington, then to make sure the motel lobby was still there. The spider never moved. Maybe it was dead. I thought of tapping on the window, but that wouldn't have been fair.

Just before four o'clock in the afternoon the phone rang. It turned out the Lady knew someone...who knew someone...who put her in touch with Celia Cunningham's lawyer. Arrangements had been made, for the next morning.

"You're amazing, Helene."

"Yes, well, you've been retained by Dr. Cunningham's attorney to discuss with her the community service requirements of her probation. She's getting out of prison in about a week. Of course, you needn't report back to him unless there's some reason to. You're to meet her at ten o'clock. Not an ordinary visitation time. But Celia Cunningham's a rather special person—even in prison, I'm told."

I hung up the phone. Back at the window, the web was empty. Had the spider caught what it wanted and gone away? Or had something bigger eaten the spider and gone away?

THE FEDERAL DETENTION CENTER is northwest of Lexington, out past the VA hospital and the Coca-Cola plant. It might have been a small college nestled among the rolling Kentucky hills, if it weren't for the double rows of chain-link fence and the shining coils of razor wire. The guards were expecting me. They took me through a series of locked doors, the last one opening onto an exercise yard the size of several football fields.

She sat at a picnic table off to the right, the only person in the yard, gray hair almost to her shoulders, longer than I'd have thought prison regulations allowed. Her hands rested on the pages of a book that lay open before her, but her head was raised as though she were studying the fences in front of her and the green fields beyond. My shoes crunched on the gravel path. She looked my way, then closed the book she hadn't been reading, slid to the end of the bench, and rose.

"Dr. Cunningham?"

"Just Celia," she said. "Not *doctor* any more."

The book on the weathered wooden table was a thin paperback. T. S. Eliot's *Murder in the Cathedral*. The air was warm and sunlit, and smelling like wet wood. Groups of small gray sparrows wheeled back and forth across the yard and chattered at each other. Sometimes they paused in one of the maple trees and sometimes they sat in the openings of the inner chain-link fence around the yard. They never sat on the loops of gleaming, razor-sharp wire that coiled around and topped the outer fence.

When I gave her my name, she nodded but didn't extend her hand. She was tall, an inch or two short of six feet. Though slim and pale, she was not unhealthy looking, in white sneakers, blue sweat pants, and a green nylon windbreaker.

"Won't you sit down, Mr. Foley?" Her voice was pleasant and her eyes, deep-set and gray-green under dark brows, were not a prison inmate's eyes. They lacked the required suspicion and hostility. They were mainly curious, but with a touch of melancholy.

"They say my lawyer sent you," she said.

"Yes, Harvey Traffinger."

We sat down and looked at each other across the picnic table.

"I can't imagine why Harvey would ask you to see me."

"Actually, he didn't. I asked him. That is, a friend of a friend of mine asked him for me. My friend's name is Helene Bower."

Her eyebrows raised a bit. "Lady Helene Bower?"

"Do you know her?" I asked.

"Not really. I know of her. And I'm sure we've met somewhere." She looked straight at me. "But why..."

I gave her my card. "I'm here on behalf of a client. Maybe you know her." I paused. "Her name is Harriet Mallory."

The sparrows still chattered. The air was still warm and bright, still smelling like wet wood. Nothing changed, except melancholy turned to sadness and crowded the curiosity out of Celia Cunningham's eyes.

"I...could say that I don't know any such person, I guess. But that wouldn't finish it, would it?"

"No."

"Well then, what do you want of me?"

"I've done some checking. You have two children. A daughter, Noreen, and a son, Kevin Peter, about ten years younger. So far, that's what I know. But what I think I'd find out, if I kept digging, is that Kevin was adopted."

She lifted the book from the table and held it in front of her with two hands and stared at the cover for a long time. The silence was shattered by a long, harsh bell, like a school recess bell. I jumped. Celia stared at the book, motionless.

About two dozen women filed into the yard. A few sat at another picnic table, while the rest headed for the cinder track that circled the yard inside the inner fence. No one came near us.

Celia's eyes stayed on the book. "Are you familiar with T. S. Eliot?"

"Enough to know you won't find *Murder in the Cathedral* in the mystery section. As I recall, it's a play about the killing of an archbishop. It has that famous line...about doing the 'right deed for the wrong reason.'"

"My goodness. You're right." Her eyes lit up with surprise. "Imagine, at my age, and I've just discovered it for the first time. Before you arrived, I had just reread something...let me see..." She opened the book. "Here, listen to this: 'Only the fool, fixed in his folly, may think he can turn the wheel on which he turns.' It seems...appropriate somehow. When I was younger, I thought we all had so much more control."

She set the book on the table and placed both hands palms down on the cover, as though drawing strength from it. She looked at me across the table. "What do you want?" she asked. "That is, what does *she* want?"

"She doesn't know who adopted the boy. She wants to know who he is, and that he's all right. That's all." *Or*, I thought, *at least that's what she says.*

"I don't know her. But I've kept track of her. She's known as *Happy* Mallory, I understand."

"Yes. I think of her as Harriet."

"Kevin doesn't know. That is, he's always known he was adopted. He even knew his natural father was dead. But he never asked about his...his birth mother. I've always wondered about that, if maybe it wasn't part of his... Anyway, he never wanted anyone else to know. He said we—my husband and I—were his *real* mother and father. I don't think any of his classmates ever knew." She paused again, then looked up at me. "I suppose you'll tell her?"

"Yes," I said. "I will."

"I don't want Kevin hurt."

"There's no reason to think he'll be hurt, even if he finds out who his birth mother is, which won't necessarily happen. She doesn't even want to meet him. She just...she says she just wants to know he's OK."

"And why should she think he's not OK?"

"She didn't say she thought he wasn't OK. She just..."

"What is Lady Helene Bower to you?"

The quick switch took me a little by surprise. "The Lady? She's...she's a good friend, maybe like an aunt, or a big sister." The question wasn't easily answered, but for some reason I wanted Celia Cunningham to understand. "We're very close. I mean, I'm married—sort of—and it's not that kind..."

"I understand. There are many ways of being close."

"Yes. I've helped her, when she needed it. More often, she helps me."

A look of recognition came across Celia's face. "Why, of course! You're that lawyer. The one who went to jail?"

"Not a lawyer now. My license was suspended, indefinitely, until further order of the Supreme Court. I'm not holding my breath."

"Because you wouldn't reveal what a client told you. You were protecting him."

"Protecting him wasn't the point," I said. "We'd all have been better off with him on another planet somewhere. A rapist for sure, and maybe killed two cops. But the point was the attorney-client privilege. He believed whatever he told me was confidential, privileged. I'd promised him it would be. The court said the privilege didn't apply and held me in contempt."

"They put you in jail until you'd tell what he said. I remember reading that."

"Yes, Cook County Jail. Not a nice place. That's where the state's attorney—and the cops—wanted to keep me. The Lady helped get me moved to a jail downstate. Finally...well, they let me out. But no law license. Anyway, it's old news."

As I talked, I could see the lines in her face relaxing. They were deep lines, nice lines, looking as though they were ready to smile. But instead of smiling, she said, "You don't know who Kevin is yet."

Around the yard a few of the women were smoking and I realized I didn't smell cigarette smoke so often anymore. "There are lots of Kevin Cunninghams in the phone book," I said. "No telling whether he's one of them. I don't even know that he's in Illinois."

"And if I don't tell you?"

I shrugged.

"You'll find him," she said.

"A matter of a few days. I'm saving time coming here."

She studied my face as she spoke. "And is time so important?"

"To Harriet Mallory it is. More important than money, it seems."

"I wonder why," she said in a soft voice.

I didn't say anything. It wasn't a question. And if it had been I wouldn't have had the answer.

"I used to have what I thought was a lot of money," she said, looking down at the book on the table again. "Now I have about ten dollars to my name. To my surprise, I haven't found that to be a problem at all. Except once in a while—like now." She paused, then finally said, "I want to hire you, Mr. Foley."

"I already have a client."

"I'm not trying to interfere with your duty to your client. She wants you to find her son. I want you to see he doesn't get hurt...after you tell her who he is.''

If there was a conflict of interest hidden somewhere in there, it was one I was willing to overlook, for the right price. "How do you know I can do that?"

"I don't. But Kevin has no one, you see. When he was ten years old, Patrick—my husband—left. That is, I finally put him out for good. Kevin worshiped him, but we hardly ever saw him again. He showed up last about six years ago. He'd been drinking. He was always drinking. That's the last we heard from him. And my daughter, Noreen, she was like a second mother to Kevin, but she was killed not long ago. That hit him very hard. So...I don't know what you can do for him, but this sudden interest of Harriet Mallory frightens me." She finally smiled. "Besides, who else can I ask?"

The smile did it. "If you can spare one of those dollars," I said, "you've got a deal."

The recess bell rang again, and the other women in the yard moved slowly toward the building. The ones who'd been smoking carefully tamped out the butts and took them inside with them.

"We still have a few minutes," Celia said. "Not time for everything, but let me tell you what I can. Kevin's...well...he has a few problems."

Somehow, that didn't come as a surprise.

SIX

IT WAS FRIDAY NIGHT and the Pavillon Room at the Bismark Hotel was jammed. It was another cocktail party for Joe "Camper" Campden, and they told me Harriet Mallory would be there. Camper had been a member of the state legislature longer than most of the people at the party had been voting. Why he kept needing to build up his campaign chest was beyond me. But I try not to think about politics.

One thing I knew. The real movers would be at any fund-raiser for Camper, scattered among the hacks and hangers-on. As for me, elbowing and hip-checking my way through the raucous, back-slapping crowd, I couldn't tell the movers from the losers. Certainly no one in either category was quick to grab my hand and pump it.

I'd made the rounds three times and was about to head for the piano at Miz Becky's Tap when I spotted Harriet. She was off in a corner of the room, in animated conversation with two men. She was smiling like she was enjoying herself, so I put the two smooth-looking characters in the "mover" category.

Harriet must have had her radar on. As I approached, her face started scanning the crowd. She finally got a fix on me and, by the slight shake of her head and the look in her eyes, made it clear I should pass right by.

I walked up and put out my hand. "Am I glad I caught up with you. We have to talk."

She took my hand as though wondering what to do with it. "Well..." she started.

One of the two men broke in. "Friend of yours, Happy?" Without waiting for an answer, he turned his deeply tanned face to me and broke into a convincing smile. "I don't believe we've met, sir. I'm Cleveland Richardson." The name was very familiar; he was one of the top personal injury lawyers in the state, the kind of guy for whom multimillion-dollar verdicts have gotten boring.

He wrapped a large hand around mine in a firm, well-practiced grip. He had lots of curly, snow-white hair and earnest blue eyes.

"Malachy Foley," I said, extracting my hand. "Pleased to meet you, Mr. Cleveland." I turned to Harriet. "I didn't mean—"

"It's Richardson, Mr. Foley, Cleveland Richardson." He chuckled but didn't sound amused. "And this is Representative Sam Drake."

The representative was pink and chubby and had much thinner hair in person than in the photographs that turned up in the papers so often. I shook his hand, too, and we told each other how delighted we were. Then Richardson said, "Well, Happy, Sam and I have to run. But let's stay in touch. I think we're on to something here."

Harriet glowed "good-byes" to them. When they were gone, she turned to me. "My God, Foley, you're obnoxious."

"Just trying to blend in," I said. "Anyway, I've got an answer for you. Where can we talk?"

Her face crashed, as though I'd mentioned something she'd forgotten. "Not here, certainly. I'm meeting Jerry for dinner at the Nikko in half an hour. You can join us."

She moved away to shake a few hands. There was politics in the air.

"ABSURD," Harriet said, choking on a mouthful of bean sprouts. She managed to complete her swallow before she went on, "...absurd and impossible. It can't be true."

The three of us were at a corner table in the least Japanese of the several restaurants in the Hotel Nikko, on the north bank of the Chicago River. They were already eating when I joined them. After I ordered I told them what I'd found out. It ruined Harriet's meal. There wasn't much to ruin, actually, just a healthy-looking salad and a glass of Perrier with a slice of lime.

"Absurd, I'll give you. Not impossible," I said, "because it's true. The boy himself has no idea who his real mother is." I retraced my steps for them, ending with Celia's confirmation that Kevin Cunningham was Harriet's son. I didn't tell her Celia had hired me. I skipped the blue Bonneville too, for then.

Jerry Wakefield washed down a chunk of aged beef with a swig of a burgundy that cost more by the swallow than a whole bottle of the stuff on my kitchen counter. He looked like he might burp, but managed to keep it inside. He waved his glass at Harriet. "This is some kind of a joke, babe," he said. "I told you we oughta use one of my people."

"No, darling," she said, sounding as though she meant both words, "we agreed it was my choice...and my money, of course."

I lifted the bottle of burgundy from the wine bucket. It was wrapped in a white linen napkin that I tried not to drip on as I poured myself a glass. It tasted better than the wine on my kitchen counter, too. I decided I'd invite Cass to dinner at the Nikko, before I ran out of money. She might even say yes. And I might remember the name and year of the wine. Maybe. And maybe afterward Cass would come back home. And maybe then the Cubs would win the pennant. And maybe Jerry Wakefield...

I looked at Harriet. "Maybe we should talk alone for a few minutes."

"Mr. Foley," Harriet said, "Mr. Wakefield is my husband. We don't have secrets." She looked at Jerry. "Do we, darling?" When he didn't answer, she turned back to me. "Anyway, whatever you have to say can be said in front of him."

Darling kept quiet and forked another chunk of beef.

"Fine," I said. "Look, there's no doubt in my mind that this Kevin Cunningham is your son. I've seen his picture and I can get one for you. Taking a look at him in person might help convince you. I'll give you copies of the hospital records. I suppose you could talk to Celia Cunningham yourself. She's not lying. She'd be happier if no one found out, including Kevin. Of course, there are sealed adoption records that'd prove it for sure, but you said you don't want him to know, and..."

"No," she said, a little too loudly. "That is, I...I might look at the hospital records. But I don't think I'll need that much convincing. You see, I know this...this man, at least by sight. And the more I think about it, the more persuaded I am that you're probably right. It—"

"You gotta be kidding," Jerry interrupted. "This guy doesn't know what he's talking about."

I drank some burgundy to placate myself.

Jerry continued. "You can't be serious, Happy. I mean...*your* son? A priest? A goddamn Catholic priest?"

"Please, Jerry. Just calm down, will you? I don't know what to think yet. It's...well...not what I expected."

"Well," I said, "it could be a lot worse. I mean your son could be a dope dealer, or a pimp...or a divorce lawyer or something."

Jerry glared across the table at me, then got to his feet. He leaned over and gave Harriet a brushing kiss on the cheek. "Listen, Happy, I can't take this crap. I gotta make some calls. I might be awhile." He stalked away, but not without a last toss of burgundy.

Harriet held her Perrier in her left hand. With her right forefinger she swirled the lime slice around in the glass. "Did you have to *try* to infuriate him?"

"I'm sorry," I said. "But sometimes I can't help it. He's the way he is. I'm the way I am."

"And me?" she said. "What am I? A mother. Hard to imagine." She sipped her Perrier and nudged the salad around on her plate awhile. I went to work on my lamb chops, thinking maybe there was a human being across the table from me, after all.

"Yes. Well, along those lines, I've got a couple of questions," I said. "First, what did you mean about knowing Kevin—*Father* Cunningham, I guess—by sight?"

"That's one of the things that makes this so bizarre. I mean, it's bad enough he's a priest and I'm...well, I suppose I'm an atheist or an agnostic or something. I've never given it much thought. But besides that, this... Father Cunningham...is violently antiabortion, which makes him antifeminist, antiwoman, antihuman rights, anti...oh, I don't know...anti*freedom,* for God's sake."

"Violently?" I asked.

"OK," she said, "I don't know that he himself is overtly violent. But a lot of these sanctimonious bastards go around bombing clinics and shooting doctors and...well, what's the difference? That's how I know him, anyway, because I've seen him at antiabortion rallies. He might even have been in court the day you walked in, for all I know." She paused. "You said you had two questions."

"I do. But the second question is a bunch of questions. Why are you looking for your son? What kind of trouble is he in? When are you going to tell me what this is all about?"

She sighed. Sometimes people do that when they're trying to think of what to say, and how to make it sound true. "It's not *about* anything, other than a mother's natural desire to learn something about her son. I told you that, right from the start."

"Yes. You did. And I didn't believe you, right from the start." I held my hands out, the backs toward Harriet. "And if I had any doubts, they were scraped away."

I told her then about the Bonneville and the two punks, including the warning that I shouldn't get "even close" to her. "So, tell me. What's going on? Maybe there's something I can do. And no extra charge, believe me."

"I... Oh, I don't know...maybe I..." Her face sagged a little and her eyes lost their toughness. She still didn't look fifty years old, but she looked like someone who might need help—someone who might be somebody's mother.

She was *that* close to telling me something. I knew it.

But it didn't last. Jerry Wakefield was coming across the dining room and when she saw him she was good old Happy Mallory again, toughest lady lawyer in town. As Jerry sat down, she reached into her purse, pulling out a checkbook and a pen. "So...that's it, then. You've done your job and it's over. I'm convinced you're right, although I can't say I'm satisfied."

"Are you sure there isn't something else you want me to do?" I asked.

"Jesus, Happy," Jerry broke in, "Didn't I tell you this guy'd come after you for more money?"

She was writing in her checkbook and didn't look at either of us. "Jerry darling, I'd appreciate it if you'd just shut up. And you, Mr. Foley, I said your job is over."

"Fine," I said, watching Jerry reach for the burgundy. "Make it payment in full, though. You don't get a discount for clergy."

Nobody laughed. Harriet gave me the check. Jerry put the meals on his tab and they left.

I stayed and finished my butterfly lamb chops and the burgundy.

After that, I thought about Cass and had a glass or two of Grand Marnier and, for dessert, a dark chocolate specialty of the house that was on fire when they brought it to the table.

And after that, I had indigestion for about eight hours.

SEVEN

THE WEEKEND didn't amount to much. I talked to Cass's machine the first four or five times it answered, and slammed down the receiver when the machine kept answering after that.

The usual crowd showed up at Miz Becky's Tap Saturday night and, inspired by the tuned-up piano and a steady flow of Miller's Draft, I convinced myself the stride style I'd been working on really did sound a lot like vintage Fats Waller. Not that anyone else in the place paid much attention.

Sunday was pretty much my basic Sunday—a headache in the morning and moping around in the afternoon wondering whether to read the newspapers or be satisfied with the depression I already had. I did check the sports pages and learned the playoffs were underway. The Bulls were on the road. They'd be on TV at six o'clock.

SLAMMER'S is a sports bar north of the Loop, just off Ohio Street. An hour later the place would be jumping with lawyers, commodities traders, and other paper pushers high-fivin' each other and screaming obscenities at the referees on the big-screen TV. But Jerry Wakefield was early for the game, like Harriet had said he always was, and I'd been able to maneuver him to a quiet end of one of the place's three bars.

The squat little bartender had a head the size, shape, and color of a bowling ball—the old-fashioned black kind. He brought us our drinks and padded off.

Jerry Wakefield lifted his Chivas and picked up the conversation where we'd left it. "Like I said, it's none of your business, Foley. But you're right. I tried every way I knew to keep Happy from looking for her kid. The past is dead and the only smart thing is to let it stay dead. I told her if she found him it'd bring her nothing but grief. And it will, you know. It's gonna screw up her whole life.''

"Not so good for you, either, is it?''

"Sure. When Happy's not... Wait a minute! What are you talking about? What difference do you think it makes to me?''

I poured, and when the Sam Adams wouldn't all fit into my glass, I drank the remainder from the bottle. "What difference? Oh, I don't know, other than that you're Harriet's husband and only heir. As far as you knew when you married her, she had no living relatives. Now?'' I set the empty beer bottle on the bar to my left. "Now she suddenly has a son. Seems like a big difference to me, Jerry. You're almost ten years younger than she is. She has a lot of money. You—''

"What are you getting at, Foley?'' He'd swiveled on his stool and was leaning close to the right side of my face. Without turning to look at him, I guessed he was using the menacing glare he used with opposing counsel in his divorce cases.

"What I'm getting at, Jerry, is one of the oldest games there is.''

He almost lost it then. Rolling his formidable shoulders under his shirt, he stood up beside me, his fists clenched tightly at his sides.

I turned my head and lifted it to meet his glare. My right hand was palm down on the bar; my left was cupped around the empty Sam Adams bottle, lifted about six inches above the bar. "Relax, Jerry. This isn't your arena, and you know it.''

He was a big man, and used to intimidating people. But he had to think twice about going up against me and Sam Adams. Even if he won, there was nothing in it for him. If either of us had any doubts about that, they vanished when he sat back down on the bar stool, his finger in my face notwithstanding.

"Look,'' he said, his voice shaking. "Happy's my wife. She's the best thing ever happened to me, and money's got nothing to do with it.'' He paused for a moment, long enough to finish his scotch.

"Jerry,'' I said, staring down at the picture of Sam on the bottle, "money's got something to do with just about everything.''

He leaned close, then, so close that the breath of his harsh, near-whispering voice brushed across my earlobe. "You listen to me, you cheap, fucking jagoff. You did your job and you got paid. Now I want you to stay far away from Happy, you hear me? I mean it. Don't fuck with me. I got friends, you hear? You fuck with me and they'll make you wish you never heard of me."

"Jerry," I said, shaking my head, "it's too late for that. I already wished I never heard of you before I ever heard of you."

The conversation, not surprisingly, was over. He stormed across the room and out the door.

When I finished my beer, the bartender was there in an instant. "Another Sam Adams, sir?"

"Why not?"

He set the beer in front of me and I asked, "Mr. Wakefield come in often?"

"Oh, yes, sir. Couple, three times a week. Game nights, mostly. Good customer, Mr. Wakefield."

"And he has...*friends,* I hear."

He tilted his round head to one side. "Sorry, sir?" If he hadn't been a bartender, you'd have thought he didn't know what I was talking about.

"Nothing," I said. "It's just that he told me to put the drinks on his tab, and I wanted to be sure it was all right."

"Oh, sure. That's fine, sir. No problem."

Driving back north to Miz Becky's Tap, I knew I was far from finished with Harriet's boy.

IT WAS LATE when I got home that night, and I didn't return Cleveland Richardson's message until the following morning. Still, he arrived promptly at eleven, striding across to my table by the window at Barrister's Restaurant, a favorite hangout for payrollers and real politicians alike, not far from City Hall.

From his polished black wing tips up, his appearance was impeccable. Blue pinstripe suit freshly pressed, crisp white shirt, tie the latest style with just enough red to make a statement. White hair glowing, tan face smiling to show perfect white teeth. Shoulders back, head high. Authoritative, yet at ease. Artificial.

"Don't get up," he said.

I didn't.

The waiter, who'd vanished immediately upon taking my decaf order, suddenly rematerialized. Richardson flashed him the famous Richardson smile—the one they say turns juries into packs of happy puppies, anxious to chew their way into those bulging corporate wallets for Richardson's injured clients.

More power to him, even if it didn't mean I had to like him.

We said hello, then sat pretty much in silence until the waiter brought our coffees and left.

"I appreciate your meeting me on such short notice, Mr. Foley. Now then, we're both busy people, so why not cut right to the chase?"

"Why not?" I agreed, thinking I ought to look up the derivation of that phrase.

"You'll remember we met Friday night when you approached Happy Mallory at the Pavillon. I did a little checking on your...ah...background, and on what you're up to these days." He drank some coffee and gave a nod and a wave through the window to a couple of pinstripes walking by.

"Fine," I said. "Then why don't we cut right, as they say, to the chase?"

"Yes." He smiled again, and I swear something in me started to melt before I could catch myself. "Well, I must tell you," he said, "I'm concerned. It has to do with Happy and...well, let me level with you. We—that is, some of us who are active in political matters—think Happy has a great future. We're making plans and, quite frankly, they include her. She could go a long way in this state"—he nodded solemnly—"and possibly even farther, if you know what I mean."

"That's terrific," I said. "So...why are we sitting here together?"

"Because you've been doing some work for Happy." He sipped his coffee and didn't smile.

"If you want to know what it's about, you could ask her."

"I did, and she told me it was business, nothing to do with her personally. But we're still concerned."

"So you want me to tell you."

"That would be helpful, of course, but I don't have much——"

"Right," I said.

"So instead, I want to be up front with you, confide in you, expect you to keep this between us, and see whether we might...cooperate to the extent possible."

"I'll listen. I'll keep quiet, within reason. I don't know that I'll cooperate."

"Fair enough." He leaned forward, exuding earnestness. "Look, we think Happy's a winner. But, as with every possible candidate, certain things bother us. For instance, this abortion clinic case. It makes her an appealing women's rights candidate, of course, but it's too controversial."

"That's not it," I said.

"No, just an example. And we can live with that. There's something more personal that's of greater concern." He stared down into his empty coffee cup. He was either a great actor, or else he was telling the truth. Or both. With a good trial lawyer, who knows?

He seemed to be waiting for me to say something, so I said, "Why not cut right—"

"Jerry Wakefield," he interrupted. "He's the concern to my people. My guess is he's become a concern to Happy, too. I think that's what she has you working on."

"Look, I told—"

"No." He looked at his watch. "I don't expect an answer. If it *is* Wakefield, I want you to know we're worried too. For Happy's sake, of course, but also for the sake of the...bigger picture. Frankly, I don't want the party embarrassed. My point is that if it's Wakefield, or anything else in which I can be of assistance, I'll be there. I'm not expecting you to report to me. I just want you to know, I'll help however I can."

Fortunately, he was on his feet and out of the restaurant before I had to say anything intelligent in response.

EIGHT

THAT AFTERNOON, the soft spring sunshine bathed even the West Side battlefield around Madison and California in deceptive tranquility. In front of Saint Ludella Church, two black girls strolled together, laughing and chattering. Both looked about fifteen years old. One carried a baby in her arms, wrapped in blankets.

Next to the church was a three-story building with RECTORY carved in stone above the door. Lest that sign be over the heads of visitors in more ways than one, someone had added a small plastic one below the doorbell: PRIESTS' HOME. Two teenage boys lounged on the stone steps, pretending to ignore me as I climbed between them. It probably took both of them to lug around the enormous boom box that was yakking rap, but at a surprisingly low volume. I pressed the doorbell.

The man who answered was an easy six foot five in his stocking feet—which is what he was in, along with faded black pants, a faded black shirt with short sleeves and no collar, and a faded black crew cut over a very large, very rugged face. He looked like Lech Walesa's great big brother. Maybe in his midfifties, he had a body the same sturdy cereal-box shape as the federal court house, although not quite as large.

He frowned over my shoulder at the kids on the stoop. The radio went off. The big man breathed a tired, but obviously good-natured, sigh. "Andrew. Curtis. It's one o'clock. Why the hell aren't you at school?" He sounded more like an old-time beat cop than a priest.

One of the two spoke up. "Shoot, Father Casey, man, I mean...well, you know, we were on our way and...well...we had a little problem, you know, and we thought we best go hang by the rectory. Maybe stay out the way awhile. I mean, I could explain, but...uh..." His voice trailed off, as he nodded, just slightly, in my direction.

"Yeah, well, all right," the priest said, resigned. "But go 'round back, would you? Jeez, you think I want a truant officer on my damn doorstep?''

While the two scrambled to their feet, the priest turned his attention to me. His eyes were brown and touched with a softness that didn't match his appearance, or his vocabulary, at all. ''Safe to say you're not a truant officer, huh?''

''Right.''

His wide face cracked into a grin. ''Not sure there even are any. You wanna come in?''

''Thanks.''

We passed through a small foyer, its floor made of those tiny white tiles our parents used to see in public washrooms, and then down a long, dim hallway that smelled of boiled coffee and old waxed woodwork and sauerkraut. Long-dead bishops or popes or something smiled coldly down at us from the walls until we turned into a square, high-ceilinged room. Cardboard cartons and piles of folded, used clothing sat along two walls and covered the top of a huge oak schoolteacher's desk. There were two molded plastic chairs—one blue, one orange—that looked like they'd been stolen from an unemployment office. An old, black dial telephone sat on the floor, just below the open window, next to a pair of enormous black shoes. The shoes needed a shine.

''You don't look like a Casey to me,'' I said.

''Casimir Caseliewicz,'' the priest answered, shaking my outstretched hand. ''Sorry about the mess in here. Getting ready for a rummage sale. I'm the pastor of this establishment, such as it is. No one can pronounce my name right, even me any more. People call me Casey, or Father Casey, or whatever they're comfortable with. I'd suggest Casey.''

''Foley. Mal Foley.'' I gave him my card. It looked like a postage stamp in his palm.

As soon as I sat down in one of the two hard chairs I discovered why he'd chosen to half-sit against the window sill. Rap music passed by beneath the open window, and he nodded his head backward over his shoulder. ''Not bad kids,'' he said. ''Bright, too, you know?''

''I noticed he said rectory, not priests' home.''

''Huh? Oh, yeah...right. Like I say, plenty smart. But, man, what a damn tough life those kids lead. Sometimes I wish...'' He shook his head, his face sad for an instant, then breaking into a smile again. "They thought you were a cop. You do have that look, you know."

"Probably genetic," I said. "My dad was a cop."

"That right?" His eyes lit up. "Mine too. Twenty-seven years. Then took a couple slugs in the chest trying to talk some boozed-up steelworker out of blowing away the guy's wife's boyfriend. Got a hero's funeral."

"Yeah...well...what mine got was indicted and thrown off the force."

"So..." He spread his hands out, palms up, and lifted his huge shoulders in a shrug. "Anyway, what can I do for you?"

"I came to see Father Kevin Cunningham."

"Kev? Not here. Almost never here."

"His mother said he lives here."

"Kev's mother? I thought she..." His voice trailed off.

"Right. Lexington. She'll be out any day. She's worried about Kevin. Asked me to...to check on him, see how he's doing."

He stared at me for a long moment, trying to decide whether to talk to me.

"Look," I finally said, "Kevin's mother is Celia Cunningham. She's an ophthalmologist. I visited her in prison. She told me Kevin doesn't have many friends, but that you've been good to him. She said you call him Kev, and he always calls you Father Caseliewicz. She said when he introduced you to her the first time he described you as a very *priestly* priest, whatever that means."

That tipped the scales.

"Yeah, I remember that. That's Kevin all right. Kind of stiff and old-fashioned for a young guy." He shoved my card deep into his shirt pocket, behind an unopened pack of cigarettes. "Kev's been here almost two years—not full-time, but as what we call a 'resident.' His main job's teaching undergrad theology at Loyola. Says Mass here on Sundays and, technically, lives here. But he's not here much during the week. He's got a room at Loyola."

"I called Loyola. He's not there. No classes this week. Exams or something."

Standing up, the priest turned and stared out the window, apparently to see what he could learn from the brick wall that was about ten feet away. "Actually, it's kind of hard to pin down where Kev is at any particular time. I...uh...I think he likes it that way." He turned back to me. "He never misses a Sunday here. The people like him OK. I try to get him involved in things around the parish. He'd like that better than teaching. I heard he had a gift for working with kids. I could use that around here. I'm too old to relate to kids like those two you met out front. But...I think what Kev really likes is the freedom to come and go."

"So? Any idea where he's gone?"

He fished my card out of his pocket and stared at it some more, still struggling with whether talking to me might hurt Kevin somehow. I liked him. Anyone would have.

"Look," he said, jamming the card back behind the cigarettes, "is there some problem or something? I mean, I like Kev, and I hate to...Jeez, I don't know."

"Look...ah...Casey, certain things have been happening, things that make Kevin's mother think he might be in some kind of danger. I'm sure she'd appreciate any help you can give. Maybe you'd give me the names of some of his friends, someone he might be staying with."

"Well...that's one of the problems. As far as I know, Kev doesn't *have* any *friends*. I mean, people like him, but he just doesn't seem to make friends, you know? He's very...closed in or something. I'm the only friend I know about. One thing, though, about a year ago Kev bought a place—a cottage—up near Bullhead Lake. I asked him how the hell he had money for that. I mean what he earns teaching isn't much, and he doesn't take any salary from here. He said he gets a little money from a trust his mother set up years ago. Anyway, I think he runs up there a lot. It's not much more than a couple hours or so away. Kev took me once to see the place. Gave me a key, told me to go up whenever I want. Never do, though. It's all right, I guess. One of those places where there's about a million lookalike cottages around a lake."

"Is he...drinking?"

The priest frowned. "His ma told you about that too, huh? Well, far as I know, Kev's been dry—oh, four, five months anyway. But he won't go to AA. And without that, it's only a matter of time till the next binge.'' The frown turned to a smile, as he poked a huge thumb at his chest. ''Take it from the voice of exper—''

A harsh buzzer jarred the office.

The priest looked at his watch. ''Damn! Must be the rummage sale ladies, to sort through these clothes.''

''Hold on, Fath—...uh, Casey. Does this cottage have a phone?''

The priest was jamming his feet into his shoes. ''Nah. Kev told me he didn't want one.''

''Look, I'm going there right now. Can you give me directions?''

''I guess I could tell you the area. But jeez, you'd never find the right cottage. I'd probably have a hard time picking it out myself.''

The doorbell rasped through the room again.

The priest yelled loudly, ''I'm coming, ladies! I'm coming!'' Looking at his watch, he added, for my ears only, ''What the hell, ladies, you're only two hours late, for God's sake, on what's supposed to be my damn day off.''

I followed him down the hall. When we reached the front door, he stopped and turned. ''Say, if you wanna go to the cottage today, and come back tonight, I'll go with you. I think I can pick out the place if I see it. How'd that be?''

''Well,'' I said, ''I really should leave right now.''

''That's fine,'' he said, and opened the door.

The three elderly black ladies on the stoop were full of hellos and smiles and apologies for ''bein' a bit late, Father Casey.''

The priest told them he didn't mind, and that pretty ladies aren't expected to be on time, kidding them on down the hall to the clothes. They gushed and giggled like schoolgirls and promised to answer the phone and the door until someone named Edna got back at three o'clock. They adored him. No doubt about it.

He grabbed a tan jacket from a hook near the front door, and we headed for the Cavalier.

''ACTUALLY, I'm not sure this is such a good idea, your coming with me,'' I said, thinking of the warnings I'd received to stay away from Happy.

But by then we were already on the entrance ramp to the Eisenhower Expressway. I used the excuse that he'd save me a lot of time finding Kevin's cottage. That was only part of the truth, though. Another part was he was so anxious to go. And on top of that, I looked forward to his companionship on the ride. He seemed like an unusual priest. Not that I knew many priests.

"Whadda ya mean, not a good idea?" he said. "If Kev's in trouble, I wanna help." He didn't ask what the trouble might be—which was just as well, since I didn't know. "Besides, Monday's supposed to be my day off, and most the time I don't even get my butt outta there. So, lemme tell ya, this is a *great* idea!"

At the end of the entrance ramp we were swept into the endless stream of cars. The priest fiddled with the radio until he found some Mahler on WFMT, then turned it low and settled his big frame deeper into the seat.

Getting to Bullhead Lake, and then finding the right cottage, took the better part of that warm, sunny afternoon. Casey ignored the radio and talked a lot. He laughed a lot, too, at himself and his own corny jokes. Yet he never got tiresome. He talked about the West Side, his work there, the people of Saint Ludella's. He called the parish his "assignment." He made his work sound interesting and challenging, occasionally even dangerous, but always satisfying. To him, anyway.

I told him if it was me, I'd rather be "assigned" some place a little less depressing. He just laughed.

"I admit, though," he said, "when I first saw all those damn housing projects and burned-out buildings, and the vacant lots full of broken glass, and heard people yelling and sirens screamin' all night...well, I tried to pray, but what kept coming out was, 'Holy shit, Lord, what the hell am I *doin'* here?' But hell, that was eight years ago. It's different now. I mean, the neighborhood's not any different. But I'm different, I guess. You know what?" He reached across and touched me on the arm for emphasis. "Now I thank the Lord that I am where I am."

His mix of street talk and God talk was new to me. But he meant what he said. This was a guy who didn't need a career counselor.

Steering the conversation back to Kevin, I asked, "You known him a long time?"

"Hell, I never even met him until someone from the Chancery Office called and told me the cardinal wanted Kev to live at Saint Ludella's. Before that, everything I knew was picked up at priests' meetings and conferences and stuff. The word was that in the seminary Kev was a star in everything—studies, sports, everything. When he was ordained—six years ago—a lotta guys figured he was bishop material, all right. And he had plenty of ambition. But there's a lot about Kevin that's...I don't know...puzzling, I guess. People like him, but like I said before, he's...withdrawn or something."

"Has he been a teacher ever since he's been a priest?" I asked.

"Nah. He just started that last fall. His first assignment was a big suburban parish," Casey said. "Up near Wheeling somewhere. Weddings, wakes, funerals, baptisms—nonstop, a real sacrament factory. Lotsa young people. They say Kev was great with the kids. All kinds of programs going, even interracial stuff. Then, all the sudden, in less than three years—bang! He gets transferred to the southeast side, nothin' but empty steel mills and a few old Polish people pissed off at all the Mexicans and Puerto Ricans moving in. No one said why he got moved. Most guys think he musta had a fight with the pastor, kind of an old-fashioned fart—pardon the expression—but with a lotta clout downtown at the Chancery Office. But when you think of it, Kev's old-fashioned himself, sort of. So me, I think it was probably the booze."

"I guess he didn't last long at the second place, either," I said.

"About a year or so. Then he had the accident."

"Accident?"

"Hell, yes. Big scandal for a while. Kev was coming back on a Saturday night from this parish fund-raiser at a restaurant way out in the south suburbs someplace. The dinner got over about ten-thirty, but it was way past midnight when he shoots through this red light at about fifty miles an hour. He swerved away from a car bearing down from his right, and wham!—right into a light pole.

"When the cops got there, they found Kev with his seat belt fastened, out cold, drunk as a skunk, not a scratch on him. Bad part was, there was a woman in the passenger seat. She went through the windshield face first. Died on the scene.''

He went on to explain that Kevin eventually pleaded guilty to driving under the influence, and the prosecutor dropped a reckless homicide charge. Kevin was ordered into an alcohol program and transferred to Saint Ludella's.

"But of course," Casey said, "Kev didn't buy into the rehab program. Still hasn't. He's a drunk, you know, and until he admits that to himself, well..."

"And...uh...you're an alcoholic yourself?"

"You got that right," he said. "With a capital A and that rhymes with *J* and that stands for 'Jesus, am I ever.'" He grinned. "Sorry about that. But don't worry. I got lotsa bad jokes, but that's my only poem.''

NINE

THE SUN WAS a ball in the west, glowing red in my rearview mirror when I turned off West End Road onto North Lake Drive, at Bullhead Lake. Vacation cottages lined both sides of the narrow asphalt road. Here they were a little larger and not as close together as on West End, but most didn't look "winterized." There were only a few cars by the cottages, and not a single person in sight. The season wouldn't start till Memorial Day.

"Hold it, Mal. Slow down along here." The priest peered out the window toward the lake side of the road. "Somewhere along...Wait a minute. Hold it! I think this is it, right here."

I turned into a gravel drive, about three car lengths long, that dead-ended at the huge stump of what must once have been a towering oak tree, about ten feet short of the northwest corner of a gray-shingled cottage. The back of the cottage faced the road; the front faced the lake. Tangles of untended bushes, birch trees, and evergreens separated the cottage from its neighbors on both sides.

Pulling to within inches of the stump, I cut the ignition. The place looked disappointingly deserted.

"Are you sure?"

"Yeah. Well...I think I am," Casey said. "I mean, the trim's been painted green. But I think this is it. Can't hurt to knock on the door, anyway."

So we did.

First, the back door. No answer.

Then around to the lake side. There was a screened porch and a ragged lawn that sloped some twenty yards down to a narrow sand beach. A rowboat rocked gently in the slight breeze, tied to a pier that poked like a blunt white finger out into the lake. Inside the porch we knocked on the front door. No answer.

"I shoulda taken time to find my goddamn key," Casey said, after we tried both doors.

We circled the cottage. Every curtain at every door and window was pulled tight.

Just around the corner from the back door, snuggled close against the east wall of the cottage, were two upright liquid propane gas tanks. The valve that controlled entry of propane into the cottage from the tanks was open. Next to the tanks, the wheel on the electric meter was just barely turning.

"Gas and electric are on. Boat's in the water. The place has been opened for the summer," I said. "No one here, though."

"Looks that way, but I think he's around somewhere. I just got a feeling. Maybe he went out to eat or something."

"Yeah, maybe."

We were back at the front door. There was a welcome mat but no key under it.

"Why don't we try a window?" Casey said.

"What? You mean break in?"

We found an unlocked window on the east side of the cottage. I looked around. No one could see us, as far as I could tell. "Casey, how sure are you that this is Kevin's cottage?"

"Well, ninety percent sure, anyway. Tell you what. I'll go in first and check. If it's not Kevin's, and I get caught...what the hell, I'm just a big dumb priest making a mistake."

"Wait a minute, Casey, this might not..."

But his mind was made up.

"What they gonna do to a priest, anyway," he said, hoisting himself up to the window sill, "shoot me or something?"

He disappeared through the curtains.

"Holy shit!"

That's all he said.

"What?" I called softly. "Is it Kevin's place, or what?"

Casey's head appeared back at the window, poking through the curtains. "Yeah, it's Kev's. No one's here. But you're not gonna believe this. Go around to the front door."

He let me in.

Casey was right. No one was there. And I didn't believe the destruction and chaos.

On the first floor were a living room, kitchen, and bathroom. There was hardly a piece of furniture left whole in the living room.

Pictures were torn off the walls, lamps smashed, upholstery slashed. But there was something even worse, more sinister. The walls were sprayed with dripping, jagged lines of blood-red paint. Not randomly, but the same two words, over and over:

SATAN RULES   SATAN RULES   SATAN RULES

Leaving Casey staring at the walls as though hypnotized, I checked the other rooms. In the bathroom the toilet bowl was shattered, the shower stall ripped away from the wall. The kitchen had broken dishes, scattered pots and pans, drawers and their contents strewn everywhere. The refrigerator stood upright and strangely untouched—except for a note stuck to its door with a little magnetic ladybug. The note was hand printed with a felt-tipped pen, on cheap white paper:

> *Those few Judas has will be all of them taken*
> *Family friends faggots and fools who reach out to him*
> *Leaving Judas alone to rot in a cage where Satan rules*
> *Not dead then worse than dead wishing dead*

I folded the paper and put it in my pocket.

Back in the living room, Casey still stood frozen in place, gaping at the writing on the walls. I went alone upstairs. There were two bedrooms, their ceilings sloping steeply with the angle of the roof. One held a small dresser made of unfinished wood, two cots with bare mattresses, and sheets and blankets stacked on a shelf in the closet. The other had a matching dresser, a double bed that was carefully made up, and some men's clothes hanging in the closet. Neither room was touched by the savagery below.

Back downstairs, I grabbed Casey's arm and pulled him out the back door. Twilight had turned to darkness. We sat in the car.

"God almighty!" The big priest's breaths were coming short and fast.

"Still wet."

"Huh?"

"The paint," I said, "still sticky."

He turned and stared at me. "I don't—"

A car, with its headlights off, swung abruptly into the driveway, skidded on the gravel, and bounced to a stop right up against our rear bumper. Twisting my head, I saw two men in the car. They seemed to have eyes but no faces.

"Ski masks!" I yelled. "Out! Run!"

I heard his door open as I opened mine and dove out onto the ground. Half rolling, half scrambling on all fours, I made it around the corner of the cottage.

Gunshots exploded. Just three, in quick succession, followed by a quiet, angry voice. "You dumb shit."

The shots echoed, again and again, across the lake. Then there was silence.

Standing out of their sight, in the narrow space between the corner of the cottage and the propane tanks, I thought of the Beretta. It was a nifty little semiautomatic with a seven-round magazine. Just then it was carefully wrapped in a rag and tucked under the front seat of the Cavalier. It might as well have been tucked under my pillow in Evanston.

Shoes crunched on gravel. Only a few steps. Two voices spoke in hushed tones.

I leaned closer to the corner, straining to hear, catching fragments of sentences.

"...tole you, asshole...quiet."

"Yeah...but bananas at big breeze...right?"

"Dust bin...mist inna trees...gone."

"Yeah, well...uh...disjunctive holy scar."

That's what it sounded like, anyway. And I remembered it. Then there was more, even less audible, but as though arguing about what to do.

What to do was on my mind, too. I could run for it, with a good chance of getting away. I'd have to come back for the car sooner or later, but I could bring the law along. The problem was, I didn't know where Casey was. I couldn't just leave him there alone with them.

While they talked, I climbed up on the propane tanks, using the electric lead-in conduit that ran from the meter up the side of the cottage to hoist myself up. I stood precariously, one foot on each tank, my back pressed against the shingled cottage wall, and waited.

Footsteps again on the gravel, closer. Voices still hushed, but I could hear better now. The plan was they'd split up and circle the cottage from opposite directions. I heard one depart around the west side of the cottage, leaving the other by the back door, out of my sight, maybe fifteen feet away. If he stayed where he was, the man circling the cottage would eventually come around the lakeside corner and spot me for sure, darkness or not.

For a couple of long seconds, I silently urged the man by the back door to come my way, meet his partner. What good is a plan, for God's sake, if you don't follow it? Finally, there was a cough, and then footsteps coming my way. With the footsteps came a soft metallic sound—the sound of a man checking the magazine of his pistol.

He came around the corner, gun in hand—but not carefully enough. My toe caught him under his chin, snapping his head backward. With the swing of the kick, I lost my balance and crashed to the ground on top of him.

While I scrambled to my feet, he was still rolling on the ground, clutching at his throat with both hands. His gun wasn't in sight. He tried to shout, and the rasping noises that came out were loud enough to alert his partner that something was going on. I didn't bother with him. The Beretta under the front seat was my goal.

Both front doors of the Cavalier were still open. Crouching on the ground, I reached under the driver's seat and, after an eternity of groping, found the packet of rags I knew held my gun. I pulled it out, keeping my eyes on the corner of the cottage. The man I had kicked was on his hands and knees now, breathing in angry, terrible gasps and scratching frantically through last fall's leaves for his gun. Then his partner appeared, going down on one knee beside him.

Fumbling clumsily with the rags wrapped around my gun, I watched the man I'd kicked gurgle horribly at his partner and point my way. I still hadn't gotten the Beretta free, and I scrambled into the front seat, pulling the door closed behind me. Shots rang out, pounding into the side of the car and shattering the front-door window. I dove through to the other side of the car. With the

Beretta freed and in my hand, I moved forward and crouched beside the front tire, then fired three times over the hood of the car, keeping my head down and aiming in the direction of the corner of the cottage. Time passed with no shots fired. Suddenly, the driver's door of the car behind mine opened and slammed shut and the motor roared to life. One of them had made it to their car.

As I crouched beside the Cavalier, a voice called from the thugs' car. "C'mon, let's get outta here, get your fuckin' throat looked at."

A hoarse voice answered from the corner of the cottage. "But they said some in the boat and the rest—"

"Forget that. We don't need this shit. Plus, we don't gotta do everyone in one night, for chrissake. Let's go."

I lifted my head above the hood. Shots came again from the corner of the cottage and I dropped back down. The car behind mine was backing up. I raised my head again. This time I saw the second man, running from the cottage toward the moving car. The shots he sent my way as he ran disappeared into the trees behind me, but they kept me pinned down. These guys weren't beginners. He made it to their car, and it was almost to the road.

I stood up. Their car stopped and a shot pinged off the side of the Cavalier. I decided it wasn't worth it and dropped back down. There was still Casey to think of.

"Who are you?" I called out.

"Fuck you, asshole," came from the car. Then, in a sly, coldly quiet tone that froze the blood around my heart, he added, "But...ah...maybe you oughta check out the boat."

There was the spinning of tires on gravel, then a squeal as they bit the asphalt. I followed the sound of the car to the end of North Lake Drive and lost it somewhere down West End.

They couldn't have been been there much more than five minutes. I breathed a deep sigh and stood up. Something moved in the bushes behind me.

I dropped flat and rolled to the side.

A thin voice squeaked, "It's me."

The squeak didn't sound like Casey. But it was him all right, leaning heavily against one trunk of a split birch.

"Casey," I said, "don't sneak up on me like that."

He opened his mouth, but no words came this time, only a frightening wheeze. A terrible shudder racked his body. His legs gave way and he sagged slowly, till he was kneeling on the ground. Stretching his arms out toward me as though pleading, he fell forward on his hands. His head hung down, almost to the ground.

Kneeling beside him, I saw the bullet hole in the back of the tan windbreaker, to the right of his spine, below the shoulder blade. I laid my arm gently across his shoulders.

His voice came out as a thin whisper, his face to the ground. "All these years a priest...hospitals...wakes...funerals. Now, my turn. I oughta be prayin', but..."

Sirens whined in the distance, coming closer. Someone must have heard the shots.

Casey twisted his head slightly toward me. "Mal?"

"It's all right. Just take it easy. You don't have to talk."

"No. I gotta say it. I...I'm afraid...you know? I'm afraid to die. Do you think I'm gonna die, Mal?"

I wanted to lie to him, but I couldn't. "Just let yourself down easy," I said. "It's OK. I'm right here with you."

"Yeah, I know. But I'm a—" His arms crumpled and he fell, heavy and wooden, flat on his face in the damp, decaying leaves.

TEN

THE AMBULANCE roared off into the night, carrying Casey to the nearest hospital with a trauma center, in a town called Shiloh. I stayed behind and talked to the cops.

They introduced themselves as Sergeant Conroy and Officer Willis and were probably forty percent of the Bullhead Lake Police Department. I showed them my private investigator's license. They stopped calling me "sir."

They didn't push too hard. They were short-handed, the rest of their people out directing traffic around an arson and triple shooting at a liquor store in Fox Lake. There wasn't much I wanted to tell them, and they didn't want to hear much. What they really wanted was for the shooting of Casey to have been a random act by a couple of hopped-up crazies, out trashing and burglarizing empty cottages. A convenient explanation, but it didn't sound right, and it didn't really account for the painted words: SATAN RULES.

I didn't press the point.

And I didn't mention the note I'd taken from the refrigerator door. Maybe I should have, but I didn't.

I did suggest we look in the rowboat. In fact, I insisted.

The three of us walked silently together down to the pier. It was very dark on the lake, no moon, a few tiny pinpoints of light flickering on the opposite shore. A far-off fisherman's outboard chugged lazily, then faded away. A couple of hundred yards to the east and out from shore a tiny red safety light bobbed gently, and transistorized "golden oldies" drifted softly our way from an almost invisible boat. Otherwise, the lake was still and black.

At the end of Kevin's pier, the metal rowboat sat nearly motionless in the water. Willis swept the inside with the beam of his flashlight. A couple of inches of water covered the bottom of the boat. There were two oars and, for an anchor, a cement-filled coffee can attached to a thin chain.

That's all there was.

"So what'd you think there'd be, Foley," Willis said, "a footprint or something?"

"I just told you the man said to look in the boat, that's all. But...the way he said it made me think we'd find something—something bad."

"Yeah. Well, dopeheads, you know. Say anything. This used to be a nice area, you know? But now? Shit, might as well be the fucking goddamn city of Chicago."

We walked back to the cottage.

"Well," Conroy said, "let's lock up the doors. Not much we can do here tonight. We'll give the sheriff's office a call. I doubt they can shake anyone loose from that liquor store tonight, but they'll have a couple of dicks here in the morning, look around a little."

They turned toward their cars.

"What about me?" I said.

The sergeant climbed into his squad car and looked back at me through the open window. "You mean will the sheriff's dicks want a statement? Hell, I don't know. They'll have our reports. If they want you, they'll find you. Up to them."

Willis drove off, while Conroy watched me back out and turn toward West End. Then he drove away in the other direction.

From a nearby gas station, I called Shiloh Hospital.

"Father's condition is critical and he's undergoing emergency surgery. We've notified the archdiocese and we're trying to locate relatives. That's really all I can tell you, sir."

Not much sense in my sitting around the hospital.

There was a kid putting gas in his car at one of the self-serve pumps.

"Where's the closest restaurant?" I asked.

"Well, there's a tavern about a mile out on Seventeen. They got hamburgers and frozen pizza and stuff, I guess. Place called Groper's. You can't miss it. Probably a bunch of cars in the lot."

IT WAS GROUPER'S, actually, and it was nearly deserted, only a middle-aged couple nuzzling at the far end of the bar and a bartender blowing cigarette smoke at a tiny black-and-white TV. I sat in a booth with two bottles of Miller and waited for my Tombstone pizza.

I unfolded the note from the refrigerator door, laid it on the table, and sat there staring at it.

Who was "Judas"? Kevin, maybe. But why "Judas"? Who were the "family friends faggots and fools"? How would they be "taken"? Why? Where did Satan rule? Why would Judas wish he were dead?

Seven questions. One answer, maybe. Hitting below even my average.

I reached absentmindedly for one of the Miller's. Empty. I reached for the other. Empty. I didn't remember either one of them.

"Hey, mac, this here Tombstone's gettin' cold," the bartender called. "You want me to nuke it again or what?"

I picked up the pizza and a coffee and returned to the booth to consider my options. I could go sit in the hospital and beat myself up for bringing the priest with me. Or go home and wait for the sheriff's detectives to drag me back up for a statement. Or eat my pizza and wait for something else to come to mind.

I ate the pizza. What came to mind was to call the Lady. Sometimes she has good ideas. And even when she doesn't, talking to her seems to help. I got a refill on the coffee and took it to the phone.

She answered it herself. "Hello?"

"It's me, Helene."

"Malachy! How nice to hear from you!" She always sounds like she means it. That helps.

"Thanks."

"Are you well? You sound...distressed, or something."

"I've only said four words, Helene."

"Yes. And you sound distressed. Is it that Cunningham matter?"

"Why do you say that?"

"I thought of it earlier. There was something on the evening news about that Happy Mallory person. She may run for... what?...solicitor general?"

"Maybe attorney general?"

"That's it, attorney general. The commentator suggested she might someday become governor."

"Wonderful. But I want to run some things by you. Do you have a few minutes?"

She did, and it took more than a few minutes. Memory is one of my strong points, and I reviewed the entire day, in as much detail as possible, right up to the Millers and the Tombstone pizza and the refill on the coffee. When I finished she was silent a moment, then wanted to hear again what the two goons had said after the first shots were fired.

I repeated the phrases as I'd heard them. "Frustrating," I said. "I can't get any meaning out of it. But I remember exactly what it sounded like."

"Are you sure you have it right? *'Bananas at big breeze'?* I don't—"

"Bingo!" I said. "I got it!"

"Got what?"

"What the guy said. When I heard you say it on the phone, I got it. 'But that was that big priest.' That's what the guy said. They knew it was Casey that ran into the trees. *'Mist inna trees'* meant they thought the shots missed him."

"I don't see how they could have known who he was, Malachy, but I suppose you're right."

"And if they knew Casey, maybe they knew me, too."

"So…*'disjunctive holy scar'*…"

"'This junk is Foley's car,'" I said. "It's obvious."

"I don't know how *obvious*. But we can certainly assume they knew who both of you were."

"But if they knew who he was, then why shoot Casey?"

"Well, I don't know the ultimate answer. But doesn't he fall into a category described in the note? A friend of Kevin Cunningham?"

"I guess he does. But you don't think someone's really planning to kill all of Kevin Cunningham's family and friends, do you?"

"I know only what the note says," the Lady answered. "Family, friends, faggots, and fools who reach out to him."

"But…" I was wishing I'd reordered beer instead of getting the coffee. "How many is that, for God's sake?"

"The note says 'those few,' and your Casey said he was the only friend of whom he was aware. There must be others, of course, and—"

"And there's Celia Cunningham," I said.

"Yes. And then, who else? The Mallory woman? Does she qualify?"

"Only if whoever it is knows about her."

"Of course."

"So, there's Casey, and Celia, and possibly Harriet. I wonder who else cares about Kevin, would reach out to him."

"We wouldn't know without asking Kevin himself. Although, I suppose..." Her voice trailed off.

"You suppose what, Helene?"

"Well, there's you, Malachy, isn't there?"

TWENTY MINUTES LATER, I parked the Cavalier on the shoulder of North Lake Drive a hundred yards east of Kevin's cottage, and walked back. The high cloud cover had cleared, and a tiny sliver of moon showed up in the sky.

The cottage was deserted. The window Casey had gone through was still unlocked. I hadn't reminded Conroy about it.

Inside, I lowered the window behind me and pulled the curtains closed. I wondered how many laws I was breaking by poking around the cottage. And I wondered what I was looking for.

In the kitchen, the contents of cabinets and drawers still lay scattered everywhere. By the back door, a white plastic garbage bag lay on its side, tied shut with its own built-in yellow ties. I laid the lighted flashlight on the floor, untied the bag, and dumped out the garbage. It stank. Coffee grounds, eggshells, empty wrappers, uneaten food. A couple of day's worth of garbage for one person? One day's worth for two? I couldn't tell. Where's a good detective when you need one?

I had the same luck in the living room. The beam of my flashlight swept shadows across furniture that still lay trashed and strewn everywhere. SATAN RULES still screamed silently from the walls.

The bathroom was even smaller than the one in my place. At

least I have a tub. Standing in a puddle of water from the shattered toilet bowl, I tugged on the mirror over the sink. The medicine cabinet's contents were untouched, and about what a single male occupant would ordinarily need. Under the sink a plastic waste-basket stood at an angle, wedged between the wall and the U-shaped trap. I pulled it out and shined the light inside. Nothing but wads of tissue. At least it didn't stink. I stuck my hand in and rummaged around. One of the wads was folded rather than balled up. Within the folds was a small plastic device—a tampon insertor. Not what a single male occupant would ordinarily need.

I rewrapped it and put it back in the wastebasket. Then I took it out again and, still wrapped, put it in my pocket. It may not have been the smartest thing to do, but if Kevin was Judas, my promise to Celia made me one of the fools who'd reach out to him.

Upstairs, the bedroom with the unmade cots told me nothing. In the other bedroom, an open canvas duffel bag sat on the closet floor. There were also two well-polished black loafers, with a black sock stuffed into each shoe. Four hangers hung from the rod. One was empty. One held a white shirt with French cuffs and no collar. The third hanger held a black biblike affair, topped by a starched, white roman collar. Beside that hung a black suit, lightweight wool. In the left jacket pocket was a pair of cuff links. In the right pocket was a white-and-yellow photo developer's envelope and a bunch of snapshots.

I spread the photos on the bedspread and scanned them in the light of the flashlight. Of the eighteen prints, fifteen were of Kevin's cottage, the pier, the rowboat, and the view across the lake. There was one picture of another lakeside cottage, painted blue. Finally, there were two shots of a young woman in white shorts, blue sweatshirt, and a captain's cap. In one, she crouched on a wide, white-painted pier, above a fiberglass outboard runabout tied to the pier. The other, apparently taken from the pier, looked down on her standing at the wheel of the outboard, the cap tugged low over her eyes. She was laughing and peering across the bow as though headed out to sea.

I fished the strips of negatives out of the envelope. They were numbered, four to a strip. The first shot on the roll was blank, overexposed. Number two was the blue cottage. Three and four were the woman. After that, Kevin must have rushed through shooting the rest, anxious to get the roll developed. I looked at the woman's picture again. I'd have done the same thing.

I put the prints of the blue cottage and the woman, and the matching negatives, in my shirt pocket. The rest of the photos and negatives went back into the envelope and back in the jacket pocket.

The three dresser drawers were empty. I dumped the contents of the duffel bag on the bed. Men's shorts, socks, a couple of paperbacks—a mystery by someone named Delano Ames and a Dylan Thomas poetry anthology—and a small canvas shaving kit that held a disposable plastic razor, some shaving cream, a comb, a bottle of aspirins, and a little red box of three Trojan supersensitives. The box of condoms was still sealed shut.

I replaced everything in the duffel bag as I'd found it, except for the little red box. My pockets were getting full.

I sat on the bed with the flashlight off and tried to think. Most of the thoughts came out as the same questions I had at Grouper's. Now there were a few more. Who was the woman who had been in the cottage so recently? Was she the woman in the snapshots? Did the condoms mean Kevin was involved with her? or with someone else? or hoped to be? How bad was Casey? Would he die? Why was I sitting on Kevin's bed in the dark with my pockets stuffed full of evidence? Evidence of what?

The questions all bothered me. But one other question was especially a burr in my brain. Why did the man in the ski mask say to look in the boat? There was nothing in the boat.

Or was there?

Downstairs, I made sure all the windows and the back door were locked, and pulled the front door locked behind me. Better that it looked like the police had been the last ones inside, in case anyone noticed anything missing.

When I walked across the lawn, down toward the pier, frogs started to chirrup back and forth through the darkness. Maybe I was making them nervous. Maybe they were making me nervous. Something sure was.

The lake was still quiet, although brighter now in the pale moonlight. A breeze rippled the surface of the black water. The rowboat rocked gently, bumping against the end of the pier. I looked down into it. A little muddy water, a coffee can anchor, two oars. I stepped down into the boat and poked the beam of the flashlight up under the seats. Other than old webs and dried-up spider egg sacs, there was nothing.

But there had to be something.

I sat in the rowboat and breathed in the odors of water and fish. A dog barked in the distance, just twice, the sounds carrying across the water. The red safety light still bobbed on the boat out on the lake to the east, and the soft music continued. The outline of the boat itself showed now in the pale moonlight. I listened to Neil Diamond and marveled at the patience of people who fish. But...

There was nobody fishing. The small, sleek outboard looked empty.

Thrashing around clumsily in the rocking rowboat, I got it untied and got the oars in their locks without falling out. Then, rowing in frantic semicircles, I managed to reach the outboard, crashing into its side with a thud that echoed across the lake. Pulling the rowboat alongside with my hands, I peered down into the runabout.

It was the same boat I'd seen in the snapshots, its anchor chain disappearing into the water.

And it was the same woman, her body sprawled awkwardly on its back on the bottom of the boat. She was dressed only in blue jeans pulled over a one-piece bathing suit. The top of the suit was pulled down, leaving her naked to the waist. Her skin was pale white, so pale it seemed to glow with a blue tint. Several inches of water washed around her in the bottom of the boat, lifting her hair up and out from her head, then dropping it again, in time with the rocking of the boat. The water looked gray and murky in the moonlight. I knew it was actually rusted with blood. Scratches and slashes crisscrossed the skin above her breasts, and her throat was slit crudely from ear to ear.

The portable radio, a black plastic rectangle, sat on the boat's cushioned driver's seat, and the endless flow of "classics" continued—Barry Manilow, the Supremes, Cat Stevens. How long I stared at the woman's mutilated body, or what thoughts went through my mind, I have no idea.

Suddenly the station was signing off for the day, with the solemn, honeyed words of a generic prayer superimposed over the soft strains of "God Bless America." "Lord," the praying voice intoned, "thank you for this day, and the many blessings it has brought us. We ask you..."

I discovered then that the two boats had drifted a few feet apart, and that I held the radio in my hands.

"...forgive those who do us harm, Lord, and..."

I wanted desperately to shut the voice off, but my brain couldn't seem to tell my fingers how. Frustrated, I finally just let go and dropped the praying box between the boats. At first, it kept on praying at me, floating on its back on the water. Then one end slowly sank, swinging the other end—still broadcasting—at an angle above the surface.

"...and finally, for those who this day have joined the ranks of our beloved dead, we offer this prayer..."

The black rectangle slid beneath the surface of the water, a miniature Titanic, taking its prayer for the dead down with it.

ELEVEN

DEPUTY CHIEF WENDELL CURTIN was lean and tough and, as he'd said about five times, "so disgusted with those stupid fuckers I'd like to kick their goddamn asses inside out." Curtin was head of the Lake County Sheriff's Criminal Investigations Division and the "stupid fuckers" were Conroy and Willis. Their failure to call the sheriff to Kevin's cottage immediately was a threat to what Curtin kept calling his division's "ninety-three percent homicide solvability factor."

Right now, though, he looked as tired as I felt. It was midmorning, and none of us had gotten much sleep. In addition, although Curtin's fury and disgust with Conroy and Willis were genuine, it must have occurred to him by this time that their blunder would be a convenient excuse in the all-too-likely event that this proved to be one of his unsolved seven percent.

Whatever the reason, he was winding down, his voice going into a monotone. "I know you told us already, Foley. But tell us again."

So I told them again, Curtin and his two homicide investigators, how the words of the man in the ski mask—about looking in the boat—kept echoing in my brain. I explained again how I'd gone out to look a second time at the empty rowboat, and how I'd noticed that the other boat out in the lake hadn't moved, and how I'd rowed out and found the woman's body.

I even admitted again how stupid it was to drop the radio in the water, but how I'd lost control for a while. That much they knew was true. They'd already seen the vomit smeared on my clothes and floating on top of the muddy water in the bottom of the rowboat.

They put me down as an incompetent meddler—but not a murder suspect. The medical examiner's preliminary report suggested the woman must have been dead before Conroy and Willis had been there the first time.

Curtin stood up and looked out the window of the tiny Bullhead Lake Police Station, and one of the others took up the questioning as though on cue. "...and so you and this Father Caza...whatever...wanted to talk to the other priest, so you came up to the lake, right?"

I decided not to complain, just to repeat. "I wanted to talk to Father Cunningham. The other priest came along to show me the way. It was his day off, you know? I think he...he just wanted to get away for a while."

"Yeah, well, he got away, all right."

My blood froze. "What do you mean? Is he..."

"Nah, not dead. At least, not as of about a half hour ago. Bad, though. Fuckin' shame, you know?" He shook his head. "You Catholic?"

"I...uh...I'm not..."

"Forget it," Curtin interrupted. "Let's get back to the point. Why was this Father Cunningham so important to you?"

"I didn't say he was so important. I'm working on a case. He was a possible witness. I can't tell you who the client is."

"That's bullshit. We can get that information and you know that."

I shrugged. "Maybe so. Not from me, though. Not yet, anyway."

They let it go.

They were assuming the dead woman had lived in one of the cottages around the lake, but hadn't yet identified her. "And you don't have the slightest clue who she was, right, Foley?"

"Never saw her before in my life. Never saw Bullhead Lake before in my life." I stayed away from the "slightest clue" part of the question.

I didn't tell them about the snapshots or the note from the refrigerator or the other things I'd taken from the cottage. Or how, before I called the sheriff, I drove till I found an all-night convenience store and bought some plastic sandwich bags and hid the photos, the note, and the folded tissue under a rock down the road from Kevin's cottage. Or how I tossed the box of condoms in the well with the spare tire in the trunk of the Cavalier.

As it turned out, all of that proved unnecessary. They didn't search my car. In fact, they lost interest in me after my third or fourth retelling of the events.

Kevin, now, that was a different matter. If not technically a suspect, he was at least a potentially interesting witness. Curtin, too, would have preferred the local cops' original "drug-crazed trashers" theory, which is what he gave the press. But he knew that was stretching it, and the longer it took to locate Kevin the more interesting he would become.

AN HOUR LATER, at Shiloh Hospital, they let me look at Casey through a glass wall beside the nurses' station. There wasn't much to see but tape and tubes and plastic bags full of fluids, and machines with monitor screens that meant nothing to me. I couldn't even tell if he was breathing.

A doctor who was far too young to be as worn looking and stooped over as he was verified my identity and tried to explain Casey's condition. He talked about the bullet going in the back, hitting some ribs and bouncing around through Casey's liver, and then colon, and then lodging in the "anterior abdominal wall." He'd needed massive transfusions, because of blood loss from the liver, and they were worried about infections. They also worried about his other internal organs failing. It was "respiratory distress" that required use of a "ventilator" to do Casey's breathing for him.

The doctor asked if I had any questions. When I just stared at him, he said he was sorry and walked away. I stood there a long time, looking through the glass.

A nurse came along. "If you'd like to talk to Father's family, Mr. Foley, they went to the coffee shop. His mother and two sisters. They should be back any minute."

"Thanks," I said. "I...uh...I'll go look for them."

But I didn't. I walked past the sign to the coffee shop, through the lobby, and out to my car. I didn't want to talk to the family. They might have asked why I brought Casey with me to the cottage. Hadn't I suspected there might be trouble? I didn't need to hear those questions from outside my head, too.

I drove back to Kevin's cottage, retrieving the photos, the note, and the wad of tissue on the way. The property was cordoned off with plastic yellow ribbon. Sheriff's investigators and an assortment of technicians were wandering around with videotape cameras and evidence bags, writing things down in important-looking loose-leaf notebooks.

Sergeant Conroy was there too, standing alone by the side of the cottage, below the window that Casey—and later I—had climbed through the night before.

"Can't stay away, huh, Foley?" Conroy said.

"Just wondering if anything turned up."

"Some reason why I should tell you?" He was still upset because he knew he should have called Curtin the night before. But he wasn't stupid and he also knew that he owed me for downplaying what I'd told him the night before, which gave him at least a bit of an excuse.

"Just curious," I said. "It's not every day I find a woman out on a lake in the middle of the night with her throat cut."

Conroy was staring up at the window.

"I just thought," I went on, "that if you found something, it might jog my memory into thinking of something I forgot."

He turned around. "Yeah. Well, if there's something you... forgot, you better come up with it quick. In the meantime, this here's the window the priest climbed through, right?"

"That's right."

"And it was unlocked?"

"That's right, too," I said.

"It was locked when the sheriff's boys got here after you called. But I don't remember locking it when we left the first time last night."

"I don't remember either," I said, trying to look pensive. "But I'm sure you and Willis would have secured the premises before you left."

Conroy didn't say anything.

"Or," I suggested, "maybe Father Casey locked it himself before he let me in."

"Maybe," he said. "Anyway, they ID'ed the victim. Pamela Masterson, twenty-six years old, single, unemployed. Raised by a maiden aunt who had a cottage about a half mile down North Lake Drive for years. Aunt died a while back, and the girl inherited the cottage. Trying to find some next of kin right now." He stared at me. "Am I jogging anything?"

"Not a thing," I said. "You sure that's all?"

He frowned thoughtfully at me. "I don't say you've done me any favors, Foley. But lemme propose you a hypothetical that Curtin hasn't given—hasn't proposed, I mean—to the press. What if Curtin's boys had found a nice-sized bundle of coke taped up underneath something in the victim's boat? Suppose that? Would that jog anything for you?"

"Sorry, nothing yet." It was my turn to frown. "Any sign of the priest?"

"Not yet. But his clothes are here. He'll call. And if he doesn't, Curtin will find him." Conroy turned to go, then turned back. "And if you find him—"

"If I find him, he'll call."

"Yeah. For your sake."

That was all I'd get out of Conroy. So I drove to a phone and called my answering machine. Four calls. The first two disconnected without messages.

The third was from Cass. "Thanks for the daffodils," she said. I thought her voice was a little shaky, but maybe I just needed to change the tape on my machine. "I saved them long after they wilted, and...well...I was finally throwing them out today, and I was thinking. Why don't we have a talk? Maybe...well, anyway, let's talk."

Other than the message on her own answering machine, I hadn't heard her voice in months. It hit me harder than I thought it would. I almost hung up and missed the fourth message.

The caller spoke slowly, deliberately. "This is Father Kevin Cunningham. I'm calling for Mr. Malachy Foley. I obtained your name from my mother, Dr. Celia Cunningham. I'm on my way to the home of Lady Helene Bower, in Evanston. I'll be there." He paused, then added, "I may have a problem."

I didn't recognize the voice, but I was more than familiar with the halting pace and the exaggerated diction. He had more than one problem—and one of them was booze.

TWELVE

FIVE MINUTES LATER, I was headed for the Tri-State Tollway and home.

I could have called Cass. She wanted to talk, and I'd been anxious for that. But now, what if she wanted to come back home? Would she be in danger? The slashing of Pamela Masterson, the bullet in Casey's back—people close to Kevin Cunningham weren't doing well at all. And someone—Jerry Wakefield, and maybe someone else, too—didn't want me "even close to Happy." But I didn't intend to stay away from either one of them. I couldn't, not now, not after what I'd delivered Casey into.

So I didn't know what to tell Cass. Maybe I'd call her when I got home.

Meanwhile, there was Casey. Yesterday he's a big happy guy, maybe working too hard, but enjoying every minute of it—worrying about the teenagers on his front porch, kidding the rummage sale ladies, telling corny jokes, climbing through windows like a kid. Then some soft-shelled beetle slithers out from under its rock and puts a bullet in his back.

I'd seen people die before, some of them good, some even innocent. But Casey...This was worse. I barely knew him, but he'd trusted me. He'd trusted me with the truth that he was afraid. If *this* guy was scared to die, what about the rest of the world? In other words, what about me?

What sense did it all make? Who were these people who knew they'd been shooting at "that big priest?" Who recognized "Foley's car?" Who was threatening everyone close to Kevin, "family friends faggots and fools?" What did Harriet have to do with it? What was it all about?

Whatever it was, I'd have to watch out for myself, as well as for—

Hard to believe, but it took me that long to realize Casey was still in danger—if he wasn't dead yet. I swung off the tollway into the next "oasis," a rest stop with an Amoco station and a Wendy's.

Calling Curtin was no use. The sheriff wouldn't put a guard on Casey on my say-so. I'd just raise questions I had no answers for, and didn't want asked. So I called my ex-partner, Barney Green.

There was a wait, but he finally came on the line. "I guess you must be working on something. You haven't asked for a favor in months." Barney can be a little cynical at times.

"I haven't even said hello yet, Barney. Maybe I just wanted to touch base."

"Yeah, that could be, I guess. So...how ya doin'? How's Cass? You guys back together?"

"Cass is great. We're...talking. But right now she's pretty wrapped up in a grant proposal, I think. Anyway, the reason I called, I'm working on something."

"I'd never have guessed," he said. "And...?"

"And I need a favor."

"Right."

Barney's a personal injury lawyer. He hires private investigators all the time—to take pictures, interview witnesses, gather documents. But in a city like Chicago, there are always people with "special needs." And Barney knows people who can meet those needs. He agreed to arrange twenty-four-hour protection for Casey. It would be that night before the first man could get there, and whoever it was would have to do their own explaining to the family, and work it out with the hospital.

"It'll cost plenty, Mal, the kind of people you want."

"I'm good for it. Thanks. And...uh...we oughta get together some time."

"Sure," he said. "You name it. But I gotta run just now. Couple calls coming in."

With a cheeseburger and a root beer to go, I headed back to the Cavalier and the tollway, thinking I ought to cultivate my few friendships more carefully.

I'd met Barney in law school. When we were admitted to the bar we both went to work for his dad, Art Green. Art was divorced and Barney was his only child. A sole practitioner and a good trial lawyer, Art's true gift was "client acquisition." He knew how to go out and get cases, and how to weed out the "good" cases from the mediocre.

I didn't like the work much, but it was how I met the Lady. She and her husband had come from London for a six-month stay. Sir Richard Bower, a renowned surgeon, was lecturing around the United States, and they'd chosen Chicago as their home base. On a foggy November Saturday, Sir Richard was returning from the International Conference of Neurovascular Surgeons in Lake Tahoe. As his small chartered jet approached O'Hare, there was a close call with a jumbo jet taking off for Orlando. There was no collision, but Sir Richard's plane dipped first one way, then the other, then plummeted five hundred feet to a concrete runway.

How Art heard about the fatal crash, arrived at O'Hare within an hour, and managed to "sign up" Helene Bower as a client, I never asked. But the case was a "good" one all right—in fact, a personal injury lawyer's dream. There were eventually nine defendants, including the aircraft manufacturer, the manufacturers of three component parts, the owners of the charter service, the airline company whose plane went on to Orlando, and some others whose roles never were clear to me.

Art put my name and Barney's with his on the retainer contract with the Lady. We'd help him "work up" the case, and help try it if it couldn't be settled. Suit was filed within a week and Art threw himself into the case as though it were his life's work, with us muddling along beside him. The Lady, who was childless and had never done much of anything but socialize and do charity work during the twenty years of her marriage, stayed on in an apartment in Chicago.

With each defendant well insured, and each insurance company anxious to avoid a hit for total liability, they all got together pretty quickly and made an offer to settle. The seven-figure offer blew my mind away, even if it was structured to be paid out over twenty years. The Lady was stunned also. Art told us all to be patient, and he was right. Eventually there was a higher offer. It was in writing and came just a few days before Art, watching a Bears game and reading depositions in his office on a Sunday afternoon, suffered an infarction and dropped dead.

Barney and I met with the Lady the morning after the funeral.

Barney wanted to reject the offer, go ahead with the suit, and bring in an experienced lawyer to help try the case. That was vetoed by the Lady. She wanted to put her husband's death behind her. He'd been well insured and, with the addition of the settlement money, she was more than satisfied. As for me, over the months I'd come to be more a friend than a lawyer to the Lady, so I stayed out of the discussion. I'd have voted her way.

So the Lady had a guaranteed income for life. For lots of reasons, among them British tax laws and the chance for a totally fresh start, she decided to remain permanently in the United States. She purchased a large home Cass and I helped her find, on the lakefront in Evanston.

Barney poured his share of the fee into his law practice. I gave half of my share to my mother, who died a year later with a will that split it up among her children—except for me. My half went into a trust, set up so I couldn't touch the principal even if later I changed my mind and wanted to. It paid me a little something each month, not enough to live on, but a cushion that gave me a sense of freedom. I started spending more time practicing the piano and less time practicing law. I'd handle a criminal case now and then, until my license got yanked. After that, I got into the kind of work I was doing now—when I felt like it or needed the money. The fact is, I was usually broke, but far better off than ever before.

So I drove home from Bullhead Lake thinking things could be worse. It was another bright, warm day. Traffic was light. The drive made me optimistic.

I'd go home, take a shower, walk across to the Lady's house, and talk to Kevin. We'd get him a lawyer and he'd give a statement. Between the hospital staff and family, Casey would have plenty of company until the bodyguard arrived. Then he'd recover and go back to Saint Ludella's.

Meanwhile, Harriet and I'd work together on whatever the problem was that she hadn't told me about. We'd bring in the police if necessary, and make the problem go away. After that, Harriet would stop beating people up in the courtroom, and concentrate on scheming with the likes of Sam Drake and Cleveland Richardson to make the world a better place. Maybe she'd decide to meet Kevin, maybe not.

Kevin would get active in AA and turn his life around. Celia Cunningham would get out of jail and wouldn't change a bit. I'd play four nights a week at Miz Becky's Tap, and Becky might even put a sign in the window identifying the piano player.

Like I said, the sun was shining and the drive home made me optimistic. Or maybe there was something in my root beer.

I TURNED INTO the crushed stone drive to the Lady's mansion and parked the Cavalier in my section of the garage under the coach house I lease from her. Retrieving the little red box from the trunk, I went upstairs.

After a shower and a change of clothes, the fatigue really hit me and I was afraid to sit down. I picked up the phone to call Cass, then decided I'd call her later. I went downstairs, walked to the end of the drive, and twisted the old-fashioned bell in the center of the Lady's front door.

After about as long as it would take to check things out through the peephole, the door was opened by a tall black woman. She wore a long dress with huge yellow and red flowers on it, and a bright red scarf wound around her head like a Masai princess. She might have been pretty, even elegant looking, despite the jagged scar on her left cheek. But there was an ugly sneer on her lips, a cruel, steel-cold glare in her eyes, and a Louisville Slugger in her hand.

"What's your name, man?" she demanded, in a tone that might have saved her life more than once on the street or in some lockup.

"Foley," I said, "Malachy P."

She smiled, and the pretty woman suddenly appeared. Her eyes brightened, even sparkled. "Oh good," she said, and sounded like a schoolgirl. "That's what I thought. But..." She held up the baseball bat and waved it good-naturedly. "Can't be too careful, you know." She leaned the bat carefully in the corner beside the door. "The Lady was thinking you'd come. Follow me. They're in the front parlor. She and the father, 'cept he don't...doesn't...look like a father to me."

Part of the Lady's program—though she wouldn't like to call it a program—is to provide a comfortable, frugal way of life for the women she shelters. Most of them stay in a big house she bought in Uptown, but some live for a while at her Evanston home.

She's not successful with all of them. But sometimes she is, and often enough to make you wonder. A cowering wife finally takes the kids and then follows through with the divorce. A beat-up whore pawns her glow-in-the-dark hot pants and goes to court-reporter school. Everyone says they're miracles. The Lady says no, they're just some women "waking up." But whatever they are, they can make your heart ache, in a nice way. As I followed her down the hall to the parlor, I pegged this one as a miracle waking up.

The Lady was sitting in one of those ancient wing-back chairs that dare you to try to slouch, having coffee with "the father."

When she saw me, she set her cup down and stood up, nodding toward the man who was rising clumsily from the chair opposite hers. "I don't believe you two have met," she said.

I'm not sure there's a way priests are supposed to look. But the Lady's doorkeeper was right. Whatever the profile, Harriet's boy didn't match it—not just then, anyway.

He was close to six feet tall, with unruly brown hair and plain features. He'd have been a little underweight, except that his gut was pretty far out of control for a man of thirty-one. While his right hand shook mine, his left hand kept struggling with the collar of a brown tweed sport jacket. When he gave up, the collar was still turned up in the back. The tails of a white dress shirt were tucked into his pants in a way that showed a triangle of pale belly above his belt buckle.

"Mal Foley," I said. "You must be Kevin Cunningham."

"Father Cunningham," he answered, the accent clearly on the *Father*.

"Oh? Well...Father, then."

"I was just saying, Mr. Foley, that it was time I was leaving."

"Yes. Well then, so long...uh...*Father*. Have a nice evening."

Don't ask me why, but I resented his insisting on "Father." He wasn't my father—although the two shared a certain affinity for the sauce. In fact, his cardboard manner reminded me of how my father used to act, when he was trying hard to hold himself together.

I'd been searching for Kevin Cunningham for over a week. I'd promised Celia I'd look out for him. Now, here he was. And all I could think of was the woman with her throat slashed and the priest with a bullet in his back, how badly I wanted to go to sleep, and the hell with Father Cunningham. I went to the coffeepot on the table against the wall and poured myself a cup.

"Malachy..." the Lady said.

"What?" I asked. But I knew she meant I was being foolish.

"You know what."

The Lady seldom scolds anyone, even me. She was worried. Whether I liked Kevin Cunningham or not, she did.

"OK, Helene, I'm sorry," I said, taking the coffee I'd poured and setting it next to Kevin's chair.

The Lady relaxed and spoke softly to the priest. "Sit down, Kevin dear. Drink some more coffee."

He'd run out of whatever had fueled his brief show, and he sat down. I got another cup of coffee for myself, and pulled up a chair.

He drank, and his cup clattered as he put it carefully back on the saucer. He seemed to study the sound for a while. Then he said, "I'm a mess, aren't I?"

"Well," I said, "you need a shave, a shower, some clean clothes, a square meal, and a good night's—"

"No, it's more than that." His voice trembled.

"You've seen today's papers," I said.

For an answer, his lips bubbled out and in a few times. Then the sobs started, and the tears ran out of his eyes. He didn't cover his face. He just stared into his lap and cried, his shoulders heaving up and down.

I looked at the Lady. She looked at Kevin. "Well," she said, her voice soothing and gentle, "that's a beginning, isn't it?"

THIRTEEN

PRIEST OR NOT, he cried like any one of a dozen other lonely, frightened drunks I'd seen do the same, and long enough for the Lady to leave the room and come back with a box of tissues.

When the sobs died out, he wiped at his cheeks with the palms of his hands. "Sorry. I...." His voice trailed away as he fumbled unsuccessfully through his pockets.

"Kevin," the Lady said.

He looked up, startled. "What?"

"On the table, dear, beside your coffee."

"Oh," he said, reaching for the box of tissues. "Thanks." He wiped his face and blew his nose, wadding the tissues clumsily and stuffing them in his jacket pocket.

"No, I haven't seen the papers," he finally said, looking at me. "But I saw the news at noon. I was getting a...a sandwich, at the Billy Goat, on Lower Wacker, and they had the television on and...Father Cazeliewicz, is he...?"

"Casey? He's alive," I said. "Not conscious, but alive."

"Thank God," he said. I gave him credit for not correcting my informality. He picked up the cup from the table beside him and held it, without drinking. "They said my cottage was...vandalized."

"That's a way of putting it. The interior, downstairs anyway, was pretty well destroyed."

"You...you were inside?"

"Yeah, I was inside all right. So was Casey."

He sipped some coffee, probably thinking he was gathering his wits. "And you found a woman, dead, in a boat. That must have been awful. I...I don't remember what they said her name was. But the police think whoever did it was—"

"No good, Kev," I said.

He sipped again from his cup, still trying hard to be slick. "What do you mean?"

"About not remembering her name. It won't fly. I've seen the snapshots. The blue cottage, the pretty woman—first on the pier, then in the boat."

His head jerked. "Did the police...?"

"No, the police haven't seen them."

He stood up and took off his sport coat, laying it carefully on an empty chair, then sat down again. "I spent part of the morning with her. We went for a ride in her boat. I helped put it in the water a few days ago. But then we had a fight...an argument, I mean. I drove back to the city."

"Where was the argument? At your cottage?" I asked.

"Ah...no. I mean, I don't know. Actually, she's never been in my cottage. It was outside, by her place. And...and then I left."

"What was the argument about, Kevin?" The Lady asked that question.

"What was it about? I mean...it wasn't about anything. It was just..."

"Kevin," the Lady's voice was gentle, "please, we want to help you."

"Well," he said, "she...she wanted to go out to dinner that night and I said I couldn't. I...well, I thought she was forgetting I was a priest and I couldn't get involved, you know, in a serious way. Anyway, she got mad and I left."

"Are you sure you weren't already involved...in a serious way?" I asked.

"What are you talking about?" he snapped. "Of course we weren't. I helped put her boat in the water and we went for a ride in it. That's it. Period. Nothing else."

I passed up the obvious Shakespearean quote. "She wasn't in your cottage in the last few days?"

"No. Nobody's been in there since I opened it a few weeks ago. Nobody but me."

"All right," I said. "So when you left, where did you go?"

"Nowhere. I mean...just back to the city. I went to a place called The Good Doctor's Inn, on Halsted south of Wellington. A friend of mine tends bar there. I talked to him for a while, and then...well, I don't really have a clear recollection. I woke up in my car this morning somewhere on Lincoln Avenue. I drove to the lakefront and sat there. Then I decided I'd go downtown, to the lawyer's office.''

The Lady had gotten up to draw the drapes. "A lawyer?" she asked. "Why, Kevin?"

"My mother's lawyer. She's due home pretty soon, and I thought I'd ask him when. I had nothing else to do, so I drove downtown. His office is just north of the river. I was hungry. I went to the Billy Goat and...and I saw the news on TV. Then I went to the lawyer's office." He nodded toward the Lady. "My mother had given him your name...in case I had any problems. Your name, and Mr. Foley's."

"So," I said, "how well did you know Pamela Masterson?"

He flinched as though I'd slapped him with the name. "Not well. I already told you that."

"I know," I said. "Now I'm asking you again."

Standing, he walked to the table and poured more coffee. "I didn't kill her," he said.

"No one asked that. How well did you know her?"

"We met last summer. But we only...really got to know each other a few weeks ago. We went out a few times, dinner, a couple of movies. But...you know...nothing else, if that's what you mean."

"What I mean is that her throat was slashed from ear to ear."

A shudder went through him. "Surely you don't think I could..."

"I think just about anyone could do just about anything."

"Yes, but..."

"So it wasn't you. But you lied to us. And you keep on lying." He started to protest, but I cut him off. "Forget it. We'll get to that later. You didn't kill her. But listen, Kevin. Whoever it was, they killed her because of you."

Kevin stared at me. His hands started trembling again.

"And whoever killed Pamela shot Casey. That was because of you, too."

"You're crazy," he said. Then he turned to the Lady. "This man's crazy."

"No, Kevin," the Lady answered. "I'm sorry, but he's right."

"The words 'Satan rules' were spray-painted all over the inside of your cottage."

"I know," he said. "That was on the news."

I took the paper out of my pocket, unfolded it, and handed it to Kevin. "This wasn't on the news. It was taped to the refrigerator. The police haven't seen it."

He tried to hold the paper steady with both hands as he read it. "My God," he said, his voice barely audible. "What is this? 'Those few Judas has will be all of them taken...Leaving Judas alone...where Satan rules.' What's going on?"

"We don't know," the Lady said. "Has someone been threatening you?"

"Not at all. I don't have any enemies. I just don't understand."

"I don't either," I said. "But the note's coming true. Pamela Masterson was a friend—maybe more a friend than you've said. Her throat was slit. Casey was another friend. And he was shot in the back."

"What you're saying is impossible," Kevin said. He stared down at the note in his hand. "'Family friends faggots or fools...' Doesn't make sense. No, the police must be right. Those guys were drunk, or on drugs or something. They probably didn't even know what they were doing."

"Kevin," I said, "I was there. I saw them. I heard them. The police will believe what they want to believe. But those two were as sober as you and...well, as sober as I am."

"I, for one, take that note very seriously," the Lady said. She did, too. Although I questioned its efficacy, I'd never known her to keep a baseball bat by her door before.

I took the note back from Kevin. "The important question is—who's next?"

"I...I don't know," he said. "I really don't have many friends. Casey, Pamela, really, that's—"

I interrupted. "You said you had a friend that's a bartender."

"What? Oh, you mean Carl, Carl Hemming. He's a writer, or wants to be. Science fiction. Gay science fiction, I think. Anyway, he gets tickets to Cubs and Bulls games, from some guy who comes in the bar. I've gone to a couple of games with him. I

mean, yes, he's a friend, now that I..." He stopped. "I
mean...we're not..."

"Who else are you close to?"

"I don't know. I can't think of anybody." He shook his head.
"Kind of sad, isn't it? I had a sister. She lived out in the southwest
suburbs, Palos Park. She was...she was killed in a robbery about
a month ago. She worked in a Seven-Eleven and a couple of guys
came in and... Well, anyway, the only other possible person would
be...would be my mother. You don't think it's possible anyone
would hurt her, do you?"

"Yes," the Lady said, "I think it's very possible. And what
about your father?"

"It's been six years since I've seen or heard from my father."
He studied his shoes for a minute, then looked up. "I thought he
was dead. I—"

"*Thought* he was dead?" I asked.

"I still think so. But a couple weeks ago, I got a message that
someone called and wanted to talk to me about my father.
Wouldn't leave a number. Said they'd call again. But...they never
did. I finally decided it was someone's sick idea of a joke."

The Lady looked at me. Someone else to add to the list. Then
there were the unnamed persons—friends and fools. Like me, for
instance. Maybe Harriet too, assuming whoever it was knew about
her. And they did. To think otherwise you'd have to think Harriet's
newfound maternal instincts and the events at Kevin's cottage
were purely coincidental. Like thunder and lightning are coincidental.

Like the call about Kevin's father was coincidental—or like
some armed robbers shooting his sister was coincidental.

FOURTEEN

IT WAS LATE when Kevin and I left the Lady's house and walked down the drive to my place. We hadn't told him about Harriet.

Once he was bedded down on the couch in front of the fireplace, I called Shiloh Hospital and got the usual answer, "stable but critical, sir."

I needed to call Cass. But it was awfully late. I set the timer on the coffeemaker and went to bed.

By eight o'clock the next morning the coffee was ready, but my mind wasn't any clearer on the Cass question. Besides, it was early and I had other calls to make. With Kevin's snores floating softly into the kitchen, I sat at the table, a hunched shoulder pressing the phone to my ear, and sopped up soft-boiled eggs with a slice of rye toast. Outside the wall of windows, more leaves were appearing every day between my apartment and the lake.

The switchboard wasn't open yet, but one of the younger lawyers at Barney Green's office answered. I told her to tell Barney I'd be in about two o'clock, and what had to be done in the meantime. Barney would pick the right lawyer for Kevin.

A call to Shiloh Hospital got me the same response as always. I looked at the clock. Cass teaches undergrad English Lit Wednesday mornings at Northwestern. She'd have left home already. So I called. "I'll be in and out a lot," I told her answering machine. "But I do want to talk to you. Keep trying, please."

Cowardly, of course, but nothing better came to mind.

It was just eight-thirty. My resolution of a minimum one hour a day at the piano, even on "work" days, had been taking a beating. I closed as many doors as possible between Kevin and the studio beyond my only bedroom. I could have used the electric keyboard with a headset, but I felt like banging away out loud, and figured Kevin would sleep through a sousaphone quartet. And if he didn't? What the hell, let him take a shower and get his act together.

I needn't have closed any doors. At ten o'clock it took some pretty vigorous shaking just to rouse Kevin enough to tell him I'd be gone for a while, and to stay put until I got back. He didn't look up to going anywhere, even if he wanted to.

It's a good two-mile run from my place to Dr. Sato's Academy. He's Japanese and his name isn't Sato. He adopted that name years ago when he came to Chicago and discovered everyone thought his real name sounded Italian. What he's a doctor of, who knows? His students don't ask. He can take a man two-thirds his age with a thirty-pound weight advantage—me, for instance—toss him around like a rag doll, and not even breathe heavy. So Dr. Sato's students don't ask about his credentials. We just go in, take our lumps and some gentle verbal abuse, pay a modest fee, and go away wondering if we'll ever please him.

I changed, bowed deeply at the doorway, then slipped out of my sandals and stepped onto the spotless mat that covers nearly the entire floor of the large, bare room over Jackie's Cleaners on Central Street. No one else was on the floor. Dr. Sato sat in his glass-walled office in one of the far corners. He stubbed out his cigarette before he came out to greet me.

"Good morning, *sensei*," I said. "You're looking well."

He returned the bow. "Thank you, Malachy. It has been many days."

"Yes. Well, I've been—"

"Certainly. So, warm up, please. Ten minutes for the mind, five minutes for the body, and I will return."

He walked back to his office, sat down with his back to the room, and lit another cigarette.

Ninety minutes later I was both exhilarated and bone tired. Two other students, both Evanston cops, had come in. We'd worked out and then practiced throws and holds together and with Dr. Sato. When the session was over, the three of us swept the dust from every inch of the floor with straw brooms, while Dr. Sato sat in his office and smoked cigarettes.

When I bowed my good-bye, Dr. Sato spoke to me. "There is something occuring with you, Malachy?"

"Yes, *sensei*."

"Still, there were moments today when you were present, mind and body as one. More than usual. Maybe as many as five minutes. That is good.''

I grinned. "You know, *sensei,* that's the first time you've congratulated me on anything, ever.''

"Do not misunderstand, Malachy. I do not *congratulate.* To say that good is good, that poor is poor, is not praise or blame. It is fact. You could do better. Do not seek praise. When you do, you look beyond yourself. That is not helpful.''

"Yes, *sensei.* I understand.'' Which I didn't. He knew I didn't, and he wasn't going to lose any sleep over it.

Five minutes. He'd given me credit for five good minutes. On the way home, I tried hard not to feel good about it. Maybe I'd understand some day.

KEVIN WAS SITTING at the kitchen table. He was buttering a piece of rye toast when I came through the door from the back stairs to the coach house. He stood up. He'd showered and shaved and was probably wearing the clean underwear and socks I'd laid out for him in the bathroom. He looked different than he had the night before. He stood a little taller, held his stomach in, and had a certain air about him. *Dignity* came to mind. Or at least a sort of stiff imitation of it.

"You don't mind, do you?'' he asked, holding up the toast and the butter knife.

"Help yourself. But you missed the best part.'' I pulled open the refrigerator door and took out a squat glass jar. "Homemade jam, from fresh strawberries. The Lady made it.''

I'd eaten all the eggs, and there wasn't much else in the refrigerator. Between the two of us, we finished the loaf of bread. While we ate, and then on the drive downtown, I tried to make small talk, but Kevin was somewhere else.

Barney met us at his office and, before we had time to speak, marched us back out into the hall and down one flight of fire stairs to the suite of offices just beneath his, where Kevin's lawyer was expecting us. She was barely five feet tall, fiftyish, and very businesslike. Barney handled the introductions. "Renata Carroway, maybe you know Mal Foley, my former partner.''

While we shook hands, agreeing that we'd never met, she kept her gaze on Kevin.

"And Renata," Barney said, "this is the individual I told you—"

Kevin stepped forward and stuck his hand out stiffly. "Father Kevin Peter Cunningham, Mrs. Carroway. I'm sorry if you've been put to any trouble. I have nothing to hide, so I don't need a lawyer. Furthermore, if I did need a lawyer, I'm perfectly capable of selecting a competent one for myself or, if necessary, the archdiocese would certainly provide me with excellent representation."

"Well," she answered, "I'm not a *Mrs.*, but I'm pleased to meet you, Father. I must say I've rarely heard anyone make so many ignorant and naive statements in one breath." With that, she took Kevin by the arm and moved him toward her inner office. "I've canceled everything else I had this afternoon. You and I can confer while we drive to Lake County. I'll drop you off in Evanston when we get back."

TWO BLOCKS NORTH and thirty-five stories up, I had to face R. Pennington again. She came out to the reception area. "There's nothing more to say, Mr. Foley. Miss Mallory is simply not in." Coldly dismissive. She certainly had an air about her. I just couldn't see her as a secretary. Maybe a headmistress. Her authoritarian tone made me want to hang my head and shuffle back across the thick carpet to the elevators.

But I held my ground. Even if I wasn't working for Harriet anymore, she had a right to know what was going on. Besides, I was determined to learn the real reason she had hired me to find her son.

"I need to talk to her right away. Where is she?"

The already chilly Pennington tone got ten degrees cooler. "I'm sure I don't know. But I don't expect to see her today. Would you care to leave a message?"

"If she calls in, tell her I need to speak to her at once. I'm on my way to Mr. Wakefield's office. She can try me there, or leave a message on my machine where I can reach her. It's important. It's about...about a family matter."

"Fine," she said, humoring me and making sure I knew it.

"How about Corinne Macklin?" I asked. "She still work here?"

"Of course she does. But I can tell you Miss Macklin's not in either." When I didn't turn away, she sighed. "Would you care to leave a message for her also?"

"Corinne? Just remind her it'll work better if she says *and*, not *but*."

She didn't bat an eye. "I'll see they both get your messages. Good-bye." She turned and marched away.

J. Birnbaum, the receptionist, rolled her eyes, as though to say that she couldn't stand Harriet's secretary either. "Is she always that pleasant?" I asked.

"Honestly," she said, "I don't know *where* they ever found that woman. I spoke to her once myself about her attitude. Just about bit my head off. Said she didn't need this job in the first place." She shook her head. "But they say she's terribly efficient."

Down thirty-five floors, a block west, a few blocks north, up eleven floors, and the door had THE LAW OFFICES OF JEROME C. WAKEFIELD, ESQ. in heavy brass letters on dark oak. I figured I looked more like Wakefield's type of client than Brothers and Cruickshank's type. The woman at the desk beyond the door certainly looked more like my type of office help, right down to the garish lipstick and the left forefinger unconsciously twirling a lock of otherwise straight blond hair.

"Hi," she said, looking up from her Avon Products catalog. "Can I help you?"

"Mr. Wakefield, please."

"Gee, I'm sorry, but he's not in. Not all day. Maybe one of the other attorneys can help you, though. Is it a divorce case? That's all they do here, you know." She seemed actually interested in being helpful.

"I'm really looking for Harriet Mallory."

"Mallory? We don't... Oh, you mean Mr. Wakefield's wife? Gee, I don't know if she's ever been here. I mean, I've never seen her myself, and I've been here over a year. You wanna leave a message or anything? Or...let's see...we got a directory here of all the lawyers in the whole state. It's called *Sullivan's*. I could look up her phone number for you.''

"No thanks. I'll call back."

"OK by me," she said. "But if you need a divorce, you know, this is the place to come. Great lawyers. Especially Mr. Wakefield."

"Really?"

"Oh yes. He did my sister's divorce. You should see him in court. My ex-brother-in-law's lawyer was one of those screamers, you know? But Mr. Wakefield handled him easy. Very smooth, very professional. But the other lawyers we got are good, too." She cocked her head to the side and winked. "I gotta warn you, though, they're kind of expensive."

"I'll keep that in mind."

"So, have a nice day." She smiled a real smile and went back to her catalog.

R. Pennington could have learned a thing or two from her.

FIFTEEN

THERE WAS A PHONE in the building lobby. She picked up on the first ring. A good omen. Or maybe not.

"It's me." I swallowed involuntarily and discovered my mouth was dry. "Um...how are you?" Real savoir faire, that's me when the pressure's on.

"I'm...there are people here," she said. "Some of my students, I mean."

"Cass," I said, "it's been a long time. Can we...? How about dinner?"

"I'd love to Mal. I really would." She meant that. It was clear in her voice. "I could meet you in, say, an hour and a half or so, if it's somewhere nearby."

We decided on Los Magueyes, on Chicago Avenue in Evanston. It had been easy. A phone call to my wife, for God's sake, and I'd been worried for weeks what I'd say. But in the end it was simple. We'd meet for dinner. We'd talk—maybe about what counted, maybe not. But then there'd be another dinner. We'd take it step by step. Simple.

Meanwhile, there was time to stop at The Good Doctor's Inn on the way.

Lake Shore Drive north to Belmont. West to Halsted. Two blocks south is Wellington, and a little south of that The Good Doctor's Inn was tucked between a used-book store and a dead-end alley. There hasn't been a legal parking place available on the street in that neighborhood after 3 p.m. in fifteen years. That day there wasn't even an illegal spot. So I parked in the alley, snug against the outside wall of the tavern, just below the No Parking sign.

The blue Bonneville that had been with me at least since I left the Loop continued south on Halsted.

The Good Doctor's Inn was too small to become more than it had always been, a neighborhood bar. It was dark inside, and smelled like damp dust and stale beer, like taverns are supposed to smell. Three customers sat apart from each other, evenly spaced along the bar that ran the length of the right side of the room. It was past five o'clock when I slid onto the first stool near the door. Behind me, four women filled the front booth by the window. Judging by their conversation, which you couldn't ignore if you wanted to, they were nurses at a nearby hospital. Judging by the volume of their laughter, they'd been in that booth quite a while. The other six booths were empty.

On a high shelf above my end of the bar, a television set was tuned to a game show with some people sitting behind screens making faces while other people who couldn't see them jumped up and down. I couldn't get the point, because the sound was turned off. I ordered a Miller's from a pale pretty woman with frizzy, shoulder-length red hair and large, blue-framed glasses.

"I can change the channels on the TV," she said, as she set the bottle on the bar in front of me. "But there's something wrong with the sound. It doesn't work."

"That's all right," I said. "Actually, I'm looking for one of the bartenders, Carl Hemming."

"You and me both," she said. "He's supposed to start at five. He'll be along, though. Sometimes he forgets to check the clock. I can use the extra hours anyway."

Twenty minutes later, the manic nurses were gone, Carl hadn't shown, and I was getting impatient. "Is the manager here?" I asked, ordering a second Miller's.

"Gone home to supper."

When the beer arrived I laid a ten on the bar. "Where does Carl live?" I asked.

The redhead was startled. "I...I don't know."

I laid a second ten beside the first one.

"Really," she said, "I don't know. Keep putting bills out there and I might make something up. But the truth is, I don't know." She thought for a moment. "I can give you his phone number, though."

I left both tens on the bar. From a pay phone on the wall between the front door and the bar, I called the number.

"Hi. This is Carl. I'm not here just now, but leave your name and number..." I didn't. The Name and Address Service told me the number was unlisted and they couldn't give out the address.

At five-forty-five the bar was filling up, but still no Carl Hemming. I didn't like it.

I also didn't like it that I'd be late meeting Cass. I drained a third beer and headed for the open doorway at the far end of the bar. Beyond was a hall with two doors on the left, labeled MEN and WOMEN respectively, and a door on the right that said EMERGENCY EXIT ONLY. I selected MEN and went in.

When I came out, I went through the exit into the alley. Not an emergency, just a shortcut to the Cavalier. Outside, darkness was falling fast. Across the alley from me, a fan over a closed door exhaled the hot breath of an Asian restaurant—Korean was my guess—into the alley. Apparently, the Koreans hadn't paid their scavenger's bill. Bulging, leaking garbage bags sat on and around the wheeled, overflowing refuse bins. The pavement was slick beneath my feet and I didn't care to check what caused the wetness. The shadows—and the gloom that rolled across my mind like a dense fog—turned the dark plastic bags into huge, bloated rodents on a digestion break between courses, urine seeping from beneath their shiny haunches.

To my left the alley dead-ended. To my right was trouble.

A dark-colored Ford sedan sat nosed at an angle into the alley, blocking the way to the sidewalk and pinning my car in the alley. The door that had just closed behind me had no handle on the outside. The only way out of the alley was to squeeze past the two men who leaned with practiced carelessness against the side of the Ford.

The steady glow of the street lights and the ceaseless passing sweep of headlights on Halsted Street combined to throw crooked, moving shadows across their faces. They looked as hard and slippery-smooth as the alley pavement beneath my feet.

I didn't know these two, of course, just the breed. They didn't need to turn their heads to know I was there. They hear like coyotes and see to the side like lizards—survival skills in the job we pay them for. Every day, they wade around in perversity, up to their necks and beyond. The strong ones escape being poisoned by the muck. But these two?

They were in civilian clothes—maybe Violent Crimes, maybe Vice, maybe Narcotics, who knows? It was me they were waiting for. That was in the air, stronger than the odor of fetid garbage in the alley. It's happened before, this threat from the very ones sworn to protect, and it never brings out the best in me. Waves of anger and revulsion washed over me—and with them fear. It's probably the fear that turns me brash, and petty, and stupid.

There were only two choices. I could either wait for them to come in after me, sitting on my haunches like a cornered garbage bag, or I could go forward and meet them closer to the public eye.

So, hitching up my psychological gun belt, I strode jauntily toward the two men. Whistling a happy tune would have been overdoing it, even for me. As I turned sideways and eased between the building and the front end of the Ford, the nearer man swung his head, lazily, and focused tired eyes on me.

I grinned. "Uh...excuse me," I said. There was no way I could get out to the sidewalk without brushing up against him. "May I get by, please?"

"Whatcha been doin' back there, pal?" He sounded bored, and his eyes had puffy bags under them like he didn't get enough sleep. Taking his hands from the pockets of his tan windbreaker, he crossed his arms across his chest. Just beyond him, right on cue, the second man uncrossed his arms and stuck his hands into the pockets of his own windbreaker—this one dark blue.

"Hey," I said, "you guys really got this routine down. Who does your choreography?" I couldn't keep my mouth shut.

"Amusing," the first man said, turning his head slightly to the left. "But I thought I asked the man a question, didn't I?"

The second man said nothing. To look at him, he might not have been listening.

"Yessir. A question. You sure did," I said, talking as rapidly as possible. "You asked what I was doing in the alley. Well, sir, it's dark and kind of scary back there and there's these huge rodent-type things that look like they're...uh...like they're pissing on the pavement. You oughta go look." I moved sideways, brushing past the first man. "Might even be relatives of yours I think but I gotta get outta here before I get hurt because...oooof..."

The second man had glided suddenly in front of me and planted his fist, with no apparent effort, deep into my solar plexus.

I straightened quickly from a doubled-over position, spreading my hands, palms out, in front of me. No one moved while I recovered enough to speak. "What the hell," I gasped. "Cops, Jesus...getting as bad as political candidates. Can't take a little kidding around. What's your unit anyway? Narcotics? Vice? Vio—"

"That your car there under the No Parking sign?" the second cop interrupted.

"Traffic?" I asked.

"Is that your car?" he repeated.

"Well, officer, yes and no. That is, it's titled in my wife's name. But I use it. Of course, if you mean...ooof..."

Another easy fist to the belly, placed a little lower. This one from the first cop, the one with the tired eyes, who had finally lifted his buttocks off the side of the unmarked squad car.

"You can just fucking park anywhere you want to, huh?" he asked. "You don't have to obey the law like the rest of the goddamn mopes in the world, I guess."

"OK, OK, you're tough." Between gasping for air and swallowing down the vomit that wanted up and out, I could hardly form the words. "Now...you got something to tell me? Then skip the bullshit lecture on the law."

They tossed me in the backseat of the Ford. The two of them sat in the front. The one behind the wheel faced straight ahead toward the dead end of the alley, while the other turned and leaned over the seat back toward me.

"So," I said, "what's the point?"

"Look, Foley. We don't like you and we don't dislike you." As he spoke, he pulled on a pair of thin black leather gloves. "You're like dried dog shit. Avoid it if you can, but even if you step on it, it's no big deal."

"You got a great gift for metaphor," I said.

He reached out with his gloved right hand then, and slapped me, hard, across the face. My brain rattled, and the sting brought tears to my eyes, but I stared straight at him. "Like I said, what's the point?"

"The point is...someone doesn't like you messin' with something you're messin' with. Someone says they told you before not to get close to happy, but it seems you didn't get it clear. You should get it clear this time, 'cause there won't be another time.'' He reached out and slapped me again, harder this time. ''No more warnings. You stay close to happy, you're dead meat. That's the point.''

If I'd have been smart, I'd have bought some time then, told them I'd quit, acted afraid. Hell, I *was* afraid, so that part would have been easy. But I was angry and humiliated and I couldn't do that, not even with bells clanging in my head and tears streaming down my cheeks.

''That's the point, huh?'' I said. ''Don't stay close to happy. What the hell does that mean?''

The blank look in his eyes told me he had no idea what it meant. But what he finally said was, ''I don't answer questions, mope. You don't understand, that's your problem.''

''It's like I thought. You don't even know what it is you're telling me. But I understand perfectly. You tell your Mister Someone I got it clear last time, and I got it clear this time. Then you tell him I said he can go back home and diddle with himself some more. I do what I want to do. You tell him he's bought himself a big problem. You tell him all that, OK? From me.'' The words came out, but I couldn't keep the trembling from my voice.

The cop shook his head, almost sadly. ''You really are a piece of work, Foley,'' he said. He hit a button, and the rear door locks popped up. ''We don't know you. We never talked to you. And you're a damn, piss-poor pitiful piece of work. If I was you, I'd do what I was told.''

I slid across the seat, out of reach of the gloved hand, and had the door open. ''So...I should do what I'm told,'' I said, ''because that's what you'd do. Some creep pokes up out of his hole and tells you to deliver a message, one you don't even understand, what do you do? You do what you're told. Talk about pitiful...''

By then I was out of the car and the cop behind the wheel was leaning through the open window, backing the unmarked squad car slowly across the sidewalk toward the street. ''Toughest damn messenger boys on the block,'' I ranted, raising my voice, ''but still just messenger boys.''

He braked momentarily and cleared his throat, then spat. I jumped back and raised my hands, and the thick phlegm splatted against the palm of my left hand and slithered down to my wrist. He backed out onto the street, wheels spinning and squealing, and sped away.

I lowered my hand and felt the viscous glob reverse itself and slide off the ends of my fingers.

SIXTEEN

NAUSEATED AND TREMBLING, I was in no shape to drive. Back in the bar I washed my hands and ordered a Miller's. When it was gone, I called Los Magueyes.

"Oh, *si*, the lady was here, *señor*. She waited and had, I think, *dos margaritas*. She left a message, senor. I have it here. It says, 'Thank you so much for a typically wonderful evening.' I think she was not happy, *señor. Me siento mucho.*"

"Not half as sorry as I am," I said, the phone already back on the hook.

Back at the bar I switched to Dos Equis. I drank that one, and another, and ate a lot of garlic-salted bar mix from a plastic bowl and watched the network news on TV. It's just as silly without the sound.

Common sense told me it was a good thing I hadn't kept the date with Cass. Someone was too interested in me, and there was no sense dragging her into it. I went back to the phone. Common sense also told me not to call her, but...

"Hello?" Suspicious.

"It's me."

"I really don't feel like talking."

"I understand. I just want to explain. Something came up, and I couldn't—"

"Something always comes up."

It would have been smart then to apologize and say good-bye. But not me. I had to debate the point. "Not always. There've been lots of good times. I can't forget them, and you can't either. We have to keep trying."

I believed that. I wanted it more than anything. But this wasn't the time. Why couldn't I keep my mouth shut?

There was a pause, and then, "I want to try, Mal. I really do. How about...tomorrow night?"

That's exactly what I'd been afraid of, and what I'd brought on myself.

When I couldn't think of anything to say, she answered for me. "No, not tomorrow. There's something up, right?" She was angry again, and hurt, and I couldn't blame her. "Some other time then. Or...maybe not."

She hung up.

A Dos Equis later, Carl Hemming still hadn't shown up. I'd try again tomorrow. I didn't want to keep Kevin waiting too long at the Lady's. I left the redhead a generous tip and went out to the alley and my car.

But there wasn't any car. Just an empty space, and above it the NO PARKING sign—and another sign I hadn't noticed before that said violators' cars would be towed away by Wancho's Towing Service, to an address I was too mad to even read.

Two kids came along the sidewalk toward me, a male and a female—maybe. Two weird twenty-year-olds, tall and emaciated and dressed all in fringed black leather with lots of chrome buttons and hardware. Their faces were as pale as December moons and the one with hair wore it in a bouffant, half orange, half green. The other had snakes tattooed where her hair should have been.

I blocked their way. "The hell with the goddamn car," I told them. "And fuck Wancho, wherever he is."

They skirted around me warily, probably wondering where the cops were when you needed one.

I took the el to Howard Street, transferred to the Evanston line, got off at Central, and walked all the way home. No one was watching my place. I continued up the driveway to the Lady's to get Kevin.

NATURALLY, he wasn't there. He hadn't called.

We sat at the table in the Lady's huge, old-fashioned kitchen, with its Formica-topped counters and about a hundred and fifty white wooden cabinets. She sipped Darjeeling and I ate the supper she thought Kevin and I might want. It was some sort of ragout, with lots of spices I didn't recognize, and vegetables in disguise. But there was plenty of beef in it, too, and it went down well with homemade bread and the cheap red wine I'd gone over to the coach house to get.

When more than my share had disappeared, I had a cup of tea myself and brought the Lady up to date, finishing with what a rotten evening I'd had.

"I keep thinking there's no good reason not to just forget it, just leave Harriet and Kevin and their problems alone. After all, Harriet paid me off and considers my services terminated."

The Lady, silent, poured herself another cup of tea.

"And Kevin never asked for my help in the first place, and doesn't want it."

"He certainly didn't *ask,*" she said.

"Right," I said, ignoring her implication. "But what's really important is it's finally getting through to me that if I want to hold on to Cass, I ought to leave Harriet and Kevin—and all the other Harriets and Kevins that come my way—leave them all alone. There are lots of other things I could do with my life."

"The possibilities are endless," the Lady agreed.

"For one, I could tell the Supreme Court I'm sorry I stuck it up...I mean I'm sorry I thumbed my nose at them, and ask for my law license back."

She set her cup soundlessly in the saucer, and looked down into it. "Could you do that?"

"Well...maybe not. But there's still the income from the trust I set up with my fee from your case. It's not much, but I could practice the piano more and maybe pick up a few gigs. Plus I could get a job in a hardware store or something...anything."

"I agree. You could settle for any number of things." She raised her head and looked at me. "But what is it you *want,* Malachy?"

"I want Cass back," I said. "But..."

"Yes?"

"But there's still Celia. She *did* ask for help, and I agreed. And what about Casey? I'm the one who took him up there to die."

"He may not die. Besides, he wanted to go, and neither of you could have guessed what would happen."

"Great," I said. "Maybe he won't die. And maybe if he does die it's not my fault. But still, I owe him. He trusted me. When he thought he was dying, he was afraid and he trusted me with his fear.''

There were a few moments of silence.

Then the Lady said, ''So what you want is to keep going with this.''

''Yeah, that's what I really want. Maybe it's Casey, or Celia. Or maybe it's just a weakness I have. Always needing to prove something to myself, to show that I'm up to it. These...situations. They're like tests or something. There's always a fear of getting hurt, or even killed. But there's a stronger fear, a fear that if I turn away, if I let it go once I start, it might mean there's something wrong with me, that I can't finish out the game.'' I looked at her. ''I think that's kind of childish, don't you?''

''I think when you know what you want to do, Malachy, maybe you shouldn't think so much.''

So it was simple. *I can walk away anytime I want, and I choose to stay for now.*

All I had to do was discover who was out to kill all Kevin's relatives, friends, and helpers—and why. And figure out how Harriet fit into the picture. Then I had to find a way to stop whoever it was. And I had to hold on to Cass at the same time, if she was still around to hold on to.

The Lady was right; the trick was not to think. So I went home, swallowed a few antacids, and went to bed.

SEVENTEEN

"YEAAHH?"

Dragging the word out so that whatever idiot was on the phone would know he didn't appreciate being woken up that early.

"Morning, Jerry," I said. "I need to talk to Harriet."

"Jesus Christ. Who is this?"

"It's Foley. Let me talk to Harriet."

"Too late. She's gone already. You lose." What a guy, that Jerry.

"Jerry," I said, being patient, "it's only ten after six."

"I know. She's gone. Be at the health club awhile. Then at her desk a little after seven. Call her there. By eight she'll be too busy. It's that goddamn abortion thing. Probably be late again tonight."

"All right," I said, "But in case I miss her, tell her—"

He hung up. What a guy.

I took the el and by seven o'clock I was leaning against a high marble counter in the lobby of Harriet's building, sipping bad coffee from a paper cup and killing time with the security guard. He looked normal enough, but had decided to carve out a niche for himself as the world's only living being who thought Michael Jordan had been an overrated basketball player.

He nodded solemnly at me. "I mean it, man. The dude never was as good as the hype. Anyway," he looked past my shoulder, "here come Miz Mallory now."

Harriet shoved her way through the revolving glass door with her shoulder. In her left hand she had a briefcase that looked like it weighed twenty-five pounds, and a huge purse was slung over her right shoulder, her thumb hooked through the strap. Seeing me, she stopped, made a face that said, What the hell are you doing here? and after that a head gesture that said, Follow me.

I followed.

We rode the elevator in silence. She stared straight ahead and never set the briefcase down. On the thirty-fifth floor, the door to

Brothers and Cruickshank was closed. She set the briefcase on the floor while she dug a plastic card out of her purse. She unlocked the door with the key card. When she reached down for the briefcase it wasn't there.

"I got it," I said.

"Whatever." But she looked surprised, maybe even grateful. The bag weighed thirty-five pounds, easy.

We went into the suite and past rows and rows of empty secretarial stations. I switched hands on the briefcase on the way.

We finally came to the door with the H. Mallory plaque and turned in. While I sat and waited, Harriet moved restlessly around her office. She put her purse on a couch covered with papers, her coat on a hook behind the door. She went to the windows and adjusted the blinds. When she couldn't think of anything else to do, she sat at her desk and picked up a gold-plated fountain pen. She didn't say anything.

"So," I finally said, "'just a mother with a natural curiosity about her child.' Isn't that how you put it?"

She took a long breath—in, then out. "There's more to it than that."

"Really."

"All right." She paused on the edge, then dove in. "I'd put the child out of my mind thirty-one years ago. Of course, it bothered me at first, but I convinced myself it was the same as if he'd died at birth, that it was better if neither of us ever knew anything about the other. And I was satisfied with that. I scarcely thought of him for thirty-one years."

"And then?"

"And then I got a message. In the mail, with no return address. I..." She opened her desk drawer. "Here, this is it."

She handed me a cheap business-sized envelope, the kind you buy at Walgreen's, addressed to her and marked, Personal and Confidential. Inside there was a folded piece of white paper, with three typed lines:

> *Happy,*
> *Isaiah 13:18*
> *Watch and pray.*

"Well?" I asked.

"What?"

"I mean, did you look it up?"

"Of course I did. I sent Ms. Pennington to buy a Bible. I didn't tell her why, of course. I never knew there were so many versions, different translations. According to Ms. Pennington, the King James Version is pretty much a classic."

"So...Isaiah, chapter thirteen, verse eighteen. What's it say?"

She stood up and walked to the windows, staring out at the lake as she recited the verse by heart. "'Their bows shall dash the young men to pieces; and they shall have no pity on the fruit of the womb; their eye shall not spare children.'"

Looking down at the paper in my hand, I added, "'Watch and pray.'"

She said nothing.

"It scared you. And you called me."

"No, not then." She paced back and forth in front of the windows, patting her hair, checking her earrings. "It disturbed me, certainly. But I've gotten anonymous letters before, when I was a judge. And I wouldn't put it past some of the crazies who don't like me representing abortion clinics to send something like that. But, other than save the note, I didn't do anything at all." She walked back behind her desk. "A week later, the second one came."

She handed me another envelope taken from her drawer. The format was the same. Cheap envelope, cheap paper, three lines:

> *Happy,*
> *Isaiah 49:15*
> *Watch and pray.*

"And that text," I asked, "what does it say?"

She had this one memorized, too. "'Can a woman forget her sucking child, that she should not have compassion on the son of her womb? Yea, they may forget, yet will I not forget thee.'" She paused a moment. "When I read that, I knew that these messages, as unclear as they were, must be from someone who knew I had a child. Someone was warning me...about my son.''

''Who would know about him?''

''No one. I mean...that's what I'd thought. I never told anyone.''

''Jerry?''

''Not even him. Not until after the second note. Then I showed him both notes and told him about the baby. He said I should go to the police.''

''I guess even Jerry has to make sense once in a while,'' I said. Sometimes I don't know why I can't control myself.

''Please. You don't like Jerry. But I do. He's had a difficult life and still has some rough edges. But he's becoming quite respected in the divorce courts. People who haven't observed him recently are surprised. More than that, he loves me. And, whether you know it or not, I can be a difficult person to get along with. He's the best thing that ever happened to me.''

Exactly what Jerry had said about her. I couldn't tell about Jerry, but I'd swear she meant it. She wasn't foolish and she was no starry-eyed kid. She loved the man. Maybe I'd missed something.

''Anyway,'' I said, ''why didn't you follow Jerry's—''

Harriet's phone buzzed and she picked it up. ''Yes,'' she said. ''Good. Thank you, Ms. Pennington.''

I looked at my watch. ''You mean your secretary's in this early?''

''Oh yes. She knows my schedule, and tries to be here whenever I am. She's quite helpful.''

I could think of a few other adjectives, but went back to my original question. ''Why didn't you go to the police?''

''I would have, but...'' She sat at her desk and picked up her pen again. ''I have some political possibilities. There are people who have indicated a willingness to back me, with money and with organization.''

''Like Cleveland Richardson, I suppose, and Sam Drake?''

''Among others. But they're the most important. And, as I'm sure you can understand, it's a very delicate situation. Something like this—''

''I understand. You go to the police. Word gets out. The money gets scared off and you don't get elected.'' My voice rose a notch. "So you keep quiet, and if a few people get killed, what the hell? Maybe even your son gets killed...'dashed to pieces,' isn't that what it said? Hey, those things happen.'' I was on my feet by that time. "That's politics, right? Gotta take the bad with the good, right? Weigh the priorities? After all, what's a son, compared to elected office?''

"Please, look—"

"No. You look.'' I was the one walking around the room now, driven by my own anger and guilt. "There's an innocent woman got her throat slashed ear to ear, and a priest with a bullet in his back, and another one who's your own flesh and blood—"

Harriet stood up. "Sit down, Foley. Sit down and shut up!'' Her voice wasn't loud, but it cracked across my face like a bull-whip. "You're nearly hysterical.''

She was exaggerating, but not by much. I sat down.

"Now you listen to me,'' she said. "You're talking about what happened at Bullhead Lake. I heard about that. But we don't know for certain whether that had any connection to these notes. And even if they *are* connected, do you think I could have guessed something like that would happen? Or do you think for one minute that taking these notes to the police would have stopped something from happening God-knows-how-many miles from here? I didn't even know who my son was, for God's sake. I started to do what I could. I called you. Then you found him and...and I didn't es-pecially like what you found. Then I needed time...to think.'' She was winding down, losing steam. "Anyway, don't lecture me. OK?''

"OK,'' I said. "I'm sorry.'' And I was. "But what happened at Bullhead Lake must be tied to the notes you got. You can't possibly doubt that.''

She looked very tired. "Maybe,'' she said. "But why the woman? And wasn't the priest someone who just happened to be in the way? I don't understand.''

"Forget about understanding. Take a look at this. It was left behind when the cottage was trashed.'' I gave her the paper from the refrigerator door.

She stood with one hand on the back of her chair and the Judas note in the other, and read the note. "'Not dead then worse than dead wishing dead.' My God, what sort of person is this?" She handed the paper absentmindedly back to me. "Why would anyone hate my...hate this priest so much?"

"The question is," I said, "what to do?"

"I don't know." She was back on her feet now, walking around. "But I still can't see any sense in going to the police. Say I tell them this...this Father Cunningham is my son and show them the notes. What are they going to do? Put a twenty-four-hour guard on him, and all his family and friends? And for how long? A week? A month? A year? What good would that do?"

She had a point. "I suppose they'd just drive this maniac underground until the heat's off," I said, "and then we're back where we started, only worse. He'll have had more time to think, more time to be careful."

She raised her eyebrows. "He? Why do you say he? Why not a woman?"

"The hell with that," I answered. "It's a *he,* until I learn different. Anyway, I apologize for getting carried away a few minutes ago. The fact is, I haven't taken what I know to the police either. Not the note, not about you. None of—"

Another buzz from Harriet's phone jarred the room. She jumped, then grabbed the receiver as she looked at her watch. She walked with the phone to the windows and faced out. It wasn't much of a conversation on our end. Just "yes" into the phone about five times, with a pause between each one, each "yes" a little more impatient than the one before. By the final "yes," she was back at her desk. She slammed the receiver down.

I'd been starting to learn more about Harriet Mallory that morning—that she loved her husband, that she wanted the truth and then didn't always like it, that she could be confused and uncertain like the rest of us. But when she slammed the phone down and spoke again, her voice had regained that irritating, lawyer-in-charge tone that had been missing during most of our conversation.

"I've no time to discuss this any longer. My staff is waiting. Meanwhile, you're not to do anything at all about any of this until you hear from me." She shoved the two notes back in their envelopes and returned them to her drawer. She gave me the direct number to her voice mail, in case I needed to contact her. "But you won't have to. I'll get back to you. Please ask Ms. Pennington to show you out."

I didn't have to ask. Ms. Pennington was happy to show me out. I was starting to like Harriet, but her secretary was sure getting on my nerves.

AT THAT TIME of the morning hundreds of cabs run back and forth, scooping up near-north-siders and depositing them downtown. A paying fare back north was a bonus the driver was happy to get.

"Ever hear of Wancho's Towing?"

"Not a cabbie in the city don't know Wancho's," he answered, as we pulled away from the curb. "You probably figure you had tough luck, right?"

"Yeah, I do."

"Hey, look on the bright side. You coulda been towed to a police pound. This way, you got an even chance your car won't be stripped when you get there."

He went on to relate his cousin's experiences as a police tow truck driver, but I missed most of it. I was thinking about Harriet's order "not to do anything at all about any of this until you hear from me." She'd obviously forgotten I wasn't working for her any longer.

Of course, even if I were, I doubt I'd have paid any more attention than I did.

EIGHTEEN

By NINE-THIRTY I had the Cavalier out of hock. It was still missing the window that was shot out, but with a tankful of gas and a couple of quarts of oil it was otherwise as good as ever. By ten I was on the near north side, ready for breakfast.

But first I bought seven greeting cards—section: Friendship; subsection: Miss You. With the cards, a mug of fresh-roasted mocha java, and three tortilla-sized oatmeal-and-raisin cookies, I sat near the window at Coffee Chicago, with a view of the morning people on Chicago Avenue. The coffee was great there, and you could sit for hours and no one bothered you. I'd done that myself a year earlier, several days in a row, long enough to identify which of the clean-cut kids serving coffee was dipping into the till.

By eleven, all the cards were signed—each with a note I hoped would be helpful—and all the envelopes stamped and addressed to Cass. One a day for seven days. Surely by then I'd be finished with this business of Harriet's boy, and Cass and I would have dinner at the Nikko—but the Japanese-style restaurant for us.

Then I switched to decaf and made a few phone calls that told me things I mostly didn't like knowing. I liked Casey's still being alive. But he wasn't improving, and I didn't like that. I didn't like Carl Hemming's machine still announcing he wasn't home. I didn't like Kevin's ignoring me. Celia was out of prison and somewhere in Chicago, but I didn't like not knowing where.

The "didn't likes" were far ahead, and still counting, when I paid the bill and left the coffee shop. What I didn't like most of all was continually having to look for someone following me.

Anyway, just then there was no one in sight.

RENATA CARROWAY was preoccupied and impatient. Probably no different than she was any other time. She was also abrupt, street smart, short tempered, and egotistical. She didn't care whether I liked her or not.

She was perfect for Kevin.

Sitting in her office, we talked and ate the lunches she ordered—chicken noodle soup and a small salad for her, cream of mushroom and a ham and cheese with too much mayo for me. We danced around a while, until she retained me as her investigator in the Cunningham matter. That got me within the attorney-client privilege, at least far enough to satisfy the two of us.

"Now," she said, "everything you know."

That was certainly out of the question. But keeping Harriet Mallory out of it left obvious gaps. So I told her I was skipping parts.

"For instance, how I got into this in the first place I can't say."

She didn't like it. But she understood keeping your mouth shut. Besides, what could she do?

I started with the trip to Lexington and told her everything that didn't refer to Harriet. I skipped the whole adoption business and the notes Harriet showed me.

Renata's glasses were heavy black frames around thick, round lenses. When she heard about the note on the refrigerator door, she glared at me like a caged owl might glare at a mouse it would swoop down on and kill—if only it could. She didn't approve of my not giving the note to the cops. But I hadn't been working for her then.

The sheriff's police insisted he wasn't a suspect, but Renata hadn't let Kevin give a statement about the Masterson killing.

"I know that makes him look suspicious." She paused to drink the last of her soup from the Styrofoam cup. "But the problem is, Kevin's not telling the whole truth."

"You're kidding," I said. She was right on the button.

"No, he's lying all right, at least about his relationship with the dead woman. He told me she was just a neighbor and he'd helped put her boat in the water. But I'm sure there was more to it than that. And if that's so, then he'd have lied to the sheriff's investigators too, and they'd find out somehow."

She'd let Kevin answer questions restricted to the vandalism at his cottage, about which he knew nothing.

"One of the investigators told me there was cocaine in the

woman's boat and that it made no sense at all," she said. "There's no hint of that in her past. He implied Kevin must have put it there. But the very idea of Kevin slitting that woman's throat is ludicrous, and they know it. When we left, he wanted to go visit that other priest, Kozlowski or whatever. We called and found out he'd had more surgery and wasn't conscious, so we drove back to the city. Kevin refused to go to your friend's home in Evanston. He thinks you're trying to control him and he wants to be a big boy. He insisted on going to Loyola to pick up his car. If you'd told me about the note, I wouldn't have let him do that."

"Yeah, well..."

"'Yeah, well...'" she repeated. She was great at sarcasm. "Anyway, after talking to you there are other things that worry me, even more than they did before."

"What things?"

"Kevin is a very fragile person at best, and he's been terribly shaken. First by his sister's homicide. And now, well, I don't know which hit him harder, the priest's shooting or the Masterson woman's death. He's very mixed up. Told me he used to love working with young people but doesn't do that anymore. Strange...And there's something else."

"What's that?"

"His father. Out of the blue he said he ought to go look for his father. It seemed a strange—"

"Look for his father? Where?"

"How would I know? If you'd have told me more in the first place I'd have been more concerned about it, that's for sure. All in all, I'd say this priest of yours is close to a nervous breakdown."

"Priest of *mine?*"

In a sudden gesture of dismissal, she snatched up the remains of our lunches and dropped them in the wastebasket. "Well," she said, "who's paying you?"

She caught me off guard. "I...can't tell you that."

"Anyway," she said, "I'm not."

"Fair enough."

"Something else no one told me." She turned the owl glare on me again. "Kevin looks to me like an alcoholic. He denies it, of course. I asked him."

AT THE GOOD DOCTOR'S INN, the manager wasn't worried about Carl's not showing up the night before. "Not scheduled to work today or tomorrow anyway. Maybe just wanted to cut out early. Fact is, another guy was here yesterday, just before I left for supper, asking for Carl's address. Said they were fishing buddies or something."

"You mean you gave him the address?"

"Sure. Why not?"

He gave me the address, too.

It was a "garden apartment," the front door a few steps below ground level, under the high wooden stoop of a frame building that was originally a single-family home on Wellington, west of Sheffield. There was a newspaper in the well at the bottom of the concrete stairs. I stepped over it and rang the doorbell—too many times.

Upstairs there was no answer either. Back down on the sidewalk, I walked around the corner and to the alley that ran behind the houses. The gate next to the sagging wooden garage was unlocked. Knocking on the basement back door got me nothing. Upstairs, I roused some sort of noisy parrot or something, and no one else.

Back downstairs, the spring bolt on the basement door was easy. Inside it was colder and damper than it was outside. The back half of the basement was just a basement—washer and dryer, utility sink, furnace, baby food jars of rusting nails, dirty cobwebs, the works. The garden apartment was confined to the front half.

What little hope I had left vanished when the door opened with just a twist of the knob.

The apartment was as cold and damp as the rest of the basement. There was a musty smell in the air. Other than a tiny bathroom just inside the door and straight ahead, there were only two rooms. A kitchen to the right, and a living room to the left. I turned left. In the living room, a sofa was opened up into an unmade bed. Thin curtains covered windows set high in the walls and let in plenty of light. The cement walls were painted white, the floor battleship gray with rugs here and there, end pieces you get for a few dollars each at carpet stores. The pipes running back and forth beneath the ceiling were painted white, too. In one corner was a cheap electric heater. The plug was pulled from the wall socket.

There was another unplugged space heater in the kitchen. On the counter beside the sink were a toaster and a telephone answering machine. There were probably a stove and a refrigerator in there as well. I never noticed them. What drew my attention was the 1940s enamel-top kitchen table with its chipped red trim and rust-flecked chrome legs. There were two chrome and plastic-cushioned chairs—one at the end of the table that was cleared for eating, the other at the working end, where an electric typewriter sat surrounded by stacks of books and papers.

It was from that second chair that Carl Hemming had toppled backward to the floor after the bullet exited through the back of his skull. His body still lay there, naked except for the well-worn boxer shorts that were just a slightly paler shade of gray-white than his skin had turned.

It looked like suicide all right, with a small pillow to muffle the sound of the five-shot revolver that lay on the floor under the table. The pillow was charred and torn apart by the blast. A sheet of paper rolled into the typewriter held just one line of type: *All for you, Father. All for you.*

Type the note. Shove the gun barrel in the mouth. Don't think. Squeeze the trigger. It's over. Someone else can worry about whether the pillow will catch on fire and burn the place down. Someone else can clean up the blood—and whatever else—that splatters, then slides down, congealing on the cold, white surface of the wall.

The shivering wouldn't stop then. I stumbled to the bathroom and leaned low over the toilet. On top of the tank was a purple aerosol can that said Potpourri and, next to that, two small, clear plastic envelopes, empty. Hands shaking, I set aside the aerosol can and lifted the top from the toilet tank. There was a larger, heat-sealed plastic envelope under the tank water, weighted down with a small jar of rusty nails. The bag was filled with a white powder.

I didn't vomit; and I didn't take anything with me. I did erase the message on Carl's answering machine, though—the one that said, "Carl? It's Kevin. I have to talk to you. Call me as soon as you can."

All for you, Father. All for you.

The homicide investigators could puzzle over *Father*. Was it God? Was the note a prayer?

They might close it as a suicide when they got nowhere else with it. But they'd wonder. People who blow their brains out don't generally bother to muffle the sound.

All for you, Father. All for you.

Carl Hemming hadn't shot himself, or left any final note. He'd simply gotten friendly with the wrong person. The typed message wasn't a prayer. And I knew exactly who *Father* was.

NINETEEN

IT DIDN'T TAKE a medical examiner's license to know Carl Hemming had died long before the manager of The Good Doctor's Inn gave me his address. So, even if the cops got that far, I wouldn't be much of a suspect. On the other hand, if I'd looked for him the night before, maybe he wouldn't have died. I knew he was in danger and I could have found him. Instead, what I'd done was sit around and mope because Cass was mad at me, drink too many Mexican beers, and then go home.

That's the way I was thinking as I drove away. One part of me knew he must have been dead already when he didn't show up for work. But when I'm beating myself up I'm not one to let reality interfere.

It was a turning point, though.

I kept my eyes open and made sure no one followed me downtown. At the main branch of the post office, I dropped the first card to Cass in the box on the curb. One each day. That's what I decided.

Something else I decided was to drop out of sight. There's a high-rise motel, the Hamilton Inn, just west of the Loop. Not exactly the Ritz-Carlton but convenient to downtown and all the expressways. It was drizzling when I left the Cavalier at the curb. I checked in and called Harriet from my room. She was out, so I told her voice mail she could reach me with a message on my answering machine or at the motel.

Back outside, it was raining hard. With the Cavalier still missing a window, the driver's seat was soaked. So I drove into the motel garage, took the elevator to the lobby, and went out to the cab stand.

The cabbie wasn't happy when he heard the address, and retaliated by driving at breakneck speed all the way to Saint Ludella's. He got a good tip anyway. After all, if every client who didn't like my attitude or my work habits took it out of my fee...

At the rectory, a dark-skinned woman in a flowered apron over a faded striped dress opened the door just enough so her tall, thin body filled the space between door and door frame. "Father Cunnin'ham? No sir. He gone."

She was gray haired and solemn faced, and looked as honest as a brick.

"You must be Edna," I said.

She eyed me cautiously, head tilted at an angle. "That's right."

"Father Casey mentioned you. You're someone who can be trusted...if a person needs help." Casey hadn't told me that, and I didn't say he had. "I'm the one who was with Father Casey when he was shot."

She read the card I gave her, but said nothing. She still didn't trust me.

"You were gone that afternoon. Three women came in to work on the rummage sale. It was Father Casey's day off. The ladies said they'd answer the door and the phone until you got back—supposed to be three o'clock if I recall right. One of the ladies was very dark and heavyset. Another was light skinned and had one eye that wandered. The third lady—"

"OK, OK, I get the point," she said, opening the door wide and nodding me inside.

In an office near the front door was a desk with a telephone and three sturdy wooden chairs. We sat and faced each other stiffly. She waited for me to say something.

"Have you heard anything?" I asked. "I mean about Father Casey."

She nodded once, as though approving of my opening move. "I keep calling. They keep saying the same thing—they don't know, they don't know. But the Lord gonna pull him through. All us been prayin'. He last this long...he'll make it." There were tears in her eyes.

"I'm glad you're praying."

"So," she said, smoothing the palms of her hands down the front of her apron, "what kind of help?"

"I shouldn't have let Father Casey come with me that day. I keep feeling that what happened was my fault, at least—"

"The Lord works in strange ways. Nothing we can do about some things. 'Cept pray."

"Praying is something I'm not so good at. But I'm going to find out who's responsible. And while I'm looking for them, they're looking for me. I don't want to be found first."

"Uh-huh. So?"

"So...I want to live here."

It wasn't until my finger was on the rectory doorbell that that idea had arisen. Now the idea was growing on me.

Not on Edna, though.

"This here's the priests' house," she said. "Nobody lives here but the fathers. In the old days when it was four or five priests, they had a live-in housekeeper. But no more. I come in four and a half days a week." She shook her head. "Uh-uh. No. You can't stay here. Nope."

"It wouldn't be for long. I'd pay. I could use the housekeeper's room."

"No way. First off, I ain't in charge. Besides, Father Casey was shot way up in the country. Crazy people, on dope, police say."

"The police are wrong."

"What are you talkin' about?"

"I was there, Edna. Father Casey was shot on purpose."

Anger flashed in her eyes. "Don't you *tell* me that. Nobody that knew who he was would shoot Father Casey. No reason to. Father Casey, he talk kinda rough sometimes, but he the sweetest, kindest...That father never hurt nobody."

"It wasn't anything he did, but—"

The phone rang.

Edna answered. "Sain' Ludella." There was a pause while she listened. "No sir, he..." A longer pause. "Yes, sir...the college maybe, but...you're wel—" She slammed the receiver down.

"For Father Cunningham?" I asked.

She nodded. "Ten, fifteen calls just this day for that poor man. Newspapers, TV, 'Father This' from here and 'Father That' from someplace else. Then just nosy folks...some of 'em downright crazy. I don't wonder he left outta here." She stood up. "Anyway, you can't stay. This here's the fathers' house. Now I got work to do."

"Please. Five minutes. Will you just listen?"

"Well..."

My chances might improve if I got deeper inside. "Just time enough for a cup of coffee. Then, if you don't change your mind, I'll go. OK?"

She gave in. On the way down the hall, the smells were the ones I remembered—boiled coffee, waxed wood, the sauerkraut very faint this time. We went past the room where Casey and I first spoke, then a dining room, and on into a large kitchen.

"Coffee's ready," she said, pulling a mug out of a cupboard and pouring. "I keep it hot all day. Father Casey, he likes... Course, he's not here, but..."

"You have any milk?" I asked, staring into a steaming liquid the color of the bottom of my shoe.

We sat on tall metal stools at the counter by the coffeemaker. Skim milk from a plastic jug swirled the coffee into a slightly lighter shade of gray.

"Now," she said, "I only let you this far in 'cause Father Cunnin'ham told me about you. Said you might call. He didn't mention you stayin' here. So," she added, a challenge in her voice, "five minutes."

"First, do you want to give me your last name? Or should I keep calling you Edna, or what?"

"Fauntleroy. Edna Fauntleroy. I thank you for asking. But Edna's easier."

She'd have to know some of what was happening, feel a part of things. "All right, Edna, I'm going to tell you some things, things you can't repeat to anyone—and I mean not anyone— whether you decide to let me stay or not. Can you agree to that?"

She answered slowly, suspicion still in her eyes, but curiosity too. "I never been one to gossip. An' I never been one quick to promise. 'Specially when I don't know what I'm promisin' to." She paused. "But I will say this. If you get to something I believe I got to tell somebody...I'll stop you. How's that?"

"Good enough for me." In fact, better than I'd have dreamed. "So now, to begin with, when Father Casey was shot there were two men. They weren't doped up. They knew exactly what they were doing. One of them deliberately shot Father Casey."

She opened her mouth to speak, but I held up my hand. "Not for something he did, like I said, but...well, I don't know what reason yet. But I do know—and here's the hard part, Edna—that whoever did it has a whole list of people to be killed."

The look on her face said I was joining her own list—the "downright crazy" group.

"I know it sounds insane, Edna. But it's true."

I tasted the long-overheated coffee. It was even worse than it looked. Seeing my reaction, she instinctively got up and started making a fresh pot. The five-minute deadline was a thing of the past.

"You heard about the dead woman, Edna? In the boat near the cottage?"

"It was on the news. That, and the mess at Father Cunnin'ham's place. Only crazy people act like that."

"I agree. Crazy people, all right. But shooting Casey was no accident, and the woman wasn't just a random killing, either. She was on the list. And another person might make the news, too. Later today, or tomorrow. His name was Carl Hemming."

She stopped pouring water into the coffeemaker and looked at me. "Was?"

"He's dead. Supposed to look like suicide. But it wasn't suicide."

"He on this...this *list?*"

"Yes. There's others, too. Maybe including Father Cunningham."

She was startled. "I don't believe it. I mean, he's no Father Casey now, to be sure. He has his...ways. But I like him well enough. Fact is, I like him a lot. He reminds me of my middle boy, quiet, thoughtful, but sort of...out of place all the time. But why would anyone want—"

"All I know is, whoever's behind this must be a maniac. But he's got his reasons, whatever they are. And he has money. I don't think he's doing the actual killing himself. He hires people to do that."

"I don't know. Sounds too much like a TV show or something."

"Except it's real. Father Cunningham's cottage was trashed,

Father Casey got a bullet in his back, and a woman had her throat cut. It all really happened. And you'll hear about Carl Hemming, too.''

"Maybe. So who else is on this...list?"

"Some others, but I can't tell you. Plus, maybe some I don't know about. It's not like I've seen a piece of paper with a list on it. But there's a group of people who are all...well...related in a way.''

"And you? Are you one of them?"

"With me it's different. Whoever it is probably didn't even know who I was. But now there's a reason for wanting me dead, too.''

"What reason?"

"I got in the way. I didn't know I was doing it. But it happened.''

"And you don't know who it is?"

"Not yet. First I need to figure out the reason. Then, who it is should be clear.''

"You know," she said, "you be better off you just go to the police.''

"I can't do that. Not without proof of who's doing this, or at least why. Think about it, Edna. Are the police gonna believe me? You hardly believe me yourself.'' It was clear she had her doubts. "And what if they did believe me, and start investigating? The killing might stop for a while, and then when the police decide there's nothing to it, start up again. No, I need to at least know why it's happening before I can go to the police.''

"Well, you must have *some* idea what the reason is.''

"I've got ideas, sure. But nothing certain. That's why I need some time. Meanwhile, the killer knows who I am, where I live. I need a place to stay.''

"I don't know...I'd have to check with someone.''

"Ask Father Cunningham, then. Will he be back for supper?"

"Who knows? I gave up planning for him 'bout one week after he got here.''

"Not too dependable, huh?"

"Well, far as I know, he never missed his time to say Mass yet. But meals and things? You jus' don't count on him. Course, he's no trouble, neither. I mean, he doesn't complain, or ask for anything special, or like that. Always has a kind word or a compliment. He's kind of...well...stiff, and old-fashioned in a lot of ways. But he's still real nice—at least when he's not...not sick.''

''Let's try to reach him, so you can ask about my staying. I'll keep out of sight. I'll be gone a lot, anyway. I just need a place to sleep. And a telephone and...uh...the use of Father Casey's car, of course.''

I hadn't thought of that before, either.

TWENTY

By SIX O'CLOCK we'd reached Kevin and, while not enthusiastic, he agreed. Before Edna went home, she got me a set of keys, including keys to Casey's car. It was three years old, a brown Dodge Aries, kept in a garage built on the rear of the rectory, opening onto an alley. It needed a tune-up but reluctantly kicked over.

I took the Eisenhower Expressway east, past the University of Illinois Circle Campus, and across the south end of the Loop to Buckingham Fountain and the lakefront. By the time I got to Chapman and Tuleen's on North Dearborn, the rain had stopped.

Paddy Tuleen himself was long dead, and they say there never was a Chapman—only a name Paddy picked for its nonethnic appeal when he opened his funeral home seventy years ago. Most people just called it Tuleen's, anyway.

It would be a one-night wake, and a private burial. That was it for Pamela Masterson—a spin around the lake in a nifty little outboard on Monday, and into the ground on Friday. For no reason other than her friendship with "Judas." Maybe it made some crazy kind of sense to whoever slit her throat. But it made no kind of sense to me.

Chapel B was small and pretty well filled by the couple of dozen visitors. All of them were standing except two who sat next to each other opposite the door, looking bored and watching the sign-in book. I signed in with a name and address that I don't remember, and walked over to Kevin. He was turning away from a conversation with the family. He looked bad.

"What are you doing here?" he asked, barely audibly.

"Want to introduce me to the family?"

"I...I just met them, but I don't remember their names."

"And those two sitting over there, remember their names?"

"No...I don't think so. They look familiar, though. Do you know them?"

"Nope. But they're sheriff's police, I'd bet on it."

"Well anyway," he said, "I'm leaving.

"Fine. I'll meet you at the Lady's."

"Why should I go there?"

"I think it's a good idea."

"What you think is that I'm going to go out and get drunk. Everybody thinks drinking is a problem for me. It's not. I drink when I want to, and I don't drink when I don't want to."

Not having said anything about drinking, I let all that go. "So why don't we meet at the Lady's?"

"Look," he said, "I'm a grown man. I can take care of myself. I appreciate your concern, but I really don't need your help. I have to get on with my life."

Too bad Renata Carroway wasn't there. Talk about a lot of ignorant and naive statements in one breath...It was his drinking he wanted to get on with, but I couldn't chain him to his bedpost.

"Sorry," I said. "It was just a suggestion. Anyway, be careful."

He opened his mouth as if to say something but then turned and walked out the door.

Myself, I went over and stood by the coffin. It didn't look much like the body I'd seen in the boat on Bullhead Lake. For that, at least, I was grateful.

NEAR THE HAMILTON INN, I left the Aries on the street. No one had followed me.

Up in my room, I emptied the complimentary packets of shampoo and hair conditioner into the toilet, soaked the towels and washcloths, left half a can of root beer on the TV set, and rolled around on the bed a while to make it look slept in. Finally, I hung the Do Not Disturb sign on the door handle on my way out.

No more warnings, the twisted cops had said.

My gym bag, with the Beretta tucked in under the clean socks and underwear, was in the trunk of the Cavalier, in the garage on level four. I wanted it.

I went back down to the lobby. For security reasons, the elevator for the garage was separate from those for the guest rooms. Before I could press the button, the door slid open and a tiny woman in a tailored plaid suit was reaching down, ready to pick up the two huge black satchels that flanked her. She nodded gratefully when I held the elevator door open, letting her step off. I continued to hold the door as a man with a tan raincoat over his arm and a worried look on his gaunt face hurried over.

"Gee, thanks," he managed, nearly out of breath, and I followed him inside.

The man set down his briefcase and panted as he studied the array of buttons for a few seconds, then punched 3 as the door slid closed.

"Hit four, please," I said, rather than reaching around him.

"No need for that," he answered. No breathlessness now. His voice smooth and easy, matching the way he slid back the raincoat to reveal the black automatic in his right hand, pointed at my stomach.

"Shit," I sighed, eloquence abandoning me.

"Yes. But one shot, you know? It'll be over before you know it."

The elevator came to a stop. When the door slid open he grabbed the briefcase with his left hand and gestured impatiently with the gun. I stepped out ahead of him into a vestibule and started toward the metal door that opened onto the parking area.

I stopped and spoke back over my shoulder. "Maybe—"

"Forget it," he said, shoving me forward with his left fist between my shoulder blades. The briefcase clenched in his fist banged hard against my back.

I pushed through the heavy door and he followed me into the garage.

We stood in a space about as wide as two cars, with bold yellow lines painted on the floor to indicate no parking, to leave access to the elevator. Parking slots stretched left and right, filled with cars. There was a lane for moving traffic, then another row of cars parked diagonally along the wall opposite us.

An old Ford station wagon full of mom and dad and kids came along the traffic lane from our left, between the rows of parked cars. As it passed, a grinning five-year-old waved our way, then stuck out her tongue when we didn't respond. The Ford went around the corner far to the right and the sound of it disappeared gradually down the ramp toward level two.

When there was no one else in sight, no sound of more approaching cars, the man behind me whistled—long and loud and shrill. I remembered spending the entire eleventh summer of my life trying unsuccessfully to learn to whistle like that.

An answering whistle echoed through the concrete parking area, seeming to come from a long distance. A few seconds passed. It was very quiet. Then, on the level above us a motor roared into life. There was the short, sharp bark of tires against concrete once, then once again, then only the sound of the engine.

We waited. The air was damp and heavy with the odor of spilled oil, raw gasoline, and exhaust fumes.

Tires squealed down the ramp hidden to our left, and the vehicle came around the corner. It wasn't a car but a panel truck, a white minivan. I caught myself mindlessly wondering whether it was a Voyager or a Caravan.

I twisted my head to plead my case again. "Why can't—"

"Too late," he said. He pushed me forward again, as he had before, with the hand that held the briefcase. A clumsy gesture—and the announcement of just that instant of distraction.

How many times had Dr. Sato or one of his students come at me from behind? A thousand? Two thousand? With Dr. Sato, there's no praise, no blame. Only practice—over and over and over again.

It happens in tenths of a second. A slight move forward with the shove, then twist to the right and backwards, pivoting on the left foot, and drop simultaneously. Palms to the floor for an instant to reverse momentum. Then move to the right, arm outstretched, straightening the body and up and over in a circular motion. If everything goes right, you catch him moving your direction, your arm between his legs, your hand reaching up past his crotch and around toward the small of his back.

With the circular motion, with the right timing, and if he's not too heavy compared to you, he should fly right up and over you, and land a few feet ahead of where you were standing a second ago.

He did. But his head hit the low concrete ceiling on the way.

By that time the minivan was there and screeching to a stop, but still moving as the man's body slammed into the right front fender. It caught him and held him upright and spun him around along the side of the vehicle. Through it all were crunching sounds and thudding sounds, strangely audible above the roar of the motor, the screeching of brakes. Finally the van stood still, rocking gently, as he slid down its side and onto the floor.

I was running to my left by the time the driver was out of the van. Looking back, I saw he'd chosen to ignore me. He opened the van's sliding door and heaved the gunman inside. From the corner where the ramp led up to level four, I watched him toss the man's gun and briefcase inside and slam the door shut. Then, back at the driver's door, he paused and glanced around. But he climbed into the vehicle and drove away.

No matter how many times someone had come at me from behind at Dr. Sato's, each time they've been ready to be thrown. There's a mat on the floor. There's no low ceiling, and no van. Never a van. Never the terrible sad crunch and thud, or the slow slide to the oil-stained concrete floor. None of that at Dr. Sato's.

Riding the elevator down with my gym bag, I was dizzy and nauseated and tried to focus on why what I'd done was necessary. The man would have killed me. But what's necessity, anyway? I didn't need to have been on the elevator in the first place, going after my own automatic because there'd be "no more warnings." I didn't need to be running myself in circles around the city because Harriet Mallory was suddenly worried about a son she'd spent a lifetime telling herself she'd forgotten.

I didn't need to be doing what I was doing. But where would that leave Kevin? or Celia? Where would it leave Casey? No, I didn't need to be doing these things. But where would that leave me?

Outside, the white minivan was nowhere in sight. I drove Casey's Aries back to Saint Ludella's and went in through the garage. No one followed me.

But no one had followed me to the Hamilton Inn, either. So how did they find me? Canvass every motel in the city, on the chance I might check into one? Not very practical. So how did they know?

The only explanation I could think of wasn't encouraging.

There was an open bottle of white wine—"intended for ecclesiastical use,'' the label said—in the rectory refrigerator. I poured out a tumbler and took it to the phone.

Harriet picked up on the first ring.

"It's Foley. You must have gotten my message."

"What are you talking about?"

"My message—where to contact me."

"Of course I did. But I haven't called. There's nothing to talk about yet. Why are you staying at a motel?"

"I like motels. They make me feel like I'm on my way somewhere. Who did you tell?"

"Who did I tell what?"

"Where I'm staying."

"Don't be absurd. Why would I tell anyone, for God's sake?"

"Jerry. You told Jerry."

"I didn't tell Jerry anything. I haven't talked to anyone about you, or about my...about this whole thing. But I've given it a lot of thought. I need to make some decisions. I'm meeting with some people tomorrow."

"Who's that? Drake? Richardson?"

"That's not your affair. In the meantime, you're not...doing anything, are you?"

"Of course not," I lied.

"Good. I'll talk to you when I've reached a decision. Right now I'm very busy." She hung up. Whatever happened to goodbye?

She sure sounded truthful. And why would she tell anyone, for God's sake?

I prowled through the rectory, bottom to top. It was an easy hundred years old, a three-story stone battleship with meeting rooms in the basement, offices, dining room, kitchen, and housekeeper's rooms on the first floor, and living quarters for priests—God knows how many—on the second and third floors. You'd need a tank to break in.

There was nobody there but me.

And, of course, the ghosts. Whenever I stood still for more than three seconds, there was a creak from somewhere, then they'd murmur and groan, whisper and sigh. They might have been the ghosts of priests, praying. Even so, they made me nervous. Maybe they knew it was too late to pray for the man on the floor of the minivan. Maybe he was dead and they didn't like that. I knew he might be, and I didn't like it.

I lay in my clothes on the lumpy couch in the tiny housekeeper's parlor behind the kitchen. I knew I wouldn't sleep.

TWENTY-ONE

THE SMELL OF COFFEE woke me up. A shower, a shave, and a change of underwear later, I joined Edna in the kitchen.

It was your basic bacon and egg, toast and coffee breakfast. I sat at the kitchen table and looked up at Edna. She wore the same dress she'd worn the day before. It looked freshly ironed. "Meals like this," I said, "maybe I'll become a priest."

She frowned. "You wouldn't like it."

"Why not?"

She didn't bother to explain. "I been through this whole place this morning," she complained, "turning off lights everywhere. How you think Father Casey gonna pay the electric bill?"

"Well...lights make the place look lived in." *And keep away the ghosts.*

"Lights on all night? That looks lived in? Surprised nobody broke in, is all I can say."

"Godzilla couldn't break into this place, Edna. But I'll do better tonight. Any word on Father Casey?"

She sat down across from me. "I talked to his sister this morning. They just don't know. Doctor says things keep goin' wrong inside of him...even if he gets better...maybe he'll never be strong enough to come back to Sain' Ludella." She stared down at the table, her shoulders trembling.

"He'll get better," I said. "And he'll be back, Edna. He loves it here. This is his home."

She got up and started taking dishes from the table.

"Anyway, I've got a great idea."

"Oh?" She eyed me suspiciously.

"Yes. There's...uh...someone else who should come and live in the rectory for a while, too."

"Oh no," she said. It was instinctive. "It just ain't right. This is the fathers' house. One man not a priest staying here is bad enough. Two just won't do."

"Maybe so," I said. "But who said anything about another *man?*"

She set the plate down, hard. "Now you look here..."

"Don't get the wrong idea," I said. "Not a girlfriend or anything. And it's just until I can get this whole business straightened out. Besides, she'd probably even help out a little, and she'd keep you company during the day."

"I don't need help, or company."

"Maybe not. But she does." I paused. "She's in danger, and I need to know she's OK."

AN HOUR LATER Edna was fully on board. She'd listened carefully to my theory. She'd combed the *Sun-Times* and the *Tribune* and read about the "apparent suicide" of Carl Hemming. Neither paper gave it much space, but the *Times* quoted the note in the typewriter. I tore out the small article and tucked it in my billfold.

We called Kevin and told him what we had in mind.

"No way," he said immediately. "I don't want my mother in that neighborhood." Then, recalling that Edna was listening on another extension, he tried to be a little delicate. "What I mean is...well, you know what I mean. I just..."

"Yeah, I know, Father," Edna said, rescuing him. "This here's a bad area, all right. No doubt about it."

"But look at it this way," I said. "This rectory is built like a fortress. She'd be safer here than anywhere I can think of. Plus, no one will know where she is but you and me and Edna."

"Well..." he started.

"Besides," Edna said, "I'm gonna stay here all day an' all night too. So it'll be someone with her all the time." That had been Edna's idea. She seemed intrigued by the idea of staying in "the fathers' house" all night.

Kevin gave in. He'd find out from Celia's lawyer where she was staying, and call back and tell Edna.

He didn't mention Carl Hemming. So we didn't either.

After that I called the hospital. They were getting used to my calls, and told me a little more, which was more depressing than ever—talk of "sepsis," and possibly even more surgery.

Edna was going shopping. On her way out the door she said,

"By the way, this here big old house creaks and groans all the time. You just don't hear it so much till it's dark—and you're alone." She smiled. "Father Casey, he left the lights on all night too, first week or so."

WHAT PEOPLE FIND HARD to keep straight is that we have two separate judicial systems operating side by side—the federal courts and the state courts. Each has its criminal cases and its civil cases. In civil cases, where they're heard depends on the plaintiff's theory in suing the defendant, and on whether the parties to the suit are residents of the same state or not.

So, *Boulevard Center vs. Krackauer* was in federal court because Harriet's clients, the abortion clinics, claimed the defendants were violating the clinics' rights under the United States Constitution—federal law. On the other hand, most ordinary accident cases are heard in the state court.

Accident cases were what I wanted to check. I drove downtown to the Daley Center, the courthouse for state court civil actions in Chicago. The clerk's office is on the eighth floor. You have to take an elevator to seven, circle around, and go up an escalator to eight. No sense making it easy.

I was the oldest person at the public computer terminals in the noisy, bustling office. The rest were eager young law students or paralegals sent over by their employers—the ones who didn't have office computers linked to the court's docket system—to check the status of cases. One of the kids lent me a hand, and pretty soon I was scanning down the list on the monitor screen for cases against Cunningham, Kevin, in the last three years.

There were just two: CUNNINGHAM, KEVIN CHARLES, JR. and CUNNINGHAM, KEVIN, M.D. No good. But, if someone had sued Kevin for the accident in which his woman passenger was killed, they'd have sued the archdiocese, too. That's where the money was. I checked under ARCHDIOCESE, CATHOLIC ARCHDIOCESE, and CATHOLIC ARCHBISHOP, and came up with a baker's dozen. I wrote down the case numbers and moved into another part of the computer program. Half an hour later, I'd learned that none of the cases in the past three years had included Father Kevin Peter Cunningham. Too bad.

But I hadn't thought the idea—that someone hated Kevin enough to kill off all his relatives and friends because he'd killed someone dear to them in a drunk driving accident—was that great an idea, anyway.

I called the Lady to tell her that her idea hadn't turned up anything.

"Well," she said, "the woman who died must have had family, even if they didn't sue. By the way, as long as you're there, why not check Harriet's name too? Maybe *she* has enemies."

"Why would someone who didn't like Harriet kill Kevin's friends?"

"I really don't know. But it can't hurt to look."

The computer records went back fifteen years. Harriet wasn't there.

On a hunch, I called the Death Penalty Clearinghouse, an outfit that provides research assistance for defense lawyers working on death penalty cases.

"Happy Mallory?" the man said on the phone. "I used to try cases before her myself. One of the few women judges in the Criminal Division back then. She was in felony court awhile, then drug court just before she left the bench. Boy, she'd send those poor suckers away to the shithouse...wham! Not bat an eye. Consistent, though. Treated every defendant like the same piece of shit—regardless of race, creed, or place of national origin. Anyway, she never had any death cases. I'm sure of it."

So I knew that if anyone had a beef against Kevin—or Harriet—at least they hadn't filed suit. And I'd eliminated one motive for hating Harriet, whatever difference that made. I was either getting nowhere, or successfully eliminating nonproductive avenues. It's all in the attitude.

I phoned Edna. Kevin had called with the news that Celia was staying with friends in Oak Park.

TWENTY-TWO

HEAD STRAIGHT WEST from the Loop, past Saint Ludella's and the rest of the West Side, across Austin Boulevard, and you're in Oak Park. Maybe no other town in the world—"actually it's not a town but a village," they like to remind you—has worked harder at racial integration than Oak Park, or taken more abuse for its effort, from both sides. Black and white together, angry, not able to turn the wheel on which they turn.

The address was on Vidalia Street, a large frame home on a block lined with huge trees and NO PARKING signs. I'd have been the only car on the street, so I parked a block away and around the corner.

When I pressed and released the doorbell, the homely whine of a vacuum cleaner from behind the sturdy oak front door was punctuated by two "bongs," a minor third apart. A B on the press of the button and an A-flat on the release, I thought.

Celia opened the door, one hand on the now silent Hoover. I'd purposely not called ahead, but she didn't look surprised to see me. "Come in," she said. "Ed and Laura—my hosts—aren't here. They left this morning for Ireland."

Inside, we sat at a formal table in a formal dining room, complete with crystal chandelier and wood-beamed ceiling. A cool breeze flowed through the room from open windows somewhere in the house—a little too cool, really, but fresh spring air. It took me three cups of bland herbal tea, interrupted by one trip to the bathroom, to get the whole story told. Not once did she say, "That's crazy" or "I don't believe you." Maybe nothing she heard would ever surprise her again. Jail time does that to a person.

When I'd finished, I told her I wanted to move her into the rectory, and got ready to launch into all the reasons why she should. She stopped me and asked, "Are you certain Happy Mallory didn't tell anyone about the motel?"

"I'm not *certain*. But why would she lie about it? Let me tell you, Celia. She's struggling right now. She doesn't want to give up her shot at political fame and fortune. But there's something else happening, too. It's in her voice, and in her eyes. I swear she's developing feelings for Kevin. She wishes she weren't. But she is."

"I understand. And that will continue." She paused, her eyes closed for a few long seconds. "Happy's husband could have listened to her phone messages, couldn't he?"

"I thought of that. But it still doesn't really explain anything."

"So," she said, "you want me to move into the rectory."

"Yes. You see—"

"Lots of people know I came here. It hadn't occurred to me to keep it a secret."

"Why would it?" I said. "That's why you should leave."

"That will be fine."

"It will? No fight?"

She smiled. "I don't mean to disappoint you. And I certainly don't look forward to being locked away again, so soon."

"But it's for your own safety. Someone wants to kill you," I started, not willing to give up the arguments I'd rehearsed on the drive to Oak Park.

She cut me off. "I don't know that I care much whether...that is, death frightens me, of course. But it's so inevitable, anyway. However, if what you say is true, then as long as I'm alive it's not likely anything will happen to Kevin."

"That was going to be my clincher."

She smiled and stood up. "Let me pack my things—again." She disappeared up the stairs.

Five minutes later she was back. "No need to leave a note," she said. "Ed and Laura know I'm not very predic—"

B, A-flat.

We both jumped at the sound of the chimes.

As she turned toward the front of the house, I grabbed her hand. "Get down," I whispered.

She didn't move, just stared at me.

The double chimes sounded again, twice this time, in rapid succession. *B, A-flat. B, A-flat.*

I pulled her down to the floor. "It's probably nothing. But crawl to the back door and wait for me. Please."

By now the front doorknob was twisting this way and that, the door being pushed and pulled against the doorjamb. Celia dropped to her hands and knees and crawled toward the kitchen, while I duck-walked the other way, the Beretta in my hand.

The living room was a rectangle running along the front of the house. Across from me a set of bay windows bulged out in a semicircle from the street side of the rectangle. The heavy drapes were drawn aside, leaving some sort of gauzy curtains to obscure the view. I could see through them well enough to know there was a car parked out front—a dark-colored sedan. A man stood beside it.

The chimes rang again, and again, and again. Continuously now, in rapid minor thirds. Left to themselves they were genteel, subdued chimes. But the impatient finger punching the button made them angry, ominous.

The front door foyer was across the living room from me and to my left. At the other end, to my right, french doors opened into a sun room, with lots of white wicker furniture and hanging plants. I went that way.

Crouching beneath an open window in the sun room, I listened as a nearby robin sent out calls of curiosity, each short trill ending with a question mark, as though anxious at the persistence of the chimes.

I raised my head above the sill and looked out. It was the Bonneville, all right. And the man beside it, scanning up and down the street, had one hand deep in the side pocket of a brown corduroy sport coat.

The chimes kept ringing, and I kept hoping they hadn't brought a third man. If they had, by now he was crouching outside the back door.

I lifted the gun and rested my wrist on the windowsill. The man by the car wasn't looking my way. Sending thought waves at him across the yard, I willed him not to turn toward me. I begged him not to. Because if he did, he was dead.

I sighted, squeezed once, then dropped back down to the floor. The gunshot was very loud.

And then there was almost no sound at all. No more chimes in minor thirds. No more robin's questions. Only the hushed sound of the Bonneville's chassis settling down over the blown-out front tire.

Finally, a woman's voice, anxious, called out from somewhere across the street, "What's going on? What is it?"

The man near the car called loudly, politely, back to her, "Nothing, ma'am. Just blew a tire, that's all." Then, not so loud, he called to his partner, who must still have been on the front porch. "C'mon, asshole. Let's get this tire changed and get the fuck outta here."

On my way to the back door, I called 911. "Shots fired," I exaggerated, and then hung up.

THE THREE OF US had a late lunch together at the rectory. One of my favorites—tomato soup and egg salad sandwiches. We had a great time, all things considered. Celia made the egg salad. She let me add mustard and celery salt, and everyone agreed it made all the difference. Edna said a blessing. It was a little long, to my mind, and included prayers for Casey, Kevin, Celia, Edna's middle boy—even me.

When the dishes were done, Edna went home to get some things for staying overnight. She lived only a block away.

Celia and I sat alone in the kitchen with mugs of coffee. She told me again how attached Kevin had been to Patrick Cunningham, and how hard that made it for her to remove Patrick from their home. "I'm not sure Kevin has ever forgiven me," she said. "That may be why he became so attached to Noreen. Her death was so senseless, and coming when it did, on top of all the other problems poor Kevin was having..."

"Celia, I'm wondering...that woman who was killed in Kevin's automobile accident. Apparently no suit was filed. Was a claim made against Kevin? Was a lawyer involved?"

"A claim was settled without any suit being filed. Kevin didn't have his own lawyer. The cardinal's lawyers handled it. The firm was Kaluga and Dayton. Kevin mentioned a lawyer named Butterfield, but I don't think he was in charge."

"OK. And who represented the woman's family?"

"I never knew." She frowned. "There was a lot I never knew, actually. That wasn't the first problem Kevin had, and—"

"Another case? What was that one about?"

"Not a case. Not that I know of. But there was something, earlier. I only heard about it after the accident, and then only hints. It was when Kevin was at his first parish." She slid her mug around, tracing circles on the table top.

"And after that he was moved to a different church?" I asked.

"Yes. And it was around then that he seemed to lose control of his drinking. Although...maybe that would have happened anyway. Maybe his father's drinking got passed along to him, adopted or not. Kevin so adored his father—my husband, I mean. He...he never got over Patrick's being gone. We could never talk about it, you know? I—"

"Celia..."

"I'm sorry. I'm repeating myself. Well, then at the new parish, he had that terrible accident. The lawyers seemed anxious to settle the case right away. Of course, I was in jail. The woman was Mexican—I don't remember the name—and there was something about her family—"

The slamming of the front door echoed down the hall to the kitchen, followed by Edna's call, "It's just me!"

"Anyway," Celia continued, "the cardinal's lawyers were worried about the woman's family. Plus, from the little I heard, it seemed they were afraid the lawyer would somehow be able to use that earlier incident."

"To hurt Kevin?"

"Well, to help the family's case somehow. What bothered Kevin most was that his lawyers seemed more worried about the archdiocese and the cardinal being hurt than about him. Of course, it was the cardinal's money. I mean, Kevin had no money. Nor did I, by then."

Edna appeared at the door, an overnight bag in her hand. "Here I—"

I raised my hand and stopped her. "Please, Edna, give us just a few minutes."

"Well," she said, "lah-dee-dah, I'm sure." Her indignation was so exaggerated we knew she was faking it. She disappeared.

"That earlier matter, was that a car accident, too?" I asked.

"As I said, I don't know. Kevin wouldn't talk about it. But then we never did talk that much, Kevin and I, not about serious things. For example, I only learned from you that he was involved in antiabortion activities. His great love used to be working with kids. Maybe when they transferred him to the southeast side there weren't many young people in church, so he had to find something else to get involved in, I don't know. I want to help you help him—but there's so much that I don't know."

That made two of us.

TWENTY-THREE

IT WAS NEARLY FOUR O'CLOCK when I backed Casey's Aries into the littered alley behind Saint Ludella's. The warm afternoon had the neighborhood alive with shouting and loud laughter and kids I wished were inside doing homework or practicing the piano— and wailing sirens never far off. With the windows rolled up and my Cubs cap yanked down, I hoped the white guy pulling out of the alley would pass as one of the "fathers." In a few minutes I was eastbound on the Eisenhower.

Jack Butterfield would remember me. He'd been one of the few prosecutors I'd gotten along with, back when my clients might have been better served if I'd gotten along with more prosecutors. These days he was a partner and a rising star in the litigation section at the law firm of Kaluga and Dayton.

That late on a Friday afternoon in spring, though, the last thing Butterfield wanted was an unannounced visitor.

"May I tell him what it's regarding, sir?" the receptionist asked, not very encouragingly.

"Regarding information about Kevin Cunningham."

A secretary came, then, to usher me back to his office. Butterfield was standing beside his desk when we got there, slipping a pinstriped suit coat over a white shirt and stylish suspenders. He was still slim, with the lanky build of a tennis player. His thick black hair was graying gracefully in just the right places.

As we shook hands there was a touch of sympathetic condescension in his eyes. He'd made it; I hadn't. Looking around at the casebooks lying open and the reams of paper stacked everywhere in his cluttered office, I found myself pitying him in return.

We stood there, each happy not to be the other.

"I was just trying to think what cases we had against each other," he said. "Otis Ransom was one, right? Criminal sexual assault and attempted murder? Man, what a donnybrook, huh?"

"Yeah, well, you win some, you lose some." I wasn't sure which case it was, or who'd won.

"But," he said, "it was a fair fight. Neither one of us lied to the other. Well...me, but just a little." He smiled.

He was a decent guy. He'd probably won whatever case we were talking about.

"You said you have information," he said. "Have a seat."

"Not quite what I said." But I sat down.

He leaned against the side of his desk, willing to listen but not willing to give the impression he had all the time in the world.

"I'm working for someone," I continued, "who's the mother of a former client of yours."

"Sure. Father Cunningham. And his mother's name was what...Clara or something? Is she still...uh..."

"Celia. She's out." I paused. "What I'm looking at might be related to what you handled for the archdiocese and Kevin."

"He always preferred *Father* Cunningham with me," Butterfield said.

"I call him Kevin," I said. "He's getting used to it." When he grinned and nodded, I went on. "I need information. But the conversation's confidential, OK?"

"That part's not a problem." He went behind his desk and sat down. "But there won't be much I can disclose. First, it might be privileged. Second, that was a very, very difficult situation."

"Two situations, as I understand it."

He shrugged his shoulders, not denying it. "Everything touches everything else."

"I know there was a case that was settled, an automobile accident. The other matter I don't know anything about, except I think it turned the accident into a bigger case than it was worth."

Butterfield studied his hands, folded motionless on the pile of papers in front of him. Then, as the thumb of one hand began rubbing the back of the other, he looked up again. "I'm not saying I'll tell you anything. But why do you want to know?"

"Someone has a grudge against Kevin Cunningham in a very big way. And it's nothing I can go to the police with."

Butterfield reached for his phone and punched one of the buttons. "Marge? Get me Harvey Traffinger, right away." He looked at his watch and then spoke to me. "Harvey'll be in."

There was a pause, then Butterfield spoke into the phone. "Harve? Jack Butterfield. Look, I've got a guy here in my office. Says Celia Cunningham's home from the farm and he's doing some work for her. Wanted to verify that...Right...Foley...Right, I know him from way back, but I'm just covering my ass...No, that's all. Listen, you take care, OK? 'Bye."

"So, did I pass?"

He looked at his watch. "Let's talk on the way out."

I followed him all the way to the elevators before he turned and said, "I'd like to help, mostly because that priest didn't deserve all the grief he already got, and it sounds like now he's in for more. He was under a lot of stress when I knew him, and acted kind of strange, but I liked him. Thing is, I probably can't tell you much you don't already know. You're right about the death case. It wasn't worth what we paid. You've guessed there was some leverage from the earlier matter, but I can't talk about that at all. I would if I could."

"Fine," I said, "but you didn't have to call Harvey Traffinger just so you could tell me you can't tell me anything." An elevator arrived and I started toward it.

"Right." He grabbed my arm. "Stay here awhile."

What stopped me cold wasn't his hand on my arm, but something about his voice. It was more than just worry. Closer to fear.

"What is it?" I asked.

"Look, we had a situation that could have blown up in our faces in more ways than one. Fortunately, the lawyer on the other side was able to control his clients—to a degree—and was big enough that he didn't need to make a splash on this one. I mean, he worked us like a pro and squeezed us for more than his clients deserved. But he also had some sense."

"Who was this lawyer?"

"One of the best, Cleveland Richardson. The dead woman's family had a different lawyer at first, but then he got into it because he...well...anyway, he took the case over."

"You mean he heard about the woman's death and chased the case."

"All I'm saying is he got into the case and he kept the lid on everything. His people walked away with buckets of money and our people didn't get hurt too bad, other than having to fill the buckets, of course. But it could have been worse. If it hadn't been for him..." Butterfield's voice trailed off.

"Hey, Jack, come off it. This Richardson's just a very rich, very powerful lawyer, with lots and lots of friends...judges, politicians—probably popes. That doesn't make him God, you know?"

"That's right. And I didn't say I liked him, either, because I don't. He's too...smooth, too perfect. There's something strange about him. I mean, I wouldn't trust him with my daughter, you know? But he did a great job in the Cunningham matters. You can ask Harry Haskell. He was in charge for us. He was chief counsel for the archdiocese for years. Although...when I say you can ask him, that's rhetorical. He died two months ago in his sleep. I've got all his clients now."

A subdued gong signaled the arrival of another elevator. We let it come and go.

"So what are we talking about?" I asked.

"What do you mean?"

"I mean, we can't be hiding out in the hall so you can tell me how Richardson's a creep but he whipped your asses and you admired him for it."

"Right." He paused. "Put it this way. You got a wife, Mal? Kids?"

"A wife that comes and goes. No kids."

"Maybe that's good. Me, I've got a wife that stays, and three kids. I hate to say it, but me, I'd bow out of anything touching that priest."

"What are you trying to tell me?"

"I don't know what you're working on. I don't want to know. The priest was immature, a pain in the ass sometimes, but basically a good person. He got a bad deal from the start, and I...well, I participated in that. I'm not proud of it. Frankly, that's why I'm talking to you. Then the accident. No doubt about that one, of course. Maybe you can help him. I suppose what I'm doing is just...warning you."

He lowered his voice another notch as an elevator arrived and the doors slid open. ''When the second deal was done, Richardson seemed relieved everything was over. I think even he was a little afraid by that time—afraid of his own clients.'' The elevator left without us. ''All the people involved were...well...the wrong people to make trouble for.''

''All the people? Wrong people? What the hell are we talking about here?''

''We're talking about power, and money, and influence. All of them. Believe me, you don't want trouble with any of them. Not the clients, not their relatives, not even Richardson. You could...well...get hurt.''

Another gong. Another elevator. It was empty and we got on.

''If you had any sense, you'd stay out of this, believe me,'' he said.

That was stale advice.

''Look,'' I said, ''I might need one more thing.''

''That's it. I can't—''

''Not more information. Just...someone might be asking about me. I don't even know who yet. But if someone does, I want you to tell them I can be trusted. That's all. I don't care what else you say. But tell them the truth about me.''

''That means you're not going to follow my advice.''

''What advice? We never had this conversation.''

''Right,'' he said.

The elevator stopped and more people got on. We talked about the weather and Jack Butterfield's tennis elbow all the way down—then went our separate ways.

TWENTY-FOUR

SOME PEOPLE hear "ambulance chaser" and picture a plaid suit prowling the emergency room, pen and retainer contract in hand. The truth is, though, you don't need gravy on your tie to chase cases. What you need is ambition—call it greed—enough to override any sensitivity about hawking your services to people who've recently been traumatized. Bigger, more sophisticated chasers chase bigger, more sophisticated cases. Some very good lawyers are very good chasers.

Cleveland Richardson was a very good personal injury plaintiffs' lawyer. If you believed the press coverage generated by his marketing consultants, he was the best. And even if there is no *best,* most people agreed he was right up there with the champs.

Richardson would tell you his goal was fair compensation for injured persons. That's a pat answer from the personal injury lawyers' catechism. And, as far as I'm concerned, a damn good answer and a very worthy goal. Construction workers still fall off buildings; drivers still maim and kill in record numbers; home handymen still slice off body parts with power tools; toddlers still stab and choke themselves with their toys. But those things don't happen nearly as often as they would if the lawyers didn't make it so damned expensive for defendants and their insurance companies.

It's when the p.i. lawyers speak as though justice for injured persons is the *only* thing that motivates them—that's when they shatter the credibility barrier. Fair compensation is an admirable goal, for sure, but it's that contingent fee that makes a person work fifteen-hour days.

I had no problem with Cleveland Richardson's pulling down millions every year. He was worth it to his clients. Besides, trying cases takes a terrible toll, and successful trial lawyers pay dearly for their success. Actually, I'd never seen Richardson up close until that night at the Pavillon, and I'd been surprised. He looked a lot more worn than you'd expect for a man hardly sixty years old.

Successful plaintiffs' lawyers, like successful politicians, have enormous egos. That keeps them away from large law firms with their shared authority. While they're young they run solo operations, usually with a handful of associate lawyers who come and go. When they get a little older, many of them take a promising associate or two, and make them partners. Richardson hadn't done that. He was still the sole captain of his ship, Cleveland Richardson and Associates, Ltd.

Several years earlier, he'd left the Loop and gone north of the river, where he bought and renovated a turn-of-the-century three-flat apartment building, converting it into a posh suite of offices. I'd never have known that if Barney Green hadn't shown me the spread in *Crain's Chicago Business*—two full pages, with color photos—about the grand opening of Richardson's new suite. According to *Crain's,* the renovation got an honorable mention in some urban architecture contest.

Richardson made lots of money and I didn't fault him for that. And I didn't fault him for chasing that case against Kevin—which he'd surely done—and squeezing as much money out of it as he could. When a life gets snuffed out by a drunk driver, someone ought to pay—and the deeper the available pockets, the better.

But there was something about that particular case, and something about an earlier case, that I needed to know. Butterfield wouldn't tell me. And Richardson sure wouldn't, either. So there was no sense asking. But I needed to know.

THERE'S A LITTLE GRILL around the corner from the Eighteenth District Police Station on Chicago Avenue, a mile north of downtown. At the counter, drinking too much coffee and turning the pages of a day-old *Sun-Times,* I passed the time by trying to distinguish the *real* drug dealers and *real* hookers from the undercover cops. Since they're pretty much cut from the same cloth, but at a different bias, it's not possible.

Certain activities are best left to specialists. Breaking and entering, for example, should be left to people with glass cutters and suction cups and sophisticated lock-picking devices, people with patience enough to wait until 3 a.m. or so. I lacked all those things. By nine-thirty I'd convinced myself that the night people would be up and around until dawn anyway, so why wait any longer. I paid up and set out to investigate Cleveland Richardson's case against Kevin.

The building was a few blocks away, one in a row of similar renovated two-and three-flats converted to offices, set close to the sidewalk on a wide street with an alley running behind them. From the front it looked deserted. A light glowed over the door, a short flight up from street level and about as inconspicuous as the pitcher's mound on opening day.

From a booth a block away I telephoned Richardson's office and listened to a recorded message: "...please leave your name and a brief message at the tone and someone will get back to you as soon as possible."

After the beep, I said, "If anyone's there, pick up," talking through my Cubs cap over the mouthpiece. "I have an emergency message for Cleveland Richardson. It's about...uh...about Sam Drake, and about money and big trouble and...well...the Feds. Pick up the phone, goddamn it. And pick it up quick." If that didn't get a response...

No one picked up.

Just off the alley behind Richardson's building was a liquor store. I went in and bought a half-pint of Dimitri gin. According to the clerk, it was cheap—and it packed a powerful odor.

Access to Richardson's backyard from the alley was through a sturdy wooden gate, set into a slight alcove in a high brick wall. There were dim lights in the alley, but no people just then. The gate had a dead bolt that the last person through had neglected to throw, and a spring lock that I could handle. I took a mouthful of Dimitri, swallowing a little and spitting the rest down the front of my shirt, then splashed more around my face and neck like cologne. Stuffing the capped bottle down into my hip pocket, I went through the gate and into the backyard without a problem.

The yard wasn't large, but it had a tree and some bushes, and new grass growing beside the new brick sidewalk that led to a high wooden porch at the rear of the building. No lights went on, no sirens sounded. I went up the wooden steps. There were no visible security wires running around the windowpanes in the back door. If they didn't dead-bolt their gate, maybe they weren't all that security conscious. Maybe there wasn't a burglar alarm.

And maybe there was.

I began stomping on the wooden porch as hard and loud as I could, then started yelling. "Hey! Where is everybody?" Acting the drunk. Hollering at the top of my voice. "Hey! Answer the door!" Slipping into a pair of thin leather gloves. "Anybody home?"

Nothing. No sound but the same street noises there'd been all along. No lights went on in adjoining buildings. Nothing.

"C'mon! Open up in there!" I pounded on the back door with my fists and slapped my gloved palms against the glass. "Open up! I need a goddamn lawyer!"

Nothing. A long, long five minutes of nothing.

Beneath the wooden porch was a small stack of bricks, maybe left over from the sidewalk. Back up on the porch, I first shouted, "Where the hell are the lawyers when you really need help!" then paused, breathed deeply, and smashed a brick through the back-door window, the pane closest to the door knob.

The glass was still falling as I raced down the steps, out of the yard, and into the alley. Beside the open gate, I sat on the pavement, back against the brick wall, and cradled the gin bottle in my gloved hands. A car came down the alley, slowing almost to a stop as it passed. Two young couples in the car looked down on me. I toasted them with Dimitri before they sped away.

Time passed. Eventually I got up and walked, first to the end of the alley and then a slow, four-block-long square around Richardson's building, ending up back at the open gate in the alley. Everything was as it had been. No one was taking advantage of the open gate and the broken window.

Who says our city is crime-ridden?

TWENTY-FIVE

BACK ON THE PORCH, with the gate to the alley closed behind me, I reached through the broken window and unlocked the door. Stepping inside, the erratic flight of my heartbeat and the lightheadedness I felt had nothing to do with gin in my bloodstream. It might have been the high professional burglars talk about, but it felt like fear to me, plain and simple. I didn't want to go to jail, and if Butterfield was right, that was the least of my worries. What I wanted was out of there.

But I stood there and thought about Casey and talked my pulse rate down.

A dark hallway led to the front of the building, past a series of closed doors on my right. I opened each door cautiously. A broom closet. Then a room with a Xerox machine as big as my car and a sign taped to the wall saying the copier wouldn't operate without entry of the "correct employee code letters." Then a bathroom. The fourth room was larger. The thin beam of my penlight darted, like a minnow in a rocky pool, across mounds of file folders piled on two tables in the center of the room, then bumped up against rows of metal shelving that covered three walls of the room from floor to ceiling. Each row of shelves was crammed with red-brown expandable folders, most of them bulging with papers. Richardson's case files.

I removed a few files, carefully noting where to replace them. Each folder was labeled with the client's name and was subdivided into sections of manila folders with titles like PLEADINGS, CORRESPONDENCE, INSURANCE, INVISTIGATION, and MEDICAL RECORDS. Some cases fit into one expandable folder; others took up multiple folders and many feet of shelf space.

The organization of the shelves proved simple enough—ceiling to floor, left to right, Abramson to Zustro, according to Richardson's clients' names. A lot of good that did me, without the name of Richardson's client in any case against Kevin as defendant.

Sifting through and identifying the defendant in each case looked like a week's work, and my nervous system wouldn't survive an hour's worth of creeping around in that dark office, whether I found anything or not. With a fresh slug of Dimitri down the tubes—this one for real—I left the file room behind.

At the front of the building, just past another closed door, the hallway opened into the high-ceilinged, elegant reception area I remembered from *Crain's* but didn't have time to admire just then. Dim light spilled through the picture window from the street onto a curving, carved-wood staircase that led to the floors above, where the lawyers' offices must be. Clients who couldn't manage the stairs could use the ornate, open-caged elevator.

The door just short of the reception room opened into a secretarial area. I knew what I was looking for. In addition to their case files, most law offices have a system that categorizes cases according to various criteria other than clients' names—including defendants' names. If Richardson kept this data on computer only, that was the end of it. I wasn't up to trying to crack that barrier. File cards I could handle.

And file cards there were, six drawers full. The drawer labeled "Defendants" gave me what I wanted. For CUNNINGHAM, KEVIN P., there were two cards: *SANCHEZ VE. CUNNINGHAM ET AL.*, and *DRZEDZEDEVIC VE. CUNNINGHAM ET AL.* The first was identified as PERS. INJ. AUTO and the second MISC. The *AL.* of the *ET AL.* was the Catholic Archdiocese of Chicago. Both cards were stamped SETTLED & CLOSED.

Back in the file room, the Sanchez and Drzedzedevic files were easy to find. Each consisted of just one folder. It didn't take much of a run through the Sanchez file to reveal at least part of what Butterfield had been talking about. Kevin couldn't have picked a worse señorita to be caught drinking and riding around with in the middle of the night than Carmela Sanchez. She'd worked as a secretary at Kevin's parish in the shadow of the rusting steel mills. At the time of the accident, she'd been living at home with her parents, Rogelio and Rosa Sanchez. She was a month over the age of eighteen. She was also—an autopsy revealed—not quite legally drunk and about eight weeks pregnant.

The file was curiously short on information about Carmela's

family, but the MISC. folder held a clipping from a bilingual neighborhood newspaper. It was a report of Carmela's wake. Her father, Rogelio, had addressed the crowd of mourners. The paper printed his strange concluding words in his original Spanish, and then in English translation:

> The sinner who causes another to fall must know this: punishment will follow sin. This is God's just and holy will. And when God decrees that his will be carried out by the hands of us poor humans, we cannot escape this mission, any more than the sinner can escape God's will.

I folded the clipping and put it in my wallet. The words of Rogelio Sanchez were not to be taken lightly. I knew that, because I'd done some work once for a shirttail relative of his. Rogelio was a ruthless, murderous dealer in guns and drugs between the United States and Latin America.

The Drzedzedevic file was next. Richardson had represented Lawrence and Phyllis Drzedzedevic, and their son Mark. The claim was spelled out in Richardson's letter to E. Harrison Haskell, the lawyer for the archdiocese. The letter charged that Kevin, during a picnic for altar boys at his first parish, had "exposed himself" to twelve-year-old Mark, had "fondled the boy's genital organs," and had "performed other lewd acts regarding which I herein provide only a summary."

The "summary" was plenty detailed enough to make me dip into the Dimitri again.

Three days after Richardson's letter, he'd gotten a curt response, signed by Harry Haskell, telling him that "the Archdiocese of Chicago and Father Cunningham deny all liability in this matter and intend to contest these scurrilous and libelous charges to the utmost."

Three months later, scurrility and libel notwithstanding, the archdiocese paid a modest one hundred fifty thousand dollars to settle the case. The settlement agreement required "absolute confidentiality and secrecy" on both sides. Not surprising. But in addition, in a carefully drawn indemnity clause, the Drzedzedevics and Richardson had agreed to pay the archdiocese one million dollars if they ever revealed either their charges or the terms of the settlement. Richardson signed on as personally responsible, "for himself and all his heirs and assignees," even if the confidentiality agreement was breached only by the Drzedzedevics, since they certainly weren't good for a million.

I was sitting there, staring at the settlement agreement in the dim light, when the phone rang.

My heart stopped for a solid three seconds. When it restarted, I ran into the secretaries' office, where the answering machine whirred a bit more, then clicked off.

Back in the file room, I leafed through the Drzedzedevic file and found pages and pages of medical and psychiatric reports about Mark. They might have revealed why the Drzedzedevics and Richardson had agreed to the relatively small settlement and its unusual terms. But my nerve was running out with the passage of time.

I turned to the last couple of things in the file. One was a manila folder labeled INVESTIGATION: CUNNINGHAM. This contained all Kevin's grade transcripts from high school on, and a Secretary of State report of his driving record. There was also just the last page of a nine-page report from a private investigation firm. The "Summary of Investigation" wasn't significant, other than this statement: "This investigation is being terminated prematurely at the request of counsel. It should be noted that the undersigned has so far discovered no history of sexual misconduct, or any sexual conduct at all, on the subject's part."

Finally, there was a folder labeled CUNNINGHAM: PSYCHIATRIC EVALUATION. Included were just two items. The first was a demand by Richardson that Kevin submit immediately to testing and evaluation by a team of psychiatrists to be selected by Richardson, "focusing on, but not limited to, his sexual history and proclivities, including any proclivity for pedophilism." The second item was Haskell's response, which—translated from legal jargon into plain English—said, "You gotta be kidding!"

Returning the Sanchez and Drzedzedevic case files carefully to their respective places on the shelves, I went to the secretaries' office and replayed the answering machine tape. There were just two messages after mine from earlier that night. Mine had to go, so I erased all three, to avoid a gap in the tape. Mr. Hodgkins, who was calling about a new case, and Rebecca someone, who wanted Richardson to call her, would both have to call back.

I lifted a delicate, expensive-looking vase from a table in the reception area and headed for the back door. On the way, another check of the filing room assured me nothing had been left out of place. All the coffee I'd drunk, and the gin after that, urged me to stop at the bathroom, but the urge to get out of that building was even stronger.

Going down the porch steps into the yard, leaving the door with its broken glass wide open behind me, I tried to shake off the sense that I'd missed something, hadn't paid enough attention, been too anxious to get away.

Near the gate, I poured what little Dimitri was left over my head, then gently dropped the vase onto the brick sidewalk. I left the pieces there, evidence of a clumsy burglary gone sour, and went into the alley.

I'd pulled the gate closed, and was testing to be sure the spring lock had caught, when a blue-and-white squad car bounced noisily into the alley from the street. I froze there, my back to the alley, bent slightly toward the gate in its alcove. No way they wouldn't see me. Maybe they'd drive on by.

They stopped. A tired, bored voice said, from three feet behind my skull, "OK, pal, whaddaya doin' there?"

Hanging my head limply, I leaned further into the alcove and mumbled something even I didn't understand.

"I'm talkin' to you, pal," the cop said, anger edging into his voice now. "I said whaddaya doin' there."

There was only one thing I could think of to do. Letting the gin bottle slide out of my left hand onto the alley pavement, I urinated against the wooden gate.

"Aw, Jesus," the cop said, disgusted. "Let's git outta here."

The squad car roared away.

TWENTY-SIX

WHEN I WAS A KID, Wheeling was a sign along Route 45 in the middle of nowhere other than the way to my aunt's house in Grayslake. Now, at 9 a.m., Wheeling was clogging up with Saturday traffic like the rest of suburbia. Several miles north of town, East Shakerby Lane wound an eccentric circle through a housing development. It took three trips around to find the Drzedzedevic home. I could have called first, and made my chance of getting in to see them even slimmer than it was as I walked up the driveway toward the two-car garage and the front door.

The house was a typical split-level, and my ring of the doorbell drew a typical teenage response from inside.

"Hey, Mom! Somebody's at the door!"

Then, from deeper inside, a woman called, "Well, answer it, for heaven's sake."

"Yeah, but—"

"Just answer the door!"

"Oh, all right." And he did.

He was a teenager in uniform—black sneakers with laces untied, faded jeans full of ragged holes, torn T-shirt sporting the vaguely obscene name of some musical group I'd never hear of again. His red baseball cap was twisted backward on a head of straight black hair that hung long over one ear and was shaved high above the other. What got my attention, though, was the oversized book in his hand, *Understanding the Earth and Its Planetary Neighborhood.*

He looked at me curiously, probably wondering what part of the neighborhood I hailed from.

"Is your mom or dad home?" Trying not to sound like a cop.

The curiosity faded, and he called out over his shoulder, "Mom, a salesman or something to see you. Hurry up, would you? I gotta finish this book and return it by this afternoon or else I gotta pay a fine!"

Before he'd finished the sentence, though, his mother was peering over his shoulder. When she saw me on the stoop, she said, "Mark, you go on back to the family room and finish your book."

"But Mom," he complained, "the TV is on in there."

"Honey," patiently, not unkindly, but never taking her eyes off me, "you can turn the TV *off*, you know."

"Oh," he said, that apparently not having occurred to him, "OK." And he was gone.

We stared at each other through the screen door. She was fortyish, no makeup, slightly overweight in a shapeless jogging suit. She looked as though she'd been expecting me—or someone like me.

"What do you want?" she asked. She seemed afraid, even terrified.

I held one of my cards out toward the door. "I won't come in," I said. "There are some phone numbers on the back of this card you can call, to ask about me. They're all listed numbers. I've even given you the phone company number you can call to verify the other numbers."

"What do you want?" she repeated, not moving.

"I'd like to talk to you and your husband, confidentially, about...about Father Cunningham. I want you to know, right up front, I'm on his side." I paused. "But I've no reason to hurt you, either."

"I don't know," she said, "I..." But she pushed open the door a crack and took the card. I stayed on the stoop.

"Mr. Butterfield's number is there. I know he wasn't your lawyer. But maybe you trust him."

She looked back and forth between the card in her hand and the man at her door.

"Some are home phones," I said. "You could call them right away. It's...well...it's an emergency and I need to talk right away, later today if that's possible. Talk it over with your husband. Then decide. Leave a message on my machine. I'm going now. Good-bye."

"Good-bye," she managed.

As I drove away, she was still watching from the door.

"I'VE BEEN LOOKING into things a bit," I said.

Kevin sat upright beside me, silent and stiff in his spotless black suit and starched roman collar. I'd caught him finishing up a Saturday morning class. He stared through the windshield at the runners loping around the oval track beside Halas Hall at Loyola's Lakefront Campus. He could have been a figure in a wax museum but for the little vein pumping away in his left temple.

Two pretty college students strolled past, swinging short skirts behind them in the spring sunshine. Neither of our heads turned to follow them. With me, it was flat-out fatigue; with Kevin, maybe celibacy, or maybe he was mad at my showing up again. Or maybe he was too hung over. Despite the well-pressed suit and straight-up posture, he didn't look so good. The pulsing vein was probably a pounding hammer inside his skull.

"I've been looking into things a bit," I repeated. "I learned about...that altar boy...Mark...what he said."

He still didn't move, didn't say anything. But something crumpled. Deep inside the upright black suit, within the shell of his skin even, the crash of something collapsing was almost audible.

There was a long silence then.

"For whatever it's worth," he said finally, his voice thin and strained, "I didn't do it. I didn't do what they said."

"I believe you, Kevin." I wanted to anyway, desperately. And so I did.

"I don't think you do," he answered. "No one believed me. They transferred me away from the parish I loved, exiled me, told me I couldn't work with young kids, ruined me. I did nothing wrong, and not one single person who heard about it believed me for a minute."

"Oh, I wouldn't be so sure about that. You and the cardinal got out of that case pretty cheap, all things considered."

"A hundred and fifty thousand dollars—"

"—is cheap, believe me. And, apart from the amount, compare it to newspaper and television publicity, and a lawsuit, and criminal charges, and—"

"Yes. That's what the lawyers told me. They also told me the cardinal wanted to pay, and...and that if I didn't agree, I'd be on my own. I remember very clearly what one of the lawyers said, the fat one, Haskell—looked like Jackie Gleason, only in a pressed suit. 'If you don't take the deal, Father,' he said, 'the cardinal will have to cut you loose. You'll have to get your own lawyer, provide your own defense. It'll all be public. It won't be nice.' My own lawyers didn't believe me. The only one who even listened to me was Jack Butterfield. But he...even he was more interested in covering up than in getting the truth. Not that I wanted it public either, but..."

Kevin was talking now; the dam was broken. His flat, rapid speech gave the impression I could have gotten out of the car and walked around the block and he'd have kept right on talking.

"I liked that boy," he droned on, "Mark. I thought he was a decent kid. I never realized he was so...so mixed up. Of course, his parents had problems. I knew that."

"So," I broke in, "what happened?" It was time to remind him I was still there.

"What happened? Nothing happened."

"I mean at the picnic."

"That's what I mean, too. Nothing happened at that picnic. Nothing happened ever. But what's the use? You're not going to believe me."

"Kevin. I *am* going to believe you. I already believe you. Hell, believing people is what I do best. That's probably why I didn't make such a great lawyer." *And maybe not so well suited for this job either,* I thought. Aloud, I added, "That's supposed to be a joke."

There was a twitch at the side of his mouth that might have hinted the start of a smile. But it didn't last. The vein in his temple kept pounding away.

"Anyway," I said, "I do believe you. But Kevin, the kid didn't just pick the altar boy picnic out of the air."

He turned his face to me for the first time since we'd gotten into the car. "First, it wasn't just altar boys. We had both boys and girls serving Mass, and there were both boys and girls on the picnic, about twenty-five kids. And I wasn't the only adult. Some of the mothers came along, too. Mark's mother was one of them. I'd been sort of...counseling her, I guess, although I really wasn't trained for it. She was very attractive and very depressed and...well...we'd almost gotten...involved, before I came to my senses. Or maybe I just got scared. Anyway, I stopped letting her come to see me. That wasn't long before the picnic." He stopped for a moment. "This is...uh...very embarrassing to..."

"Kevin, for God's sake..."

"I know. OK. The picnic was at this private place we'd rented for the day. It was originally some millionaire's estate, up near Lake Forest. Then an order of monks bought it for a monastery. They couldn't afford to keep it up, and rented it out to groups. We were the only ones there that day. There were lots of trees and playgrounds and an outdoor swimming pool. After lunch, the kids were in the pool with a couple of mothers watching them. I hadn't brought swimming trunks." He paused. "Actually, I had the flu that day and shouldn't have gone at all. But I loved working with those kids and I was supposed to drive the bus and there was no way to get another driver at the last minute. So... Are you sure this is necessary?"

"Kevin..."

"Anyway, I had to use the washroom, so I went into the boys' changing room. It had an entrance from outside and one from inside the pool area. It wasn't designed like a public park or anything. It was just a room to change in, with some wooden partitions, and then a small bathroom with a toilet and a sink."

"Was anyone else in the changing room?" I asked.

"No. At least I didn't see anyone. So I went into the bathroom and closed the door. And I was...you know...using the bathroom."

"What?" I said. "Taking a leak? or what?"

"Yes. Just...urinating. And then the door bangs open behind me and Mark bursts in. 'Gotcha covered!' he yelled. I mean, he obviously thought one of the other boys was in there. I was...he startled me. And I whirled halfway around. And I really wasn't through going yet, so...so there he is, and...and he's got his trunks off. And he's aiming his... Then he sees it's me and not some kid, and we're both just kind of standing there." He stopped.

"And then what?" I asked.

"And then nothing. That's it as far as anything happening. Except, almost simultaneously, Mark's mother is in the changing room, yelling for Mark. She could see right into the bathroom.

She stands there a second and there's this dead silence. And then she tells Mark to put his trunks on and she takes him out to the pool area. I...well, I zipped up my pants and went out the other way. That was it."

"Did you talk to her about it later?"

"No. I didn't know what to say, so I didn't say anything. I didn't tell anyone. Then, about three months later, I got the letter from the lawyer."

"What about the rest of it?"

"What do you mean?"

"All the other things the boy said happened. None of them happened? Or anything like it?"

"No. Nothing happened. Just what I told you. I don't even know if Mark really said those things. I never talked to him again. I think they—"

"Was there a lock on the inside of the bathroom door?"

He glared at me. "You don't believe me, either, do you?"

"I'm just asking, that's all. Was there a lock on the door?"

"They told me later there was, yes. But I didn't lock it. You're going to ask me why. I don't know why. I didn't think about it. I mean, there was no one around." His voice rose a notch. "The lawyers kept asking me why I didn't lock the door. But I don't know why. I just didn't think about—"

"Kevin! Hey! Relax. That's all over now. The case was settled. It's confidential. It's over." Not entirely over, of course. But then, what is?

"Not to change the subject," I said, figuring he'd had enough remembering for now, "but where's your car?"

"What? Oh. It's in one of the faculty lots." He pointed off to our right. "Behind that building."

"Good." I started up the Aries. "It's as safe there as anywhere."

"What are you talking about? I have to be at Saint Ludella for Mass tomorrow. They'll be expecting me tonight."

"Fine. You can pick your car up later and drive to Saint Ludella's. Right now, we're going for a ride."

He turned to me. "What right have you got to tell me what to do?" His voice was strident, announcing a craving that left no room for straight thinking. "And what right have you got to poke around and dig up dirt and throw it in my face?" His hand was on the door handle.

I reached out and grabbed his left arm just below the shoulder, squeezing hard. There wasn't much muscle tone there to resist my grasp, and it hurt him.

"Hold on, Kevin. I know what you want. But not now."

"What are you talking about?"

"Just that if I were in your shoes, I'd be headed for a drink right now." And me not even an alcoholic. "But listen to—"

"Why?" He was nearly sobbing. "Why should I listen to you? Why should I do what you say?"

"Because someone killed your sister, because someone killed Pamela Masterson, and because Casey might die any minute—that's why."

"My sister's death? That had nothing to do with..." He was staring at me, wide-eyed. "And those men at the cottage were drunk, or on drugs or something. That note...that was a crazy joke."

If a drunk can deny his problem with alcohol, he can deny any problem he wants to. But it was time Kevin learned some more.

"I guess you haven't heard about Carl Hemming," I said.

"No, I haven't heard from—" He froze. Finally, haltingly, he asked, "What are you talking about?"

I had to let go of him to fish the billfold out of my pocket, but he wasn't going anywhere now.

"What are you talking about?" he repeated. "I haven't spoken to Carl. I haven't heard anything. Tell me what you're saying." He was pleading with me.

I handed him the newspaper article. He unfolded it and stared at it.

"All for you, Father," he read, in a harsh whisper. He started shaking his head from side to side, his body trembling uncontrollably. "Oh, my God," he sobbed. "Oh, my God." If this continued, whoever hated Kevin wouldn't have to lay a finger on him. He'd fall apart all on his own.

Then it hit me. That was the idea, of course. Someone was demolishing Kevin, shaking him apart, waiting—and probably watching—as his shaky foundation crumbled.

TWENTY-SEVEN

I TOLD KEVIN how I'd found Carl's body. When I finished, he sat slumped in the seat next to me, still shaking his head from side to side.

"One thing that bothers me," I said, trying to focus his attention, "is the cocaine."

"Cocaine...at Carl's apartment. And they found it in Pamela's boat, too, they said. Strange...I never heard either one of them even mention the word, never saw any sign of it."

"There's a lot here that's strange."

"I really liked Carl, but we weren't exactly close friends or anything. We went to a few Cubs and Bulls games together. He was discouraged about his writing. I'd sit at the bar and talk to him, try to encourage him. I didn't even know where he lived. He knew I was a priest, but not much else about me. Why should someone kill him? He was obviously gay, you know? And I certainly—" His eyes widened. "Oh, my God! 'Family friends faggots and fools...' This can't be happening."

"But it *is* happening. They're killing everyone around you, Kevin. If they knew about Carl, that means they've been watching you. I don't have any *right* to tell you what to do. But it seems best to keep you with me. I don't know what else to do. I'm worried about you, worried about your mother, worried about...well...a lot of people. Like it or not, you need my help. And I need yours."

There was no more argument. In fact, we barely spoke for the next couple of hours. When I told him we were on our way to see Casey, he was grateful. But then he told me "Father Cazeliewicz is a very fine priest of the Church" and went on with things like "whatever happens will be God's will" and there was "nothing to do but pray." Platitudes rolled off his tongue like credits at the end of a movie. I hadn't been through what he'd been through, and maybe that's all he had left to hang on to just then. Why it bothered me I don't know, but it did. It shut me up the rest of the way.

Then again, maybe I was just too tired to talk. Driving all the way up to Shiloh wasn't much of an idea, anyway. Casey wouldn't be able to talk to us. But there'd be a chance to check up on the security Barney had arranged.

At the hospital, though, I couldn't find any security to check up on. Casey was in a "critical care" ward, still plugged into a battery of machines that were doing his living for him. The nurses wouldn't let us very close, so Kevin and I stood across the large room from him for a while.

Finally, when we'd both had enough of there being nothing to say or do, we turned to leave, and nearly ran into a woman standing in the doorway. She had a stethoscope slung over her shoulder and a hip-length white lab coat that hung unbuttoned, loose and shapeless over a snug and very shapely red dress that ended not far below the bottom of the lab coat. She was writing on a clipboard. As we started to move around her, she stuffed her pen down into the side pocket of the lab coat, then smiled professionally. Her hand stayed in her pocket.

"Don't move," she said, her voice soft, almost a whisper.

We didn't.

The chill in her voice was as professional as her smile, and her profession wasn't medicine.

"You're Foley," she said, her eyes on mine. Then, nodding toward Kevin, "Who's this guy?"

Kevin snapped to his clerical senses. "What *is* this?" His harsh voice hit the hushed room like a donkey braying in church. "Who are...uggff..."

There'd been a few times I would have enjoyed hitting him myself, but hers was strictly professional. Just below the diaphragm, and just hard enough to take his priestly indignation and his breath away.

"Meet Father Kevin Cunningham," I said. "I call him Kevin, but he doesn't like it very well. Other than that, he's a pretty decent guy."

The three of us stepped into the hall and the woman gave me a card that said, GREAT GATSBY INVESTIGATIONS. WHEN "GOOD"

ISN'T GOOD ENOUGH, YOU NEED THE GREAT ONE. The card identified her as Cheryl Holmes, and held no address or phone number. If you had to ask, you probably couldn't afford "the Great One."

She apologized to Kevin for taking a poke at him. She called him Father Cunningham with an ease that suggested my discomfort with that was my own problem.

She certainly charmed Kevin in a hurry. He accepted her apology and kept quiet.

"I guess I overreacted," she said. "It's been very boring." Her eyes never stopped moving in a calm, sweeping way that didn't miss a thing as people came and went along the hallway. "Although some of the medical staff are...well...interesting. Take a look at this one, for instance."

A small, round man in a knee-length lab coat over a green surgical suit was hurrying down the hall in our direction. He wore green clogs that squeaked a little on the polished floor. His bald head was tilted forward, his attention buried in the handful of file cards he was paging through. If he didn't look up soon, he'd plow right into us.

"Yoo-hoooo. Dr. Marlowe," Cheryl Holmes called out, her voice lilting and warm—and just in time to avert the impending collision.

He looked up, startled. "Oh, excuse me, Miss Holmes." That's all he said. But, as his chubby body pivoted and headed into the critical care ward, his eyes stayed glued to her a few long seconds. You might say he was ogling.

Who could blame him? I was probably leering myself.

"Glad to hear you've been bored," I said. "How many of you are there?" What I really wondered was how long Harriet's advance would last.

"Three," she said. "Plus backup, of course. So five, actually." She must have seen the concern in my eyes, because she added, with a solicitous smile, "But not to worry. Mr. Gatsby's a Catholic, you know. You should get a discount for a priest." She paused, then asked, "Why don't we go to the snack bar for a cup of coffee?"

"Good idea," Kevin blurted. Maybe the look in his eyes wasn't a leer, exactly. But it wasn't altogether hormone free, either.

"Fine," I said, and turned to the woman. "But what about Casey? Shouldn't you stay nearby?"

"Oh, that's OK. I just went off duty," she said. "The next shift is up to Marlowe."

TWENTY-EIGHT

BY SIX O'CLOCK I'd dropped Kevin off at Loyola to pick up his car. I needed sleep badly, and it's surprising I checked my messages at all. I sure didn't feel like calling her back, but it was Phyllis Drzedzedevic.

I dragged myself to a Denny's up near Wheeling.

"Thanks for meeting me," I said, sliding into the smooth bench seat across the table from her. "You know, I'm not sure how to pronounce your name."

"Ignore the first 'z' and the second 'd' and you've got it," she said. "Or you can just call me Phyllis." She tried to smile, but it didn't quite work. "I spent all day deciding whether to call you. I called the names you gave me, even Mr. Butterfield. He wouldn't tell me to talk to you or not, but he did vouch for you. One of the women, Helene Bower, gave me two more names and I called them too. I even called my therapist, but she wasn't in. I dropped my son at a soccer game and—"

"It's OK," I cut in. Her speech was too rapid, too strained. "Just relax. Have something to eat."

A waitress brought coffee and left with our orders.

"I'm scared," she said, "But I have to talk to someone. I can't go—"

"Does your husband know you're talking to me?"

"Larry? No." She stirred an artificial sweetener into her coffee. "Larry's dead."

She told the story of the picnic then, and it matched what Kevin had said, right up to her supervising the swimming pool.

"All at once I didn't see Mark anywhere and I...I panicked. I was terrified he had drowned and it was my fault. I tore around the pool like a mad woman and couldn't find him, and I ran right into the boys' changing room and...there was Mark, standing there, with his trunks off. And Father was by the toilet, with...you know...exposed. And I just freaked out or something. I made Mark put his trunks on and I took him out of there and I was kind of in shock. You read these things in the paper, and—''

''You didn't say anything to Kev...Father Cunningham?'' I asked.

''No, nothing. I couldn't. At first I wasn't going to say anything to anybody. I wasn't even going to tell Larry. We weren't getting along, for one thing, and he was so...so explosive. That's why I'd gone to Father Cunningham for counseling. Then, as soon as Larry came home that night, I blurted it out. I couldn't keep it to myself. Well, he went crazy. I knew he would, but I couldn't stop myself. I told him maybe there was an explanation, maybe it wasn't what it looked like. But Larry didn't like Father Cunningham anyway and...and he was drinking, too. Larry was very unhappy and he was drinking more and more. He really hadn't been that way when we first—''

''Phyllis, please, what happened?''

''Well, it was late, and Larry stormed up the stairs and went in and woke Mark up. He was yelling and screaming and accusing Mark of...of all kinds of things, of 'letting that queer touch you' and things like that. Mark was crying. He was terrified. Finally he started to scream that it wasn't his fault, that he hadn't wanted to do anything, that Father made him do it. Then Larry—''

I leaned across the table. ''Whoa! Just slow down. Did Mark say *what* Kevin made him do?''

''Kevin? Oh, you mean Father Cunningham. I never heard him called Kevin,'' she said.

The waitress brought our orders, an English muffin apiece, and more coffee.

''No, Mark didn't exactly say. But Larry kept yelling at him, 'Did that fairy priest do this? Did he do that?' Mark would say no at first, and Larry would yell, 'He did, didn't he?' and Mark was shaking and sobbing and finally he would say 'yes' that Father Cunningham had done that. Mark would finally say 'yes' to whatever Larry kept saying. And some of the things were awful and I just didn't believe them.''

''So did you break in and say so?''

''No. I was afraid. I just sat there and kept quiet. I...I've lived with that ever since then. But Larry was...Larry could be mean, especially when he was drinking. He...in the past he..."

"He used to hit you?"

"Yes. And he was getting worse. I was working my courage up to leave him. Then this happened." She put some jam on the English muffin and set it back down on her plate. "Anyway, the next morning Larry said he'd get the best lawyer in the city to sue the cardinal and Father Cunningham for what he did to our boy."

"So you went to Cleveland Richardson?"

"Yes. Larry's father's active in politics and he knows lots of lawyers. He told us to go to Mr. Richardson. So we did. He wanted to see all of us at once. Mark's story was...well...confused and Larry kept getting mad at him and correcting him. Mr. Richardson didn't seem to think it was a good case. He said he'd get an investigator to check into Father Cunningham's background for any similar incidents, something that should have warned the cardinal about him. He told us not to say anything to anybody. A long time went by, maybe a month or more. I thought he'd eventually tell us to forget about it. That's what I hoped. Then one day he called and wanted to meet us again. It was like he was more interested in the case. He said he'd found out some things and he'd make a claim. I didn't understand it, because I was certain he didn't believe Mark the first time we were there."

"But you let him make the claim."

"Yes. I knew it was wrong. Mark wasn't telling the truth. He was just afraid to change his story once he'd told it. I was afraid, too. Not afraid so much physically. I don't know—just afraid to interfere. Larry was so excitable, and angry, and working himself into a frenzy whenever he talked about it. Mr. Richardson sent Mark to two different psychiatrists. He wasn't very happy with either one.

"Finally, there was a settlement offer. Larry said it was too small. But Mr. Richardson said we'd better take it or he'd quit the case and we'd get nothing. He said no one would believe Mark. But he said he was our attorney, so he had to get us as much as he could and that's what he'd done and if we didn't take it, no other lawyer in the city would take the case.

"He said the only way he got any money at all was by agreeing to a part in the settlement about confidentiality and a million dollars, and that we'd better not say anything to anybody because he'd be just as responsible as we were, and if he had to pay he'd get as much of it as he could out of us—our house and any savings we had, and Mark's money, everything. He got real mean when he said that and I knew he really would come after us. 'Then we won't take the money at all,' I said, 'just forget it.' But Larry told me, 'Shut up, we'll take the money,' and Mr. Richardson said we had to anyway, we couldn't turn back then. So we took the money.'' She finally paused to take a breath. "And then...things got even worse.''

"What do you mean?''

"All the money went into a trust fund for Mark and we couldn't touch it without a court order. Once Larry wanted to use some of it for us all to go to Disney World and the judge wouldn't allow it. Larry was furious. I told him he knew it was Mark's money, and anyway Mark hadn't been telling the truth. But Larry got so—''

"Wait a minute. Did Mark tell you nothing happened?''

"No. To this day, I'm not sure exactly what happened. But I knew not everything Larry got Mark to say *could* have happened. There just...well, I just don't think Mark was out of my sight long enough. Then Father Cunningham got transferred away, and I knew we'd done a terrible thing. But...'' She didn't finish.

Finally I asked, "What about Larry? What happened?''

"Larry was drinking more and more all the time. Then one night after supper, he went out to get some beer. It was raining and...and it got very late and a man came to the door and as soon as I saw him I knew something bad had happened. He was a policeman. Larry'd been driving too fast. There were a lot of witnesses. He tried to pass someone on the right and he went off the road and into the Des Plaines River and...and drowned. To me it seemed like...well...like punishment. Ever since, I've been waiting for something else terrible to happen, waiting for my turn.''

"And then I showed up.''

"Yes. Somehow, when I saw you this morning, I knew it was about this. And I was afraid.''

"Have you ever told anyone you think Mark wasn't telling the truth? I mean, maybe Larry's father or someone?"

"No. I...I'm in therapy now, though. And so is Mark. But otherwise I haven't told anyone. As for Larry's father, I've hardly talked to him since Larry died. I never talked to him much anyway. And then, well, he never admitted that Larry had a longtime drinking problem. He convinced himself that Larry got so upset about what happened to Mark that he got to drinking that night and killed himself. He blames Father Cunningham for Larry's death. At Larry's wake, he kept talking to me over and over about how 'that queer priest' took away his only son and messed up Mark for life. All that sort of thing. I warned him not to say anything to anyone because of the million dollars, and I don't think he ever has."

The waitress brought more coffee.

"My father-in-law is not a nice person, Mr. Foley. If people really knew him he'd never be elected to anything. He's very...what's the word?...vindictive. He told me that people who...who molest children don't deserve to live." She stared down at her plate. "'First we should cut off their nuts,' he said, 'then kill 'em.'"

I swallowed hard. "Your father-in-law...I mean...Drzedzedevic is an unusual name and I've never heard of anyone in politics with that name. Is he—"

"Oh, he's a state representative. But years ago, when he first ran for office, he changed his name to Drake, Sam Drake."

TWENTY-NINE

THE FOLLOWING AFTERNOON, Sunday, Harriet wasn't pleased with my suggestion.

"Absolutely not," she said, waving a manila folder she'd been shifting from one spot on her desk to another. "You agreed from the beginning not to tell him, or anyone else. That was our agreement."

"Sure. But that's when you told me about 'a mother's natural curiosity about her child'...or something like that."

"That's true. But remember, you've said since then that you didn't believe me, right from the start. And you still gave your word." She fingered one pretty earlobe, then the other. "And you promised again, since then. You're not to tell my...tell this Father Cunningham...anything about me. That was our agreement from day one. Nothing has changed."

"Easy for you to say. Plenty's changed for Pamela Masterson. Then there's the priest with the bullet in his back. And Celia, and—"

"I know all that. I know. But telling my...telling this priest about me isn't going to make him, or anyone, any safer."

She had a point there. In fact, I didn't know myself what telling Kevin might accomplish.

"Fine. I won't tell him." But I wasn't sure I could keep that promise.

I'd left Denny's the night before so tired that, Saturday or not, making the gig at Miz Becky's was out of the question. I went straight to Saint Ludella's, called the Lady, and told her everything—from Carl Hemming to Richardson's files to Gatsby's people watching over Casey. I was hoping for suggestions. Unfortunately, she'd had little to say, other than to ask how things were going with Cass, which wasn't on my agenda.

Sunday morning I'd sat in a room to the side of the altar, watching Kevin say Mass—twice. It amazed me how he moved through all those complicated prayers and rituals, looking right at home. Of course, it all came out of a big red book, except for his sermon. The same sermon twice. He wasn't much of a public speaker, and I couldn't remember what he talked about. What you couldn't miss, though, was how hard he was trying during the sermon.

After the second Mass, I'd asked him to stay put in the rectory until I got back. He wouldn't agree or disagree. I got the feeling if I could break through to him, he'd be someone I'd like to know. In the meantime, though, banging against that brick wall was wearing me out.

Now, in response to Harriet's message on my answering machine, here I was on Sunday afternoon, in the mostly deserted offices of Brothers and Cruickshank. Jerry Wakefield had been with her when I arrived. Now he was out at R. Pennington's desk, talking on the telephone. It bothered me that he was there. Harriet had a problem, and people who hover too closely around someone with a problem always make me suspicious—even husbands. Besides, maybe Harriet loved Jerry, but the less I saw of him the better.

"Do you *live* in these offices, or what?" I asked her, breaking the long silence that followed the promise I wasn't sure I could keep.

"No." More silence.

"Anyway, at least I didn't have to face that Pennington woman. I don't see how you stand her."

"Actually, she's an excellent secretary. The one before her had a nicer disposition, but announced out of nowhere one day she was moving to Hawaii. She recommended Miss Pennington and we hired her. That was about a year ago. No one likes her, that's true. But she comes in early and never misses a day."

"People like that make me nervous," I said, thinking again of Jerry.

"Well, she's extremely efficient. When you find a secretary that good, you don't have to like her. Maybe you don't know how hard it is—"

"Hey," I said, "I don't think you called me over to discuss personnel problems."

"No." She stood up and walked across the room. Unlike Jerry, her I didn't mind seeing more of.

"So here I am. At your service."

She still said nothing.

"You're pacing your cage," I said, "the way you did the first time I was here."

"I'm thinking."

Maybe so. But outwardly all she did was walk around—looking good, and making me nervous.

Finally, I got to my feet. "Well, then...have me over again one of these days. When the time adds up to an hour, I'll send a bill."

"Sit down, Mr. Foley." When I didn't, she added, "Please."

I sat. She went back to her desk and did the same.

"Do you know where he is?" she asked.

"Who?" She wasn't making it easy. Why should I?

"My...this Father Cunningham."

"Oh, him. Well, I know he teaches at Loyola, which maybe you know already, and he has a room there. Also, he stays sometimes at a church—Saint Ludella's—on the West Side."

She looked at me. "So...have you been in touch with him? Talked to him?"

"Why should I talk to him? You told me to do nothing at all. Besides, no one's paying me." She might have noticed I didn't answer her questions.

"I'll pay you."

"For what?"

"To...keep an eye on him."

"You mean a bodyguard?"

"I mean to see that nothing happens to him."

"Look, there are security firms that offer bodyguard service. They have resources, staff, sophisticated surveillance equipment. Ask Mr. Alimony out there. He'll recommend someone. Someone who's not a cheap fucking private dick."

She smiled for the first time since I'd arrived. It might have been the first genuine smile in any of our conversations. With that kind of smile she looked even better than usual. She looked like a very nice person—like a mother, in fact.

"Jerry actually hurt your feelings that first day, didn't he? I guess I hadn't been aware of that.'' She paused. ''Hard to imagine, really. But he did, didn't he?''

''You look nice when you smile. You should practice. Do it twelve times in one day and you'll have a habit.''

She frowned. ''You're a lot like me, do you know that? If things get too close, then it's time to change the subject. That's us. Never admit anything that'll let anyone know what you're feeling. You know,'' she continued, ''that's one of the things I like about Jerry. He's not like that.'' She stood up and walked to the windows, staring out. ''I'll pay you. I want you to do it. I have to take some action, but I still don't want anyone, not him or anyone else, to know that he's my son. Actually, I...I don't think I like him very well.''

''That's bullshit,'' I said, politely. ''Besides, plenty of people know already. You know, I know, Jerry knows, Celia Cunningham knows, and the Scripture scholar knows.''

''You mean whoever sent the notes.''

''Yes. Incidentally, have you ever killed anyone?''

She swung around to face me. ''What are you talking about?''

''I mean, like run someone down with your car or something?''

''No.''

''And you never sent anyone to the chair. So—''

''How do *you* know whether I did or I didn't?''

''Well, I...you'd have told me if you had. I mean, if you did, and they had relatives—parents maybe—it'd be a great motive for revenge. You'd have thought of that, and you'd have told me. Maybe your notes were threats to you, and had nothing to do with Kevin.''

She was back behind her desk now, standing, rearranging things on the desktop. She looked at me suspiciously. ''You're right. I *had* thought of that, at first.''

''And?''

''And no, I never had a death case. And I never had an automobile accident or, as far as I know, caused anyone's death in any way. I certainly sent lots of people to jail—armed robbers, burglars, rapists. All of them deserved whatever they got. I can't think of any that weren't total losers to begin with, certainly not any capable of thinking up and carrying out a sophisticated plan of revenge. Besides, the idea that those notes aren't related to what happened at Bullhead Lake is too bizarre to warrant consideration."

"Just a thought," I said. "Anyway, about this looking out for Kevin business..."

"Just for a few days, until I can figure this all out. There are too many things happening at once."

We sat there, trying to read behind the looks on each other's faces. Behind mine was the struggle to make myself tell her about the two cases against Kevin whether she liked it or not—and she wouldn't—before she got any more involved with Cleveland Richardson. Behind hers...?

I started. "Look, there's something you should—"

"Wait," she blurted, "Let me go first." She drummed the fingers of both hands on the desk, as though doing runs on a tiny invisible piano. "I...I want you to keep this to yourself."

"Hey," I said, happy that she'd grabbed the first solo, "that's what I'm good at, keeping things to myself."

She stood up and walked back to the windows. When she spoke, her back was to me. "I've told you about my interest in politics."

"We discussed it. The day I was ranting at you. You're lining up backers, money people. Someone named Sam Drake, and a Mr. Cleveland, as I recall."

"It's Richardson. Don't play with me. You recall very well. Anyway, I've told him."

"Told who? What?" My pulse kicked up a notch.

"Told Cleveland Richardson."

I stared at her. "Did you tell him...everything? I mean the Bible quotes and—"

"Of course not. I told him I'd had a child and placed him for adoption. I told him I hired you to find him and you'd done that." She paused. "Most of the rest is...mere speculation. Anyway, he said my having a son didn't change anything. After all, it's not a crime." She paused. "That's all he said—until I told him who it was."

"And then?" I asked.

"When he heard the name, he was shocked. Turns out he

knows...or at least he had a case against my...against Father Cunningham.''

"What did he say? Are you dead? I mean politically speaking?''

"Absolutely not. He repeated that my having a son, and the adoption, didn't matter. Even if it came out somehow, it wouldn't hurt anything. He thought it might even soften the opposition from the antiabortion crazies.''

"But what about his representing—''

"Everything was settled without litigation. There was a confidentiality agreement. He can't talk about it. Nothing will ever come out. I...anyway, he said not to worry about it." She paused. "Now, what were you getting ready to say?''

"Must not have been important," I said, "because I can't even remember it.''

Whether she believed me or not, she seemed relieved. "The bottom line is, they're slating me for attorney general. It's the first step. I'm going to be governor one day." She didn't sound as happy about that as you'd have thought she'd be.

I didn't say anything at all.

She was back at her desk again and sat down. "So, as I said, there are too many things happening, too fast. This is what I've been looking forward to all my life. But...just now...I need time to think. I'll pay the same fee as before." No negotiating this time. It wasn't my imagination, after all. She *was* changing, by God.

Just then, Jerry Wakefield's handsome face appeared at the door. I winced.

Harriet broke in before he could say anything. "Jerry darling. Wait a little longer, sweetheart. We'll be finished in a few minutes.'' Wakefield disappeared.

Darling? Sweetheart? I winced again. Twice.

A few minutes later, the three of us rode down the elevator and headed our separate ways. They, with their three hundred dollars' worth of coordinated gym bags, were off to the treadmills and stair machines at the East Bank Club. I, with a healthy cash advance on my new fee, was off to look out for Kevin again.

Just for a few days, she'd said, *until I can figure this all out.*
Fat chance.

There was a killer out there, and none of us was safe until he was uncovered and...what? Gotten rid of? What did that mean? I didn't like to think about it.

Anyway, I could walk away any time I wanted, and I chose not to just then. I could use the money.

THIRTY

I USED A PAY PHONE in the lobby. There were three messages on my machine.

"Give us the eye doctor, Foley. Otherwise, we'll find you, and you won't like what happens, and you'll take us to her anyway." That was all the first man said, and it must have been just to shake me up a little, since he didn't leave a number.

"I have the reports you want," the second caller said. I had no idea what he was talking about. But at least he left a phone number.

The number was on a downtown exchange, but unlisted. When I called back, he refused to identify himself on the phone, and told me only where and when to meet him for the reports.

The third caller was the Lady. She was out when I called her back.

Meeting the second caller for his "reports" might mean meeting the first caller, but not meeting him was out of the question. So, taking my time, I walked north, crossed Wacker Drive, then headed east along the river toward the Wrigley Building. I passed the Nikko Hotel, where I'd told Harriet about Kevin and where Cass and I were having dinner soon, I hoped. There was a gray mist in the air, just short of rain. At Michigan Avenue I crossed the bridge to the north side of the river. The McDonald's tucked behind the Wrigley Building was open, and nearly empty. With a cheeseburger, fries, a large coffee and a medium root beer, I took a table by the window and broke open two packets of salt.

"You shouldn't do that, you know."

I looked up. The voice I'd heard on the phone belonged to the middle-aged man sliding into the yellow plastic seat across from me. He had thinning hair and might have been in town from Des Moines for a CPA seminar, if you didn't notice the steel in his gray eyes. "All that salt, I mean," he explained.

"Life's full of risk," I said, and scattered the salt over the fries.

The card he'd placed on the table said, GREAT GATSBY INVESTI-GATIONS. WHEN "GOOD" ISN'T GOOD ENOUGH, YOU NEED THE GREAT ONE. The card identified him as John Watson, with no address or phone number.

"First Holmes and Marlowe, now John Watson. Do all you people use phony names?" I asked.

"Mr. Gatsby prefers the expression 'professional alias,'" he said.

He sipped some coffee and set the cup down. Pulling the small red tray toward the center of the table, he cut the cheeseburger neatly in half with a white plastic McDonald's knife. He ate both halves of the burger and frowned longingly at the french fries while we talked.

That is, he talked. I ate the fries and listened. He recited the information about his "four subjects" the way Kevin recited the words out of the book at Mass—easily but without a whole lot of excitement.

He drained the last of the coffee. "That's it," he said, sliding out from his chair. "At least for now. I mean, we only got the order last night. If you want more, you gotta call Herb again."

"Except I didn't call Herb."

"I know," he said. "It was a lady. Helene Bower. Said to give the info to you. You get the bill, too." He turned and went out the door.

With another burger and a root beer from the counter, I returned to the table to think. Much of what "Watson" recited I might have guessed, but coming from Gatsby's agency they were facts.

For instance, I might have guessed Jerry Wakefield was a moneymaking machine and a lavish spender, with a failed marriage, no known children, and a wide circle of female friends in his pre-Happy Mallory days. I wouldn't have guessed, though, that he was definitely a one-woman man now. As a Chicago cop, he'd been what they call a "highly aggressive" narcotics investigator. Then he'd quit the department and gone to law school. He was abrasive but very bright, and several blue-ribbon law firms had started turning to him when their best clients ran into domestic relations difficulties. Harriet must have had a hand in that.

But if he'd given up philandering and kicking ass in the ghetto, one habit Jerry hadn't shaken yet was gambling, mostly on big-league sports. He lost a lot and was often over his head to the wrong kind of people. He'd spent a night in a hospital a year ago, following a vicious "mugging" after a Bulls game. Other than bruises just about everywhere, the injuries were two broken fingers, one on each hand.

I could have guessed many of the facts about Richardson, too. A multimillionaire, he'd parlayed a string of exceptional legal fees into a string of successful real estate deals and a couple of lucrative Hollywood pictures. He owned a chunk of a resort hotel in Nassau, and a hefty share of a floating casino plying the Mississippi out of St. Louis. Married thirty-five years with two attorney children, he was known as a philanthropist and a humanitarian, with an interest in the handicapped, especially a Catholic charities facility for permanently disabled persons. His list of honors ran from a B'nai B'rith brotherhood award to Catholic Lawyer of the Year. The closest he'd come to a personal scandal was being picked up in a sweep of after-hours gay bars on the final night of an ABA convention in Seattle years ago. Never a heavy drinker, his version was he'd been "drunk out of my mind" and answering a dare to hit every open bar in town. He'd been open about the incident and played it for laughs, and it never came up anymore.

A heavy investor in Chicago politics, he enjoyed the statewide and national clout that brought. He knew all the people everyone wanted to know and, according to Gatsby's man, a number of people nobody wanted to know—except maybe the FBI or the U.S. Attorney. If you looked closely, you'd see him occasionally bump into this or that "reputed gangland figure," maybe at a black-tie charity ball, or on the pier at some posh Caribbean resort most of us never heard of. Nothing to be alarmed about, maybe. People with money do tend to rub shoulders.

Rogelio Sanchez was a very different story. A longtime drug dealer, his bread and butter was still cocaine, but he did a little business now also in heroin from China and European automatic weaponry. Rogelio's daughter Carmela had been his youngest child. His four other daughters were well married and *madres* many times over. His only son was somewhere in Mexico, hiding out—some said from his father.

Since Carmela's death, Rogelio seldom ventured out other than to church—and then only for occasions like a grandchild's baptism, or *el doce de Diciembre,* the feast of Our Lady of Guadalupe. There wasn't a law enforcement agency in the Western Hemisphere that didn't have a file on Rogelio. But so far he'd been untouchable, hidden behind just about the best security system available—mile-high walls of money.

Finally, there was Sam Drake. Smart as a whip and a brilliant political strategist, the public loved him. But by those who knew him well, he was feared for his cold-blooded approach to the political game and its changing requirements. He and Richardson were longtime associates. Like Richardson, Drake knew everyone anyone wanted to know—and, like Richardson, lots of the others, too.

Sliding the debris off my tray into the plastic bag behind the red swinging door with its yellow THANK YOU, I left McDonald's. The mist had matured into a dismal cold rain that mirrored my mood.

My thoughts were all questions. Did the "muggers" who broke Jerry's fingers ever find themselves serving rum punch on Caribbean cabin cruisers? How much did their employers contribute to whose political coffers? Who paid whom, and who washed the money? Who supplied their firearms?

And did their cousins cruise around Chicago in shiny blue Bonnevilles?

THIRTY-ONE

Two WET, DREARY BLOCKS up the Magnificent Mile to the north, I found a cozy bar in the Hotel Intercontinental and, with an Irish coffee to settle my burger, I called Saint Ludella's.

"Oh, Father Cunnin'ham's long gone," Edna said. "We kept telling him, me and his mother both, what you said about bein' careful and all. But he got a phone call and said he had to go to a meeting on the North Side, at Saint Bede's he said, and then he'd just go on to Loyola after that 'cause he has class in the morning. Left outta here a couple hours ago."

Probably just as well. Anyone watching him would lose interest in the rectory with him gone. Meanwhile, it seemed safe to assume that Kevin himself wouldn't be touched as long as there were people on the list who stayed alive.

Except the list was pretty short.

IT TOOK AWHILE to find the address in the phone book, because I was looking under *Roman Catholic,* Saint Bede's was under *Episcopal.* When I got there, the sky was a deep, dark gray, the cold rain relentless. The church looked as though it had been plucked out of St. Mary Mead and dropped a block off Broadway at the north end of Uptown. The well-varnished doors with their wrought-iron hinges were locked, but there was a handwritten sign taped to one of them:

"STOP THE KILLING" RALLY
PLANNING MEETING
4:00 P.M. CHURCH HALL

To the left of the church, there was a parking lot with about a dozen cars. Well-lighted concrete steps led down to a meeting room in the basement, where about thirty people stood around in clusters. They were all casually dressed, except for three men in suits and roman collars. Kevin's suit was black. The gray figured to be the Episcopal, but the brown tweed with a faded red clerical shirt was anybody's guess. People were sipping coffee from paper cups and munching butter cookies from the generics section at the Jewel. They might have been standing around between acts at one of the city's dozens of "little" theaters. Sedate, sober, relatively normal—none of them looked like a bomb thrower to me.

It was maybe four seconds before a tall woman spotted me as a late arrival and strode over. About forty years old, she was dark-haired and attractive, nicely filling out her stone-washed jeans and Kennebunkport sweatshirt. But she had a clipboard in her hand and a list maker's look in her eye. I tried peering over her shoulder and slipping to the side.

It was futile. She had the lateral moves of an all-pro linebacker. "I'm afraid the meeting's over," she said, her voice husky and cheerful. "But thanks so much for coming. We need everyone's help. Let's see," tapping her pen on her clipboard, "would you like transportation?...sign making?...first aid? Of course, there's refreshments, too." Her smile advertised efficiency and seduction at the same time. "But you don't look like refreshments to me."

About thirty-five smart-aleck cracks flew through my mind, but I managed to scratch them all. "I'm not here for the meeting," I said. "I'm looking for Kev...for Father Cunningham."

When the clipboard lady turned away abruptly, I thought I'd escaped.

Instead, she turned back and was suddenly at my side, slipping her right arm firmly through my left. "There he is," she said. "Here, let me take you."

Kevin was just leaving a cluster of coffee drinkers. She waved the clipboard expansively toward him and walked me across the room, her right breast bouncing jauntily against my upper arm.

I stayed right with her.

But when we reached Kevin, she removed her arm. "Father Cunningham," she said, stepping unnecessarily close to him, "there's someone here to see you." He had a cup in his hand, and she laid her fingers gently on his wrist. "Maybe you can sign him up." She turned back to me. "We especially need transportation. We don't know where, or what day they're announcing yet, but we're told it'll be this week. We need to be ready. The press will be there. Let me know, OK?''

She was gone before I knew what she was talking about, falling in with the brown tweed jacket that was just passing by, slipping her arm easily through his. I thought he leaned a little into her as she maneuvered him toward the cookie table, showing him her lists.

"I guess it's just a habit with her," I said.

"What's that?" Kevin asked.

"I mean the light stroke on the wrist, the...well...anyway, let's get out of here. Isn't the meeting over?"

"Yes." His face was drawn and damp looking, as though he had a fever. "But I don't know that I want to go anywhere with—"

"Kevin, you can't just pretend there's nothing happening. I thought we'd reached an agreement on that."

By this time I'd maneuvered him out the door to the steps that led up to the parking lot. Suddenly, on the first step, he stopped and the paper cup slipped from his hand, splashing coffee on his gleaming shoes. Bending forward clumsily, he belched, then vomited. A small amount of thin liquid came first, and then nothing at all, as his body heaved and heaved again.

"I have to go," he managed to say between gasps. "I...I don't feel well."

Helping him up the stairs, I said, "Kevin, when did you last eat?"

"I don't know. Yesterday, I guess. I don't remember. And...and I haven't had anything to drink, either. Not since Friday. I can take it or leave it."

"I didn't say anything about drinking." I walked him toward Casey's car. "But you have to eat."

"I don't feel like eating."

He got in on the passenger side of the Aries. I closed the door and went around to the driver's seat.

"I can't eat," he said, leaning his forehead on his arms on the dashboard. "My stomach's all tied up. I...I'm..."

"Go ahead and say it, goddamn it." I started up the car. "You're scared."

He turned his head to me. "All right, I'm scared. Are you satisfied? I'm afraid. Do you feel superior now?"

"Superior, Kevin? Superior? You think you *shouldn't* feel scared? What do you *think* you should feel? Don't we all get scared? Wasn't Casey scared, when he thought he was dying?"

"Father Cazeliewicz wouldn't be afraid, not even of dying. He's...he has faith, a lot more faith than I do."

"Yeah, well, I won't argue the faith business with you." We'd left Saint Bede's a couple of blocks behind by now. "But I was there, and Casey told me, straight out, he was afraid. The man was afraid to die."

When Kevin didn't answer, I tried a new direction. "Are you finished throwing up now?"

"I think so. I'm not really sick. It's just...nerves, I guess."

"There's a restaurant up ahead," I said. "Let's get something to eat."

It was a basic Greek place. Kevin had a couple of orders of wheat toast with butter and a cup of tea. I wasn't hungry, but I had coffee and a piece of strawberry-chocolate cheesecake to be sociable—and wished I hadn't. My stomach had tie-ups of its own.

"So," I said, trying another approach as he buttered his fourth slice of toast, "this antiabortion stuff, are you really into it?"

He glared across the table at me. "No. I'm not *into* antiabortion *stuff.* I'm pro-life. I think every life is important and ought to be respected, even a life that happens to be inconvenient. I'm against abortion, against mercy killing, against capital punishment."

"How about war?" I asked.

"I guess war, yes."

"How about killing someone in self-defense?"

"I...that's a tough one."

"Let's make it tougher. Suppose I could have shot that thug before he put a bullet into Casey's back. Would I have been wrong to do it?"

"Maybe you could have just wounded him."

"Sure," I said. "Whip out my six-shooter and plug him in the gun hand."

He stopped the passing waitress. "I'd like a piece of apple pie and some more tea, please." Then, turning back to me, he said, "Maybe that's a little unrealistic. Look, Mal, I know nothing is simple. It's just that—"

"Hey Kev," I interrupted, "guess what."

"What?"

"We're having a conversation—back and forth! We never had a conversation before. I mean, you even called me by my name."

He smiled. I'd never seen that before, either. "You know, I am a human being," he said. "I have conversations."

"I thought so. But back to the abortion business. What was that woman talking about, the announcement you need to be ready for?"

"It's that woman lawyer who represents abortion clinics. She's going to run for attorney general. We want to be there when she makes her announcement." He paused while the waitress set his pie and tea in front of him. "I only got involved in the pro-life movement after they made me...after they said I shouldn't work with kids anymore. I have to be active in *something*, and I've tried to throw myself into it. I'd forgotten about the meeting, but I promised to help organize a demonstration against that woman."

"Oh," I said. "Uh...what do you think of her? What's her name again?"

"Happy Mallory," he said. "I think she's despicable. And not just because her clients profit by killing unborn babies. I've watched her in court. She'll do anything to win. She's mean, aggressive, spiteful, and rude."

"The very definition of a good trial lawyer, some say."

He looked puzzled. "Why are you baiting me? Do you know Happy Mallory?"

"Not really. I've...met her. She's a real tough lady. But you know? Maybe it's all an act. Maybe under that hard shell there's a sensitive, caring human being."

He took the last bite of his pie. "Yeah? Well, she's got me fooled."

"I'll get the check," I said. "But first, I want to ask you one more thing. It's about your father."

He stiffened suddenly but said nothing.

"Renata Carroway said you had some information about him," I said.

"Why should—"

"Kevin, come on!"

"OK, you're right." His initial resistance had been instinctual. But he was opening up. "Like I told you before, I'd assumed my father was dead," he said. "He was an alcoholic, you know. In fact, that's how I know I'm not one. I mean I'm not like him. He was...well, anyway, I'm not like him."

"Of course not," I said. "I'm not like my father, either. And he wasn't like his father. None of us are like our fathers. We spend our whole lives not being like our fathers, just like our fathers did."

"I admit I drink. Sometimes too much. But I can stop whenever I want."

"Right," I said, "whenever you want. Like, I went through your cottage the night Casey got shot. Wasn't a sign of booze anywhere."

"That's because Pamela doesn't...didn't—" He stopped. "You tricked me."

"She was in there, wasn't she, she or some other woman?"

He stared at me, and there was a click of recognition in his eyes. "When I got my things back from the sheriff..." he started, then shifted gears. "Did you take something from my duffel bag when you were at the cottage?"

"Like a little red box?" I asked.

In place of an answer he said, "Pamela was there sometimes. I liked her a lot—too much, I guess. But we never...I mean we didn't...maybe we might have, but—" He was blushing.

"Kevin, that's fine. The box wasn't opened. Maybe the relationship would have gone further, and maybe not. Whatever. I don't really care. And if I had an opinion at all, I'd think it was...well, forget it."

There were tears in his eyes as he turned his head away from me. I wasn't up to getting too deep into that topic. "But Kevin, what's this news about your father?"

He was happy to turn the conversation elsewhere, too. "There was a message on my machine at Loyola. An old woman—at least

I think it was a woman. No name. Just something like, 'Your father's not doing so hot, sonny. Them vultures'll be back, and this here falcon's no good for him, anyway.' Said she'd call back and hung up. It didn't make sense. Vultures...falcon...''

"Have you tried looking for him?"

"No, I...I'd like to, but..."

"Tell you what. Why don't the two of us get together and figure out a plan to look for him?" He started to answer, but I raised my palm. "But not tonight, huh? It's late, and it's raining, and I'm tired, and you've had the dry heaves and you need some rest." He looked relieved. "We can talk about it tomorrow. I'll call you."

We drove back to Saint Bede's. I pulled into the parking lot and he opened the car door, then turned back to me. "Look," he said, "I know I can be difficult. But I...I do need help, a lot of help. And...well...thanks. You know what I mean?"

I knew what he meant. And I knew Kevin had come a long, long way just to be able to say that much. And knowing that, I knew I wasn't in this any longer just for Harriet's sake, or Celia's. And not even just for Casey, though I figured I owed him. It was for Kevin now, too.

I wanted to tell him that, but I didn't. "I'll call you," was all I said.

He got out and went to his own car. I followed him at a distance. He drove straight to Loyola, locked his car, and disappeared into the residence hall.

And me? I turned around and drove like hell to the Falcon.

THIRTY-TWO

ONE SIDE OF THE BUILDING faced Wilson Avenue across a vacant lot that was littered with plastic trash and broken glass. The painted sign still said FALCON HOTEL in huge faded letters, and below that, TRANSIENTS WELCOME. But the Falcon Hotel was a hotel like Hyde Park is a park, or Madison Square Garden is a garden. Maybe once, but not no more.

Now it was a warren of God knows how many tiny apartments, most of them "kitchenettes"—one room, with a stove, sink, and refrigerator along one wall. Rented by the week, adults only, mostly men. One unlocked plate-glass door opened into a small, urine-smelling, tile-floored foyer; then another opened into a deserted, dimly lit lobby, a twenty-by-forty-foot rectangle with threadbare gold-colored carpet. To the right, beyond what used to be a reception counter, was a wall of mailboxes. The boxes that still had doors had no names on them.

Straight ahead across the lobby was a cheap, laminated wood door with a sign stenciled in red paint: PRIVATE. RESIDENTS ONLY. Below that a thumbtack held a dirty, peach-colored three-by-five index card whose corners curled around its typed announcement: FURNISHED ROOMS AVLBL. SEE MGR. APT. 115. NO PETS!!! Above the door handle was a round empty hole that had held a lock in some earlier decade.

Pushing through, I stood inside and breathed the air of every rundown apartment building I've ever been in. The hallways are always dark and depressing, and you're ready for that. But it's the stink, no matter how familiar, that slaps you in surprise. There's urine, of course. But also the overheated, reused cooking oil, the human sweat, the long-unwashed clothes, and a hundred unidentifiable odors that mingle—always, it seems—with the charred smell of an old fire somewhere on the premises.

Common sense tells you the place should have been torn down yesterday. Then, once your nose adjusts a little, you start to hear the cacophony—the televisions and radios in competing languages, periodic bursts of raucous laughter punctuating constant hacking coughs from behind the doors. Only then you remember to ask yourself: If this place wasn't here, where the hell would all these people live?

I had two choices—up a wide set of worn marble stairs half a flight, or down a matching set half a flight. Since the top of the up stairway looked a shade less dark than the bottom of the down stairway, I went up. The wide landing opened into a narrow hall. The doors on the right side down the hall were labeled 101 and up, in odd numbers; on the left, 102 and up. Number 115 was the last room before the hall turned to run along the back of the building.

Two things happened after I knocked. The TV went silent in the middle of a Charmin commercial, and a snarling wolf threw himself full force against the other side of the closed door.

Then, over the continuous rumbling growl of the wolf, came a cackling voice—male or female I couldn't tell. "Who is it? Whaddaya want?"

"The name's Foley. I'm looking for a room."

The wolf barked then—deep, throaty, hungry barks.

"Shut up, Mitsy, damn your ass!" the voice said.

It was a woman. She opened the door as far as the security chain allowed and peered through. She wore a yellow plastic shower cap on her head and clutched her bathrobe closed about sternum high. Her upper and lower dentures were both too wide for her thin face. Behind her the wolf's low rumble continued, like a Mack truck idling outside a diner.

"The sign says no pets," I said.

"Hah!" the woman cawed, "Mitsy ain't no pet. And you, you ain't looking for no room, neither. Show me a star or get the fuck outta here before I call the real police."

I handed my card through the opening. When she reached for it her robe fell open. She had no clothes on under the robe. I turned my head away instinctively.

"Hah!" she cawed again. "Ain't you the modest one, then."

I turned my head back to her, but she didn't bother to close the front of the robe. "What's it you want, sonny? 'Sides a little nookie, that is, hey, Mitsy? Hah!''

I kept my eyes fixed on the dingy yellow shower cap. "I'm looking for a man, maybe in his sixties, seventies. Patrick Cunningham. Supposed to be living here."

"Yeah? Well, he was. But he ain't now. So get the fuck outta here.''

She couldn't get the door closed with my foot wedged in the opening. By that time there was a twenty-dollar bill in front of her face as well. Her eyes flashed—more anger than greed. "First you sons o' bitches drive that old man clean away. Now I'm s'posed to take your fucking money to help you find him? You get outta here, or I'll open the door and Mitsy'll tear off your goddamn face.''

"Wait! Hold on! I don't know what you're talking about. Read my card, would you? I'm working for the old man's son. The kid's a priest. He's looking for his father. That's all. Jesus!''

Not exactly eloquent, but there was a huge paw scratching at the toe of my shoe, and I could feel the claws through the leather.

She looked down at my card in her hand, then turned her head away from the door a moment. She seemed to be wavering on whether to believe me. Finally she turned back and kicked at the paw on my foot. "Mitsy! Go siddown. Go on!" The paw retreated out of sight. "Look mister, Pat used to live in the building. Then, a few weeks back, a couple o' hoods was in here pushin' people around, askin' questions about Pat and his family and stuff. Me and Mitsy chased 'em off. I told Pat about it when he came in. He was scared, really scared. His health ain't so good. He left, and that's the God's honest truth.''

"You got any idea at all where he went?"

"Nope," she said. She was holding her robe closed again. "But if I see him, which I don't expect to, I got your card and I'll tell him. He can make up his own mind."

"Thanks," I said, pulling my foot back. There was no sense trying for more. I turned to go.

"Hey!" she said. I turned back and she winked at me. "What the hell, I could still use the fucking twenty, you know."

I gave it to her and went back outside. Even the Uptown air was fresh, compared to inside the Falcon.

Halfway across the vacant lot toward Wilson Avenue, a thought struck me and I turned and went into the alley behind the Falcon. I went beyond the rear of the building and turned into the gangway between the Falcon and its neighbor. Blue TV light flickered from the window of what had to be 115, high above my head.

Back in the alley I found a lidless garbage can and placed it upside-down below the window. Standing on the bottom of the can, I raised my head cautiously above the concrete window ledge and peered into the apartment. The woman was sitting on a sofa watching television, absently stroking the head of a huge Doberman that lay on the sofa beside her. Across the room, ignoring the television, a terribly thin old man with stringy, yellow-white hair sat motionless on a straight wooden chair and stared down at the small white business card he held in two clawlike hands.

There were tears on his gray-stubbled cheeks.

As I watched, his chin dropped softly forward onto his chest. Maybe he fell asleep. Or maybe he died right there in front of me. Or maybe he'd died a long, long time ago.

THIRTY-THREE

SAM DRAKE'S SWITCHBOARD opened at eight-thirty sharp and everyone I was transferred to was as charming and upbeat as could be, but that didn't get me put through—until finally I approached the problem head-on.

"Tell him I have disturbing news about Mark," I said.

"Mark?" the latest charming, upbeat voice asked. "Um... would you care to state Mark's last name?"

I didn't care to, and I didn't. But within two minutes I had an appointment to meet Drake that afternoon.

I tapped out another number and talked to some people who couldn't care less about charm, and whose boss didn't want to talk to me any more than Drake did. But I had a little leverage with Rogelio Sanchez.

ROGELIO HAD A PUZZLED look on his face. We were sitting in his "Florida room," with three walls of glass overlooking a flowering garden at the rear of his rambling, multilevel brick house. The home and its grounds occupied half a city block on the far southeast side. The rest of the block held similar, though smaller, houses. They all belonged to Rogelio, and his home was placed among them and carefully designed to conceal its size and its luxury. The floors went from marble to ceramic tile to oak parquet to Mexican quarry tile as Rogelio's man led me through the foyer, down the entrance hall, past elegant, empty sitting rooms, along the side of the indoor-outdoor pool, and to the Florida room with its expensive lawn furniture and Rogelio.

After we'd both had a go at the coffee that was set elegantly on the white wrought-iron table between us, Rogelio began the conversation. "I take time with you, *señor,* only because I have not forgotten that once you were fair—even more than fair—to a cousin of my wife. What a worry that one was—and what a fool, is it not true?"

"Very true," I said. "But worries come in many forms. Not only fools...but family, friends, faggots, and fools."

That's when he got the puzzled look on his face, and it seemed as genuine as I tried to appear then, as I explained why I was there. It was the best explanation I could think of—short of the truth—although it was a pretty lame suggestion.

"So," Rogelio said, "you say the cardinal wishes to return *Padre* Cunningham to a parish where Spanish is spoken. But first he asks you to investigate whether this would be good for the priest. Is that it?"

"Not exactly. I'm told the cardinal doesn't decide these matters personally." For all I knew, Rogelio was on a first-name basis with the cardinal. "He certainly didn't ask me personally. But there's a shortage of priests and a desire to return Father Cunningham to parish work. His Spanish is fluent, and that'll influence where they send him. But...there is a fear."

"And what is this fear?" He seemed genuinely curious.

"You," I said. "They're afraid you'll cause him harm."

His eyes darkened. "Harm a priest of the church?" Not curious now but angry. "Why would someone think such foolishness?"

"You have, Rogelio, a certain reputation. Many say you are quick to dole out punishment. They say your enemies disappear—and don't show up again."

"Punishment?" He took a sip of coffee. "I am a man of business, *señor*, but I am a man of faith as well." He waved an open palm toward a corner where two walls of windows met and a fountain bubbled in a tiny pool. Above the pool, surrounded by lush green plants, stood a statue of the Virgin of Guadalupe. At the statue's feet, candles flickered in red and blue glass cups. "If there is any truth to this...reputation you speak of, it is in business matters only. But apart from business, in which of course God has no interest, I leave such things as punishment to the wisdom of God. Certainly, I would not harm a priest."

"Anyone can light a candle," I said, "but what about those threats at your daughter's wake?"

A frown came across his bronze, deep-lined face. "I do not understand, *señor*."

I handed him the news clipping I'd taken from Richardson's file.

As he read, his frown dissolved into a sad smile, a change seen only in the redrawing of the lines around his mouth, not visible in his eyes. "*Si*, now it becomes more clear." Laying the clipping on the table between us, he looked across at me. "This is why," he said, tapping his forefinger on the clipping for emphasis, "this is why one must always read the newspapers with great caution. Even when they do not purposely lie—which is sadly so often the case—they may yet deceive, by printing words and not thoughts."

"True," I said, although not sure I got the point. "But the threat to the priest in your words is clear."

"You are mistaken. I did speak that night of the *padre*, but only as the instrument of God's will. There is nothing here of threat, only a grieving father's reminder—mostly to himself—of why things sometimes happen as they do."

"You lost me there."

"This is because you do not know me, and you did not know my Carmelita. I spoiled that girl from her infancy. Everything she wanted—*el mundo*—was hers. I was foolish, deaf to the pleas and warnings of my poor wife. Then one day—as suddenly as one discovers he is an old man—I saw that my baby had become a woman. I became afraid then, and tried to rein her in. But too late. She had an untamed will. And that was my fault...my fault alone." He handed the clipping back to me. "You think I blame the priest. You even hint that I suspect him of sinning with my child. A priest of God! Why would I think such a thing?"

"It was the middle of the night. They'd both been drinking. She was pregnant, for God's sake. Your words speak for themselves, threatening the one who caused your daughter to sin."

"But you are wrong. First, my Carmelita was not so easily led. Second, I knew well who the father of her unborn child was, poor fellow. No, the *padre* had no part in that. But it was God's will that the *padre* be the instrument of her death. And that is what happened. God's will must be done."

"This is a terrible God you believe in, to punish a young girl with death, just because—"

"Ah, but still you do not understand." He shook his head sadly. "I struggled then with the mystery of my daughter's death. I thought I began to understand, and at her wake I tried to explain. It was *my* sin. I was the one being punished, and the instrument God used was this unfortunate *padre*. What I loved most was taken from me, because I had sinned. I had not done my duty as a father."

I stared down at the clipping and read it again. "Well," I said, "that's a long way from how my clients interpret your words."

He stood up and walked toward the grotto and its statue. "I have no ill feelings toward the *padre*. I swear this before the face of the Virgin. However"—he turned back to me—"not every truth makes a convincing report. If you prefer, tell your clients this: Rogelio Sanchez is a man, and it is not the way of a man to spend long days brooding over feelings of revenge. A man acts at once, or not at all. If I had thought this priest was the ruin of my Carmelita, he would have been dead—God spare me—by the time of her wake. This is perhaps a report your clients may find easier to believe."

I stood up. "I'll tell them. They'll have to decide whether to believe it or not."

"Yes, as I have had to decide whether to believe what you have said or not."

"And?"

"I do not believe your foolish explanation. I do not know why you have come here. But it has nothing to do with the cardinal, or returning this priest to a parish."

"And still you spoke to me?"

"Yes. Because, my friend, you also have a reputation. Behind your made-up stories—you are a man of truth. Now...I have business to attend to."

The man who'd let me in appeared from nowhere and led me back through the house and out to the Aries. He was still visible in the rearview mirror, standing in the street, when I turned the corner.

Who was crazy and who wasn't? Rogelio's God was just, yet

had "no interest" in Rogelio's business—a brutal business that
included selling rapid-fire guns to thugs and scrambling unborn
infants' brains with crack and China snow.

Yet I tended to believe every word he said. Who was crazy and
who wasn't?

SAM DRAKE'S RECEPTIONIST introduced me to his "aide," a pale
young man named Duayne whose every movement was nervous
and sudden, like a carp shifting back and forth in shallow water.
I followed Duayne to an office where Drake sat behind a desk,
talking on the phone and smoothing his thinning white hair. He
wore a crisp, blue dress shirt, stylish suspenders, and a red necktie.
He waved me to a seat. Duayne closed the door and stayed with
us, sitting at a small table off to my left, opening a stack of mail
and sorting it into piles, pursing his lips in and out like a fish.

Drake talked into the phone in clipped, elliptical phrases that
made it clear that he was busy about important matters. He ignored
me. Maybe he knew I never vote.

I looked around. There was lots of wood paneling, tall windows
with expensive drapes, and Oriental rugs lying around on what
might have been teak flooring. Someone had put a lot of money
into furnishing and decorating an elegant office, only to have
someone else move in who didn't give a damn what it looked like.

The place was a mass of clutter. Most of the built-in book
shelves were crammed with stacks of papers and large looseleaf
notebooks lying on top of each other on their sides. Two steel-
gray metal file cabinets sat in one corner, a large corrugated cardboard box on top of one of them, a Mister Coffee coffeemaker
and a jumble of bright-colored plastic cup holders on the other.
Drake's desk was in the middle of the room. Cords for the lamp
and the telephone ran down one end of the desk and across the
fringed rug to outlets at the base of the wall to my right. An
extension cord ran from there to the coffeemaker.

When Drake gestured impatiently, Duayne went to the file cabinet, snapped a white cup into a blue holder, and came back with
a dark, foul-smelling liquid. I set it on the corner of Drake's desk
and forgot about it.

The phone conversation dragged on. Who knows whether it was just a game, and how long he would have played?

"I'm in a hurry," I said, standing up, without a clue where I'd go if I left.

"I won't be much longer," Drake said, lifting his chin and covering the phone's mouthpiece with his hand. But he didn't hang up.

"That's the truth," I said. I went to the wall to my right, squatted down near the baseboard, and removed the phone cord clip from its socket.

Drake set the receiver down carefully and stared at me as I returned to my chair and sat down. His pink complexion reddened. He smoothed his hair again.

"Like I said, I'm in a hurry."

"Yes." He nodded his head slowly in a way that meant absolutely nothing. "OK, then, what do you want? Who is this 'Mark' you mentioned?"

"What's with him?" I asked, jerking my head toward Duayne.

"He's my employee. He stays."

"Suit yourself. Mark is your grandson. I'm told you have a grudge against the priest who—"

"Excuse me," he interrupted, then turned to Duayne. "Get outta here."

Duayne tried to hide his disappointment as he darted for the door, closing it behind him.

"That friggin' pervert priest that messed with my grandson thinks I've got a grudge against him, does he? Well, he's goddamn right. So what?"

"I didn't say the priest thinks that. I think it. 'They should cut off his nuts,' I think you said."

"You been talking to my daughter-in-law."

Drake's reputation for being savvy was well earned.

"I've been talking to lots of people. The point is you're known to have hard feelings against Kevin Cunningham. Now someone's trying to...to hurt him. I want to know if it's you."

"This is the strangest goddamn thing I've ever heard of. You're some sort of private investigator, I know that much. I remember meeting you at that fund-raiser. You think I might be up to something, but you don't know for sure. So you just walk up and point-blank ask me? Even if what you're suggesting wasn't preposter-ous, what the hell kind of investigative technique is that?"

"Beats looking for clues," I said, finding myself liking Sam Drake, despite my better judgment. "I know all about the sex abuse charge. I didn't find out from your daughter-in-law. I also know your son was drinking and drove his car into the river and drowned. You blamed the priest for that, and you made threatening remarks about him—to more than one person." That part was a guess. "Now someone's out to get the priest—and trying to kill me while they're at it. Since one logical suspect is you, asking you makes perfect sense to me."

"That's because you're a fool. My daughter-in-law's a fool, too. If she wasn't, she'd never have married my son, the biggest god-damn fool of all." He paused. "Look here, whatever I said when Larry died, those were the words of a grieving father. I don't go around threatening people's lives. When I do make a threat, it's one I can carry out—and intend to. But never a threat of physical harm. It's not my style. Now you—"

"What about Cleveland Richardson?" I asked. "Is hurting peo-ple his style?"

Drake's eyes narrowed. He could have kicked me out then, but curiosity got the best of him. "Richardson and I go back a long time, over twenty years. We're friends—in a professional sense. We share similar political ideas. He and I talked about you, you know, after you barged in on our conversation with Happy Mallory that night. I never understood his concern. I told him he was get-ting hyper, that you were working on some case for Happy or something. I guess I was wrong though, huh?"

He hadn't answered my question, and I didn't answer his. I tried again. "So, what about Richardson? Maybe he's the one with a grudge."

"If you're suggesting Richardson might be trying to harm that priest, you're nuts. What the hell does he care? All he did was handle the claim against that fucking pervert. Besides, he's so goddamn busy right now he's hardly got time to take a leak, for chrissake. What's he gonna be worried about some pervert priest that oughta have his nuts...I mean...that oughta be sent to Siberia or some place. The whole idea is ludicrous.''

''Maybe it's politics. Maybe there's some connection between the priest and Happy Mallory.''

''Christ almighty! What the hell kind of connection? That's ridiculous.''

''Maybe Richardson's gay, and—''

''You really *are* nuts!'' Drake was wide-eyed with amazement. ''Jesus, comin' up with crap like that.''

''Like I said, beats looking for clues.''

He picked up the phone, stared at it a second, then glared across at me. I got up and plugged the jack back in.

''Tell Duayne to come in here,'' he yelled into the phone, and banged it down. ''Now, Foley, if you don't mind, I got things to do. In other words, get your ass outta here, or there'll be a cop at the door in five minutes.''

I left, convinced that Drake didn't know a damn thing about Kevin's being Harriet's son—or about anything else I needed to know.

I'd have bet my life on it.

THIRTY-FOUR

I DROVE UP TO EVANSTON, and if an insight into what was going on showed up on the way, it must have been in a southbound lane. About the only useful idea I had was to call Miz Becky's Tap and apologize for missing the entire weekend—again. Becky herself answered the phone, and took the apology with a nonchalance that made me wonder if she'd noticed.

The rest of the way I thought about Cass. I drove to her place, sat out in front from then until dark, hoping she'd see me and hoping she wouldn't. I was lonely, depressed, and suddenly hungry.

There's a hot dog stand on Central Street next to Northwestern's Dyche Stadium. With two dogs, double fries, and a root beer, I sat on a stool by a narrow counter up against the windows and stared out across the alley and the empty parking lot. Beyond that, the stadium loomed dark against the night-lit sky, as big and vacant as the space inside me that hot dogs would never fill up.

I called the Lady, but she was out. So I drove to Saint Ludella's.

When I got there, Celia and Edna were in the kitchen washing dishes. Edna had to run home for a while, and Celia and I sat in the kitchen and shared a pot of decaf.

"Kevin is drinking again," she said. "Not nonstop. But I'm afraid that's on its way. I can't help him. I never could."

I couldn't help him with his drinking either, and I wasn't doing much to help him with anything else. I swirled the coffee around in my mug. "Did you ever finish reading *Murder in the Cathedral?*"

"Yes, but—"

"You read me a line from it," I said, "when we first met, in Lexington. It keeps coming back, as though it applies to me."

"I remember. And I'm sure it *does* apply to you." I must have looked startled, because her voice became apologetic. "What I mean is…isn't that why we read T. S. Eliot? Because his thoughts *do* apply to us—all of us.''

"I don't know. *I* read *Murder in the Cathedral* because Cass had it on her students' reading list.''

"Cass?''

"My wife. She teaches English Literature and I read everything on her list, thinking it might help. But anyway, that line you read me. It's been bothering me. I don't remember the exact words, but the idea was that none of us turns our own wheel, someone else turns it for us, and there's no use trying to do anything. I don't like it.''

She peered into her mug, as though reading something in the coffee. "'Only the fool,''' she recited, "'fixed in his folly, may think he can turn the wheel on which he turns.'''

"That's it,'' I said. "I don't like it. The idea that someone is turning my wheel, using me. As though it's foolish to try to do anything, useless or something. I don't like the idea.''

"You know, when I read it I didn't think that line had anything to do with not trying, or not doing. I thought it meant that the wheel of life constantly turns, that one can't turn the wheel back to somewhere it's not, back to a time that's gone.''

"'Time marches on,' or something?''

"In the play, the archbishop was being tempted. One temptation was to try to turn back the wheel, to pretend he could return to good times past, to abandon the course he'd chosen. It was the temptation *not* to go forward. That was what he rejected as foolish.''

"And in the end they killed him. I remember that.''

"Yes, they did. But…in the end we all die. While we live, we choose. We either do, or we don't do. And in the end we die.''

"In the meantime, I'd rather do than not do. But I'm trying to help Kevin, and I run from here to there. And when I get to there, I find something that's already happened. So I run and carry that news to someone else, and then before I know it something else has happened. I confront people who I think must know something and they laugh at me, or tell me I'm crazy. It's like my wheel is being turned, and I'm just riding it. I don't like it.''

Celia's eyes were closed and she sat very still. I'd been talking to myself, not paying attention to her. Finally she opened her eyes. "I haven't been much help, have I? Not to you, and not to Kevin. All I can do is think, all day, every day. Someone is destroying my son. At first I thought they wanted to kill him. But now it's become clear that death isn't really...sufficient somehow. Rather, Kevin is to suffer, suffer terribly—and not just physically. He has so few friends, so few people to cling to, and he's being crushed— psychologically crushed, crushed in his spirit—by watching them die, one by one. I think of that note. Finally, he's to be left all alone...and then to be taken to a cage, a place where Satan rules. I wonder if that doesn't mean a psychiatric hospital."

"It's crazy, Celia."

"Yes, crazy, but not haphazard. There's a plan being worked out, something we're not grasping. And I've started to wonder...I know it sounds strange...but is Kevin's suffering—his destruction—really the goal in all this?"

"I'm not sure I follow you."

"Well...why those notes to Harriet? Someone hates Kevin, so why involve Harriet? What part does she play in—"

I jumped in. "What's been bothering me is what part I play."

She shook her head slightly, as though I'd broken her train of thought. "Yes," she said, "there's your part, too. For one thing, they want me, and they hope you'll lead them to me."

"I've been careful. I'm sure they don't know where I'm staying—or where I've hidden you."

"And then, whether you lead them to me or not, they'll try to kill you."

"I'm not so—"

"You're in their way, a complication. And...there's another reason. Kevin knows you now, as someone who's trying to help him."

"One of those 'fools who reach out to him.' If I die, Kevin loses again."

"Yes. And he's close to the limit now, Mal. I know it. He's coming apart."

THIRTY-FIVE

EARLY TUESDAY MORNING Edna drove me downtown and dropped me near Union Station. I treated myself to breakfast at Lou Mitchell's before the line got too long, then walked to the Hamilton Inn and checked out.

With no rain in sight it was a good day to head for Caesar Scallopino's Body Shop, near Western and Touhy, to replace the Cavalier's blown-out window and fill in the bullet holes. Caesar's an ex-client. He wouldn't insist on an appointment and he wouldn't keep asking why I didn't make an insurance claim.

When I got there, Caesar said he'd have to replace the entire driver's door. "Won't be no problem finding one," he said, needling me. "The junkyards are full of cars like yours." It would take a couple of days, and he'd leave the car at a place we agreed on.

It was a mile's walk to the el. I rode to Evanston, and walked home to check my mail. No one was watching my place. There wasn't any mail. With no credit cards, there seldom is.

It was nine o'clock when I stopped at the Lady's. She was gone for the day, so I went on to Dr. Sato's. He wants to know when any of his students use his training outside of the dojo. I told him what had happened in the motel garage—about the shove in my back and what I had done and how the man had slid to the floor like a bag of charcoal briquets.

Dr. Sato looked up at me. "Well then," he finally said, "warm up, please. Ten minutes for the mind, five minutes for the body, and I will return."

That's all he said. Not *Good job*. Not *You could have done it differently*. Just *Warm up, please*.

LATER THAT DAY, I sat on the edge of an ancient chair in a hushed, dimly lit reception area that smelled like old stuffed furniture, notebook in hand, waiting for Sister Xavier Marie to decide what to do with me. She was maybe eighty years old and she'd been at Cardinal Stritch Home, the receptionist told me, for forty-three years. If her body was worn a little frail, her mind was clipping along just fine. That was unfortunate. It made her uneasy about me.

"Yes, Mr. Fitzgerald," she said, "you *did* call this morning. But that's still rather short notice. You can't expect us to give you a tour of our facility today."

That's what her voice said, anyway. Her eyes said something more like: *You sure don't look to me like a free-lance writer on assignment for* The National Catholic Reporter.

So it was her voice, not her eyes, I chose to answer. "Oh no, ma'am...uh...Sister. This is just a preliminary visit. You know, sort of get oriented, make a few notes. I'll have to come back, with a camera, and spend a whole day. Interview some of the staff and all. I want people to know about the work you do here. I'm putting together a series. I call it...'Finding Our Own Mother Theresas, Right Here in Chicago.'"

She wasn't buying it. And not surprising. It was pretty bad lying, after all. But locked into the sights of a shrewd old nun— it isn't easy. Besides, my gaze kept drifting over her shoulder toward the front door.

Finally, there he was. Like Gatsby's man had said: "Tuesdays and Fridays, unless he's in the middle of a trial or something."

He nodded to the receptionist and headed straight for the elevator.

"Oh look, Sister," I whispered, "isn't that someone famous? A Mr....Robertson or something?"

She twisted her head, then turned back. "Famous? Oh, my. Not that I know of. He's been very good to us, though. Mr. Richardson is one of our most generous benefactors."

"Of course!" I said. "Cleveland Richardson. The famous lawyer. I covered one of his trials when I was with the *Sun-Times*. Before the ulcer and the heart attack. These days I stick to religious stories. Less stress. And I'd like to be around to see the kids all graduate."

Sister Xavier Marie smiled a sympathetic, but still doubtful, smile.

"Anyway, Sister, maybe I could interview Mr. Richardson. Find out what makes him so generous. You know, things like that."

"I'm afraid not. Mr. Richardson doesn't wish his generosity to Stritch Home made public. He's said so himself, many times."

"Well," I said, "we'll have to respect his wishes. But...I wonder who he comes to see twice a week, anyway?"

"Why, it's Alex Boyd. Three years now. Until about a year ago a family member came too, every day. But now—" Something clicked. "Who said twice a week? I'm sure I didn't say that."

"Oh...I'm sorry, ma'am...I mean, Sister. I thought that's what you said."

It was all downhill with Sister Xavier Marie after that, and I was out of there in a hurry.

THE PUBLIC LIBRARY'S NOT BAD. But for my money, if it's not too far out of the way, the Chicago Historical Society's the place to look up old Chicago news. Of course, busloads of chattering kids come and go, nonstop, but they seldom show up in the third-floor Library/Archives Room. Up there it's quiet and uncrowded, with sturdy chairs at the microfilm machines and excellent rest rooms. Right at the edge of Lincoln Park, and free if you're going only to the third floor. Can't beat it.

Starting three years ago to the day, I worked my way backward and forward through the *Tribune* and the *Sun-Times*. In less than an hour, I found Alex Boyd, all over both papers. Headline news for a day: HEROIC MIDNIGHT RESCUE. CITY WORKERS FOIL SUICIDE TRY. Then a day or two later the *Times* had this. SNATCHED FROM DEATH...AND WORSE OFF ALIVE?

It had been a clear, warm March night. Two city bridge tenders, their shift just ended, were lifting a couple of beers beside the Chicago River before heading home. They saw Boyd climb up on the railing of the Franklin Street bridge, stand there a few seconds clinging to a steel girder, and then hurl himself down into the water. One jumped in after him, while the other ran for a lifesaving ring. They managed to drag him out and keep him alive until the paramedics arrived.

Boyd had been twenty-four years old then, and a recent graduate of John Marshall Law School. The papers printed one of those stylistically posed graduation pictures. Viewed on the washed-out microfilm screen, he could have been almost anyone. He'd passed the bar exam, but apparently was depressed because some run-in with the law kept the Supreme Court's Committee on Character and Fitness from certifying him for admission to practice law.

The tragedy was that, though Boyd's life was saved, he'd suffered a severe spinal injury. His brain worked just fine, and he could move his eyes and his eyelids. But that's all he would ever move again.

OUTSIDE THE HISTORICAL CENTER, I waved a twenty at the cabdriver. "Twenty-six hundred south California. And I'm in a hurry."

He grumbled and cursed all the way, mostly in Pakistani or Sumerian or something. But he drove like hell, and we got there at four twenty-four. I left him the twenty and dashed across the concrete plaza and up the steps.

Twenty-sixth and Cal, they call it, and it's really two buildings. One's a squat stone block that looks like a massive old courthouse. The other's a glass-and-steel high-rise that looks like a 1970s office building. They are what they look like and, together with the hideous jail that sprawls to the west behind them, they're the corporate headquarters of Cook County's most recession-proof industry—the criminal justice system.

On the fifth floor of the high-rise, a thin, pale man was just locking the plate-glass door of the Clerk's Office when I got to it at four twenty-nine. He reconsidered, opened the door, then locked it behind me. Across the room at his computer, he punched away for a while, earning disapproving looks from his coworkers—mostly women with blue-tinted hair—who were streaming toward the employees' exit. Finally, he looked up from the screen. "Sorry, sir," he said. "There is a case under that name, *People versus Alex Boyd.* But the file's in storage. I can order it. Take a week, maybe."

"You have any information about the case at all?"

"Just what's here," he answered, swiveling the screen so I could read it.

It was a two-line summary, with a case number, some dates, then a string of abbreviated entries:

PCtrSb MDSuQu/Brf/Arg/Dn PG/FG NPrCv MD1410/Dn
Pr18Mo J Mallory

"We're closing up," the clerk said. "I can print that out for you. Or do you want me to order the file?"

"I'll take a printout. Thanks."

He'd been more helpful than he'd needed to be, and he deserved a tip. But the video camera lurking up in the corner would have seen it as the payment of a bribe to a public official.

THIRTY-SIX

ANOTHER CAB TOOK ME TO Saint Ludella's. Pretty soon Edna had pork chops sizzling in the frying pan, with rice and green beans being boiled or steamed or something. There were two pork chops apiece. Edna ate one, Celia ate one, and I ate four. But they did all right; vegetables and rice have never been favorites of mine.

At six-thirty, they accused me of skipping out on the dishes again, which was true. I took Casey's Aries and in an hour I was sitting in the Lady's front parlor.

"So, it's got to be Richardson," I said, after telling her what I'd learned. "But then...since so often they know just where I am, maybe Jerry Wakefield's involved, too."

"Possibly. But none of it rings quite true. I wish..." Her voice trailed off then, as though she'd lost interest. "I would like a glass of brandy," she said.

So we drank brandy. Or at least I did. She looked very tired, which wasn't like her.

"Anyway, I've run out of ideas," I said, heading across the room for a refill. "That's why I'm here."

"You think perhaps I know what to do." There was more than just fatigue in her voice. There was a tightness, a strained sadness that caught me off guard. Then, seeing I'd poured myself just a finger of brandy, she added, "Oh, take more than *that*, Malachy. There's plenty."

The Lady never says things like that, not to me, not about alcohol. I didn't like it.

When I was back in my chair, she stared down at the floor in front of her. "A Miss Holmes called late last night."

"Holmes? *Cheryl* Holmes?"

"Yes, from the hospital. She...well, she thought perhaps I'd know better than you what to do, so she called here. I wish..." She rotated her brandy glass one way, then the other.

The silence in the room was screaming, though, and it forced her to go on. "She said...she told me Casey's family has been talking to his doctors...about...about turning off the machine, the 'ventilator' they call it. They—"

"Wait a minute," I said, my voice louder than I'd expected, and on the rise. "They can't *do* that." I drained my glass and went back to the side table, then banged the glass down, too hard, and turned around. "You *told* her that, didn't you? Didn't you, Helene? Didn't you *tell* her they couldn't turn off the machine?"

She kept quiet. Why the hell should she tell Cheryl Holmes what Casey's family couldn't do?

I didn't want any brandy. My stomach was churning. I paced in circles around the room, banging into tables and chairs, picking books up and slamming them down again. "What is *wrong* with them, Helene? Kill their own *brother?* What are they? Some kind of animals, for God's sake?"

I spun around and looked at the Lady. She was staring at her glass. It was empty.

"Malachy, you—"

"No," I said. "I don't want to hear it. Jesus, Helene, he's not *dead*. He's just in a coma or...whatever it is. I mean, Casey's as strong as an ox. He'll come out of it." I sat down, then stood up again. "Look, Helene, go *talk* to them. Please? They can't do this to me...I mean...to Casey. He's not dead. Would you just talk to them?"

She opened her mouth, but she wasn't fast enough for me.

"For Christ's sake, Helene. Don't just *sit* there! *Say* something, will you?"

So she did.

She took a deep breath and started talking. "I left at six this morning. I drove to Shiloh. I spent the entire day at the hospital. I talked to the family, and to doctors, social workers, nurses, hospital administrators."

"Why doesn't he get better?"

"Things keep going wrong—internal hemorrhaging, organ failure. He's had so many surgeries. They...none of them hold out much hope. No one is pressing the family about the life-support systems. It's just...something to be thought about. I talked for hours, *hours,* to his sisters—and his mother, poor dear. They're marvelous people. So much faith. But they kept asking me what to do. As though I knew something they didn't. It was...very, very difficult.'' Tears poured down the Lady's cheeks. ''But why me? I have my own difficulties...with believing, understanding. Why does *everyone* always ask *me*...''

She didn't finish. It was the first complaint I'd heard from her since the death of her husband. I was stunned. She sounded like me. She needed someone to comfort her, to reassure her.

But I didn't want her to be like me.

So I just kept still, not even looking at her. Finally, when I heard her take a deep breath, I said, ''Helene, did the family...is he...''

''Oh no, Malachy. No, no, no. They said they'd wait. At least a few more days. They said they'd call me before they...did anything. I asked them to do that. I don't know why, but I did. And they promised. But then...''

She stood up and went over to adjust the drapes. They were closed. They didn't need adjusting. With her hands on the drawstrings, she looked back at me and said, ''There was something the surgeon said...''

I stared at her.

''He said that even if Casey survives, Malachy, well...they just don't know. A lot of damage has been done. All those surgeries. They don't know...if he lives...how well he'll function.''

THIRTY-SEVEN

THE LADY tried to convince me to be careful, to continue to stay out of sight. But the time for that was over.

Going back to Saint Ludella's didn't seem important, and I walked down the stone drive from the Lady's house, past the coach house, to the street. I'd have welcome something just then, trouble—anything. But there was no blue Bonneville, nothing unusual. I walked back to the coach house and went upstairs. With a numbness in my brain, I sat on the sofa, knowing sleep was out of the question.

It had been wrong to take Casey with me to Bullhead Lake. I knew that when I did it. The bullet in his back, the tubes running in and out of him, the electrodes, the plastic bags collecting waste...

I sat and stared down at my shoes and hated myself because I wanted to kill somebody. And I thought I knew who the somebody was.

THE NEXT MORNING, R. Pennington, clearly unimpressed by my anger and frustration, seemed especially happy to tell me Harriet wasn't available. "Miss Mallory is engaged in an important meeting. She's not to be disturbed."

We sparred awhile, but she wouldn't give an inch.

So I sat in the reception area and waited. I'd order out for lunch if I had to. Harriet wouldn't get out of there without passing me.

People came and went. Some of them smiled nervously at the sour look on my face. Twice Ms. Pennington came out to tell me that Harriet was "still engaged. But if you want to make an appointment..."

What I wanted was to strangle R. Pennington.

Through it all, I felt my brain reaching out for something, something I knew was important. But whatever it was sat just beyond the edge of memory.

Finally the receptionist waved to me. Frustrated, and with the anger building, I strode over to her desk. She had the phone cradled against her ear and was scribbling on a notepad. When I tapped on the plaque that said J. Birnbaum, she held up her finger to quiet me, wrote some more, and put the phone down.

"That was Ms. Pennington," she said. "Happy Mallory has left the office."

"What do you mean left? She knew I was waiting for her. I've been sitting right here, so I'd catch her if she went out."

"Our offices cover several floors, sir. Miss Mallory was in a conference room downstairs." She smiled sympathetically. "Frankly, I don't know why Ms. Pennington didn't tell you that. But anyway, she said Miss Mallory and Mr. Richardson were on their—"

"Cleveland Richardson?" I swallowed hard, taking air down the wrong pipe when I did. "Where are they going?" I managed to croak.

"I really don't know. But Ms. Pennington says they left a message for you...if you're interested...?"

"C'mon, Ms. Birnbaum..."

She consulted her notepad. "They'll be tied up in meetings all day. But you're to meet them both at Mr. Richardson's office, tonight, at eight-thirty sharp. It's very important."

People were dying. Her own son was being ripped apart, and was probably scheduled to die as well. And Happy Mallory couldn't give me five minutes because she was too busy with her goddamn political ambitions—and with Cleveland Richardson.

In the lobby of the building, I started for the pay phone. Then through the plate-glass windows I saw a policeman approaching the Aries out front in the No Parking zone, just pulling his ticket book from his hip pocket. I raced for the door. One more ticket made no difference, but I wanted to yell at someone.

It felt like a five-minute push, but the slow-motion revolving door finally released me onto the sidewalk. The cop by Casey's car was middle-aged and carrying twice the weight his genes had ordered for his bone structure. He was already writing out a ticket when he looked up and peered at me through the slits in his red, pudgy face. Then, as if to prove that life weren't all bad, he *stopped writing*—repeat—stopped writing. Everyone in the world knows you're too late if they've already started writing the ticket. Cops always tell you that, even the ones that apologize.

"Just in time, pal," the fat cop said. "Better move it on out, though."

He turned and waddled ahead to the BMW parked in front of Casey's Aries. I got in the car but couldn't drive away because the cop's Harley three-wheeler blocked the way. He finished writing the ticket and slapped it on the BMW. As he headed toward the blue-and-white Harley, he bent his head toward the open window of the Aries. He chuckled. "Fuckin' smart-ass BMW's," he said, "I hate 'em."

"Me too," I lied. "Buy American, that's what I say."

He hauled himself onto the three-wheeler, punched it into gear, and was gone. He'd done me a favor, even if he did remind me a little of an overinflated version of Jerry Wakefield.

I drove straight to Saint Ludella's. Edna was in the kitchen, doing something with piles of carrots and potatoes and a chunk of pork butt, and watching a very young Mary Tyler Moore in black and white.

Celia was sitting in a room on the second floor, holding a book in her lap and looking out the window down at the street.

"For God's sake, Celia," I said, pulling down the shade, "stay away from the window, will you?"

She stared at me. "What's wrong?"

"What do you mean, what's wrong? Someone's trying to kill you and kill Kevin and—"

"No, that's not what I mean," she interrupted. "You look different. What's wrong? Has something happened?"

"Not yet. Nothing's happened yet. But...but Casey's going to die—or something worse. I never believed that before. Now I do. I need to do something about it."

"What are you going to do?"

"I don't know. Don't say anything to Edna. I mean about Casey. But you have to be careful. Keep the doors locked. Don't let anyone in. Don't call anyone. Don't take any calls."

She nodded her head, patiently. Those were the same instructions she and Edna had been following all along.

I moped around the rest of the afternoon. It didn't help when I remembered—out of nowhere—that I'd never mailed the rest of my seven cards to Cass.

Supper was a pretty somber affair. The idea of meeting Harriet and Richardson that night at his office didn't much appeal to me. It didn't make sense.

Nothing new about that.

THIRTY-EIGHT

AT EIGHT THIRTY-ONE I stood under the light at Richardson's front door. The office was dark, the picture window reflecting back the lights from the street. A brass sign beside the door directed visitors to ring the bell after six o'clock. So I did. No answer. Another ring. No answer.

The door was unlocked. Even if I'd have used my head I suppose it wouldn't have made much difference in the long run. I pushed the door open and stepped inside.

That's when the world came to an end, the whole damn show, reversing the big bang, imploding right into my left ear. It was a very loud, very bright implosion and, even if the world didn't actually end right then, most of what happened for a time after that happened without my participation. What I did was flop on my face on the floor.

When the beat of the drum woke me up, I was still flat on my face. It was a big bass drum, hitting two steady beats per second, inside my skull, on the right side, but driving viscous waves of ache sloshing up and over the top of my brain, to wash down over the sharper, more jagged pain on the left side.

I moved. My left hand felt my left ear, but my ear didn't feel my hand. I struggled to my knees, knowing I should open my eyes and investigate that sticky stuff. The eyes were slow to obey and when they did the light hurt them and they shut down again before they saw anything.

So who needed eyes? What's to expect but blood on an ear that stops a set of brass knuckles? And it didn't take eyes to know the tile floor under me wasn't the carpeted floor I'd fallen on, or that beyond the beat of the drum a radio played in the distance.

In fact, if the drum would have shut up, I'd have lain back down and gone to sleep. Instead, I lurched to my feet and forced my eyes to stay open and take an inventory. I learned I was in Richardson's copy room—just me, the photocopy machine, lots of paper in packages of five hundred sheets each, and the inside of a locked door. I learned I still had my wallet and my watch, and that it was eight forty-nine. I learned I didn't still have the Beretta. Ah, well...

By nine-fifteen, the drumbeat had eased a bit. The sound of the radio still came down the hall from the front of the building. I was sitting on the floor paging through the photocopier instruction manual when footsteps came clicking down the tiled floor of the hall. I sat and waited. The steps paused for a moment outside the door, then moved away, backtracking a few steps. A muffled splashing sound came through the wall behind the copier. A toilet flushed, and the steps returned to the front of the building.

When I finished the manual I felt qualified as a "key operator," the employee to call when the machine won't work. When the problem stymies the key operator, you call in the "certified repair technician," who probably studies a much bigger book.

By ten o'clock, even without the bigger book, I'd been able to remove one of two heavy black rollers that move copy paper from Area C to Area D inside the copier when all's going well. The roller was about eighteen inches long. It wasn't a Beretta. It wasn't brass knuckles. It wasn't even a very good club. But it was the club I had.

The ceiling was only about eight and a half feet high and, if I stood on top of the copier, I could reach out and remove the fluorescent lighting tubes from the recessed fixture. When they came to get me from the room, the light would be out. I'd be standing on top of the machine and I'd bash whoever it was on the head with the roller. Not a great plan. But it was the plan I had.

Then, staring up at the light fixture, I had another idea. The ceiling was a dropped ceiling of acoustic tile below what must have been, in this old building, ten-foot ceilings or higher. Working quietly, I stacked packaged reams of copy paper on top of the machine.

The ceiling tiles were eighteen-inch squares, laid in a metal framework suspended below the original ceiling. Standing on the machine, I pushed up a tile close to the wall and slid it to the side. Then, stepping up on the stack of paper, I was able to poke my head and wriggle my shoulders through the hole. There was nearly a yard of dark space above the dropped ceiling, criss-crossed with electrical conduits and heating ducts.

The wall between the copy room and the bathroom was plasterboard fixed to aluminum studs, eighteen inches apart. The wall stopped at the level of the dropped ceiling, while the studs continued the remaining three feet up to the original ceiling.

Reaching between the aluminum studs, I found the same type of dropped ceiling on the other side of the wall. Removal of a section created an adjoining hole in the bathroom ceiling. The bathroom was empty, the light out, the door open just a crack.

As I tensed my arms to hoist myself up into the space between the ceilings, footsteps came down the hall again. Easing down from the machine, I switched off the overhead light and lay on the floor. The steps reached the door. They stopped.

"Hey!" A man's voice. "You 'wake yet?"

"My head hurts," I mumbled, groaning and keeping my face close to the floor.

"Ain't that too bad." The voice through the door wasn't comforting, but it was better than the man himself coming through. "Go on back to sleep, asshole. You ain't got much longer to wait, anyway."

His steps disappeared down the hall. With the roller stuffed under my belt, I climbed back on the machine and, reaching out, twisted the fluorescent tubes in the ceiling fixture until they went off. In total darkness then, I reached up and hauled myself through the hole in the ceiling. For a moment, I hung with my legs dangling below the dropped ceiling, my upper body straddling the wall between the two rooms. Just the effort of hoisting myself up had exhausted me. Waves of pain started pulsing again through my head. The temptation was to hang there awhile, to rest.

Suddenly the phone rang from the front of the building and jarred me into action. Wrestling my feet up through the hole behind me, I managed to get my entire body above the dropped ceiling, lying across the framework that held the tiles.

The metal framework creaked and swayed a bit but held. Keeping my body stretched over as wide an area as possible, to spread the weight, I wormed and twisted my way forward between the studs. Finally, my feet were over the hole in the bathroom ceiling. I inched backwards then, lowering first my legs, then my trunk, through the hole. I dropped to the bathroom floor, between the toilet and the sink.

I eased the door closed and turned on the light. Four coffee mugs and four glasses were lined up neatly on a shelf over the sink. Standing on the closed toilet lid, I started tossing them, one by one, through the hole in the ceiling, sending them to the floor of the copy room. The mugs banged and bounced around as they landed, but the glasses gave the noisy, crashing effect I liked best. So I alternated—mug, glass, mug, glass.

By the second glass, steps were hurrying down the hall. Tossing one more mug for good measure, I stepped down to the floor, switched off the light, and waited. Once his footsteps passed, I inched the bathroom door open a crack.

He stood outside the copy room door, a thin man of medium height, with a gun in his right hand. He had to be alone or he'd have called for someone.

"What the fuck you doin' in there?" he called, leaning toward the closed door, head craned forward, like a weasel sniffing out a rabbit hole.

When there was no answer, he unlocked and opened the door slowly, cautiously, pushing it all the way inward. I saw him reach across his body with his left hand for the wall switch. There was a pause, then a slight hitch to his shoulders when he realized the switch was on and there was no light. He crouched slightly, chin thrust forward, the gun held waist-high in front of him.

Before he could step into the copy room, I was behind him, swinging the heavy roller down at his skull in a wide arc. Some predator's sense warned him, though, and he twisted his head just slightly, enough to cause the roller to glance off his ear and land on his right shoulder, near the neck. A solid, painful blow, but not enough to drop him. He straightened and as he tried to turn, I kicked him from behind, hard, up between his legs.

He yowled and doubled over but completed his turn, the gun still in his hand, pointed downward. There was rage and surprise in his eyes as he lifted his head and saw me. The gun hand started upward. What Dr. Sato would have done, who knows? What I did was swing the roller horizontally at his head, with every ounce of energy I had left. It caught him in the left ear. If there'd been room, it would have lifted him off his feet. As it was, he crashed into the wall and, legs crumpling, sagged to the floor.

By the time his knees hit the floor, he was already scrambling clumsily for the gun that had slipped from his hand. Why don't they stay unconscious, like they do in the movies? or like I did when they hit me?

I didn't like it very well, but I was still the rabbit and he the weasel. I brought the roller down, hard. This time on the crown of his head. This time he didn't move. I stuffed his revolver under my belt.

He was breathing when I rolled him onto his stomach, and I was thankful for that. He was nothing but bone and muscle, and the extension cord I used to tie his hands behind his back was too stiff and slippery to hold him for long. In the secretaries' area, on a shelf above the postal machine and scale, were several rolls of tape for wrapping packages for mailing. I wound the nearly indestructible tape around his hands behind his back, then yards more around his chest, fixing his upper arms to his torso.

By this time the weasel was conscious—a little woozy and a lot unhappy. Finding he had nothing helpful to say, I put his brass knuckles in his mouth and taped it shut. We walked to the front of the building. On a table where a week ago there'd been an expensive-looking vase, there was now a cheap-looking portable radio. Beside it was my Beretta.

I turned off the radio, pocketed the Beretta, and took the weasel on the elevator to the basement. I left him there, in one of the darker corners behind a case of toilet paper set on an old file cabinet, with another fifty feet or so of tape fixing him to one of the new structural steel posts that supported the first floor.

Back upstairs, wanting to leave them wondering, I raced around—retightening the fluorescent lights, replacing the ceiling tiles, reinstalling the roller, cleaning up the broken pottery and glass, and locking the copy room door. When everything was back as far as possible as it had been, I collapsed on one of the comfortable couches in the reception room.

The table lamp was off, the curtains pulled tightly across the window to the street. It was very dark, with the only light coming from far down the hall, where the bathroom door was open and the light on. I sat in the dark on the sofa to catch my breath.

It was then that the back door of the building banged open.

What followed was a nervous silence, unless you counted the closing of the back door, or the pounding of my heart and head in tandem.

A man's voice came down the hall. "Hey!" the voice called. "It's me—Runyan. We got her. There was a nigger lady too, wanted to put up a fight. But we got 'em both." The tone was triumphant. "We even left—" He stopped. There was silence, and then the voice turned suspicious. "Everything all right here?"

THIRTY-NINE

NOTHING WAS ALL RIGHT.

We got 'em both. The voice was all too familiar. It was the same voice that had taunted me at Bullhead Lake: *Maybe you oughta check out the boat.* The voice had a name now—Runyan—and when no one answered he knew the answer.

He was alone. He could have retreated out the back door and gone for help. If he had, I could have run out the front door and escaped.

But he didn't retreat, and I didn't run. Mistakes—for both of us.

I picked up the weasel's revolver from where I'd set it on the table beside the silent radio, leaving the Beretta in my pocket. Easing up from the sofa, I crept silently to my right until I could see down the hallway and still remain lost in the shadows of the darkened room.

Runyan was a wide, dark shape moving slowly toward me, still far down the darkened hall. He stopped and quietly, carefully, tried the door of the copy room and found it locked.

Raising the revolver in front of me, I saw Casey, Pamela Masterson, Carl Hemming—their features showing like slides projected on the broad darkness of Runyan's body. They faded and dissolved into the features of Celia and Edna.

We got 'em both.

He moved forward into the light that spilled from the open bathroom door and, as he did, the slides disappeared and he showed features of his own, no ski mask now to hide them. He was tall and very wide, built like a heavyweight boxer, yet otherwise ordinary looking, with a high, pale forehead and straight blond hair that fell over his collar. It struck me as odd somehow that he was older than I was, fifty easily.

He paused and twisted his head to his right to look momentarily into the lighted bathroom.

When he saw it was empty he didn't bother to switch off the light, simply turned his head and continued my way. He carried both hands oddly down beside his thighs, as though they were too heavy to lift. His huge bulk nearly blotted out the light behind him. His steps were deliberate and cautious, yet confident. He must have thought he was invincible.

We got 'em both.

Crouching motionless in the dark, both arms outstretched, I focused on his chest, sighting along the barrel of the revolver.

We got 'em both.

It was as I slowly lowered the barrel of the gun to level at his knees that he must have finally caught my movement in the shadows. I never saw him raise his arms, only saw his hands suddenly out in front of him, a gun wrapped in each fist.

Even as I dove to the side, the *thwat! thwat! thwat!* of three silenced shots pounded into the wall I'd crouched in front of. I moaned then, as though I'd been hit, and rolled farther to my left, ending on my stomach, the revolver pointed at the doorway to the hall.

He came through the door in a crouch, both hands swinging in an arc across the front of him, one high, one low, spraying the room with silenced gunfire. And as he did I squeezed off two deafening rounds in his direction from the weasel's revolver. A third shot went into the ceiling as I threw myself into another roll to my left and something smashed into the right side of my head.

The shadowed room turned red and gray and swirled slowly, the only sounds the dying echoes of the gun shots, overlaid with a horrible howling moan, like a huge yellow hunting hound I'd heard once years ago, his foreleg clamped in the jaws of a beaver trap in the Rockies north of Banff.

The howling dissolved first into a mournful groan, then a whimper. Finally there was nothing—not even the lazy red and gray pinwhirls.

THE LIGHTS ROSE AGAIN, and the screaming pain in my head rose with them. My head must have hit the corner of the glass coffee table I was using to pull myself to my knees. Once on my feet, I stumbled to the receptionist's counter. Steadying myself with my left hand sliding across the countertop, spilling piles of papers and coffee mugs and potted plants to the floor along the way, I moved sideways to my right toward where the huge, silent bulk of the man called Runyan lay sprawled on his face. Wiping the warm revolver clumsily with my shirt tail, I crouched and laid it on the floor beside him, not wanting to touch him, not needing to touch him to know the lights wouldn't rise and the pain wouldn't scream for him again—not ever.

We got 'em both.

Crouching beside the body, I searched for the car keys—Casey's keys—that were missing from my pocket.

They were in Runyan's pocket, of course, and the Aries was parked right where I'd left it in the alley. The hood was warm to the touch.

It was less than a half-hour ride, in the middle of the night, from the dead body in Richardson's glitzy office to the other end of the world.

From the empty street, the windows were dark, shades pulled tight against intruders. The usual dim light glowed high above the front door, casting sad shadows that outlined the word carved in stone. How could they have known to go to the rectory? They must have followed me earlier that day.

I remembered the cop with his ticket book and finally began to understand.

Around the corner, turning into the alley, my headlights were caught for an instant in the neon red eyes of a large gray rat loping at me from the opposite direction. The fat creature stopped, rose ominously on its haunches as though about to attack the intruding car, then turned and lumbered away—not hurrying, unafraid—into the shadows.

The garage door slid upward in front of me, then down behind after I pulled inside. With the Beretta in my right hand, I tried the door into the back hall. It was unlocked—a first in all my trips there.

I stepped inside. The hallway light was on, as always. I stood motionless for a moment, ears straining, aching with the effort to hear anything at all, but there was nothing but my own soft breathing. The sound of the overhead garage door would have announced my presence. So I stood in the hallway just inside the door, at the foot of the back stairs, and called in a voice that echoed throughout the house, "Edna! Celia!" Then again, "Edna! Celia!"

No one appeared. No one answered.

Although there were front and back stairwells to the upper floors of the rectory, there was only one set of inside stairs to the basement. There was also an exterior basement entrance, near the front of the house, with a metal-clad door that was always carefully locked unless there was a meeting in one of the downstairs conference rooms. At the top of the inside basement stairs was another solid door that could be locked or unlocked only from inside the rectory with a turn bolt. I threw the bolt. If there was anyone down there, they wouldn't easily get in.

Once again moving through the building in careful, eerie solitude—as on that first night that seemed so long ago—I went up the rear stairway. Switching on every light, trying all the doors from rear to front on the third floor, I found nothing. I heard nothing either, except—as had happened that first time—when I stopped and stood silent. Then there were the same complaining creaks and groans, the soft murmurs, the whispered sighs of all those long-dead priests, hovering just beyond the boundaries of my vision. They were the same, yet this time different. They sounded more restless, more anxious, more angry and afraid of events occurring right in their midst yet beyond their control. They sounded more like me.

There was one thing certain, though. There was someone not a ghost, someone not me, somewhere in that house. The restless clergy could feel it—and so could I.

But not on the third floor.

Taking each step deliberately—stopping, listening—I eased down the front stairs to the second floor. Methodically, not trying anymore to shield the sounds of my progress, but stopping to listen at erratic intervals, I searched from front to rear, leaving a trail of lights behind me. Once again, nothing. All the bedrooms, bathrooms, sitting rooms were empty—every closet, every nook, every hidden corner, every twist of corridor—no Edna, no Celia, no one, nothing. No sign of violence in the rooms the two of them were using. Yet no sign of them, either.

Down the back stairs from the second floor to the first, I was running now, through all the offices and waiting rooms, the dining room, kitchen, the housekeeper's room where I was living. Nothing. No one. But there had to be.

I fumbled with the lock on the basement door, adrenaline pumping, fingers clumsy. Whoever it was, they were in the basement. I could feel the presence. I pulled the door open.

There was a landing at the top of the stairs, with shelves for cleaning materials, and hooks for mops and brooms and dustpans.

He was sitting on the floor at the top of the stairs, his back against the wall, his knees pulled up to his chin. One eye was wide open and staring at me, the other swollen shut under a large purple bulge of a bruise. There was dried blood below the closed eye, and a dried trickle ran down his chin from the corner of his mouth.

His clothes were disheveled and he smelled sour and drunk. I thought he was dead.

But he squeezed his one good eye closed then, and he put his forehead on his knees and his body shook with sobs, just as it had that night in the Lady's parlor when he'd told us what a mess he was.

It was no use asking him what had happened. I left him there and searched the basement and found it empty. His sobbing had stopped by the time I returned to the landing. He said nothing while I pulled him to his feet and dragged him into the kitchen. I sat him at the table and he stared at me as I sponged the blood from his face. When I wrapped ice cubes in a towel and held them to his swollen eye, he sat there with his hands on the table until I took one of them and held it pressed under my hand to the towel and convinced him to hold the cold compress against his face.

Searching the cupboard for coffee, I spoke to him over my shoulder. "Jesus, I thought you were dead."

When he opened his mouth the voice came out as a hoarse whisper. "'Not dead then,'" he recited, "'worse than dead, wishing dead.'"

"Bullshit," I said, a little too loudly. "Living is better than dead—always." But I wasn't so sure.

When the coffee was ready I poured two cups and got a carton of milk from the refrigerator.

He stared at the cup I set in front of him. "I'd like some sugar," he said. He was in a bad way, but there was a residual toughness to him just the same.

"It's in that cabinet, Kevin," I said, wondering how well he'd do. I helped myself to milk.

He didn't want milk, but he struggled to his feet and got the sugar, found a spoon, and sat down again, holding the ice to his head all the while. As he stirred his coffee, he looked across at me with one eye. "They have my mother," he said, slowly, as though forming the words was difficult.

"And Edna?"

"And Edna, too." He drank some of the coffee. "It's my fault. When I got here, I was...I'd had a few drinks and wasn't thinking too clearly. I didn't see anyone. They must have been hiding. They came right in with me when I unlocked the door."

"And they left you here? Did you call the police?"

"No, I can't. They didn't even seem worried about that. They said if I called the police, they'd...what they'd do to my mother, and Edna, would make what happened to...to Pamela look like a kid's game. I believe them." He stared across at me, still holding the ice pack to his eye. "I won't allow you to call the police."

Celia was the mother he knew, but he was Harriet's boy, too.

"So what do we do?" I asked.

"They gave me some instructions."

"Instructions?"

"Yes, about getting my mother back." He peered at me with his one open eye, his face ashen. I wondered how long he was going to last.

"Tell me, Kevin."

He pointed to a soft brown leather attache case that lay on the kitchen counter. "They left that."

"What about it?"

He looked at the clock on the kitchen wall. It was one of those cat clocks, with bugged eyes swiveling left and right and a swinging tail for a pendulum. "I need ten thousand dollars—by ten o'clock this morning."

FORTY

PARTY LEADERS from around the state had gathered at nine o'clock for breakfast in the dining room of the Wilson Harbor yacht club. The press conference was set for ten, to maximize statewide media coverage. A live audience wasn't necessary.

About a mile in from the lake was the Falcon Hotel and the rest of Uptown, but at the harbor the scene was fresh grass and budding trees and moorings starting to fill up for the season with sailboats, a fine backdrop for the announcement of Happy Mallory's candidacy for attorney general. We left the Aries about two blocks away and walked along the water's edge toward the yacht club—the old man and I.

On the car radio, the news stations had been breaking the report of the body of a man discovered in the "elegant, near-north-side office of prominent Chicago attorney Cleveland Richardson." The victim was already identified as having vague ties to gangland figures. So far, there was no mention of another man taped to a pipe in the basement.

The air was clear and morning-cool, and smelled of freshwater fish. The sounds of the traffic on Lake Shore Drive mingled with the lapping of the water and the cries of the gulls that scoured the lakefront.

I felt like I was wearing ankle weights, and the old man who was with me had no trouble keeping up. His name was Patrick and he was sober—or as close to sober as his brain would ever get again. The building manager—maybe with Mitsy's help—was seeing to that. His mind was still there most of the time, even if he looked like the worn-out derelict he'd become. I gave him a few instructions—not very detailed, since I didn't know myself just what would happen—and left him sitting on the curb near the yacht club.

The TV crews were there, dragging cables around and taking light readings. The pro-life people were gathering too, including some I'd seen at Saint Bede's on Sunday night. Drinking coffee and passing around boxes of Dunkin' Donuts, they chatted amiably among themselves as they sorted out signs and stapled them to new pine carrying sticks: PRO-CHOICE IS NO CHOICE! NOT HAPPY WITH HAPPY! ABORTION IS MURDER!

From a private security guard for one of the TV stations, I learned that the pro-choice people had decided to stay away, to avoid a possible confrontation that might detract from the announcement of Happy's candidacy. But there were plenty of cops around, just the same, including a half-dozen blue-helmeted mounted police, their horses switching their tails in nervous flicks.

I wasn't any more interested in the abortion debate than I was in Harriet's candidacy. But the police interested me. There were so many of them—and so many in plainclothes.

When I spotted Kevin, he looked pretty good, considering he hadn't had much sleep and part of the swelling around his eye was turning yellow now, in contrast to the purple. His black suit was freshly pressed, his hair carefully combed, and he had only one shaving nick on his chin. I'd had no sleep and hadn't shaved at all, myself.

Chin held high, body stiffly erect, Kevin chatted with a couple of his fellow pro-lifers. The attache case he'd been given the night before was tucked under his right arm.

He'd told me getting the money as soon as the bank opened would be no problem. I'd told him the deal was all wrong, that no one kidnapped anyone these days for ten thousand dollars, but he insisted on going ahead. Follow instructions and deliver the money, he'd been told, and Celia and Edna would be set free unharmed, at a time and place unstated. He'd seen it as the only chance he had. There was no way to stop him, short of taping him to a pipe in the rectory basement. And then what would I have done?

It wasn't quite ten yet, and no one expected the politicians to come out right on the dot. The protesters, though, had their signs in hand and were walking single file in an uneven circle in the blocked-off roadway that led to the yacht club. Off to the side, the woman who'd led me around the basement of Saint Bede's was talking to Kevin and tapping her pen on her clipboard. The marchers' circle gradually grew as newcomers arrived. Kevin would join in the picketing soon. That was part of the protocol he'd been given.

Around at the rear of the yacht club was an open door. I went through it into a crowded kitchen, where the friendly, greasy odor of eggs and bacon mixed with the pungent smells of various melons, and coffee with a hint of chicory. There were a half dozen kitchen workers, all of them male and all wearing white pants, white shirts, and green, gauzy hairnets to protect the food.

All heads turned my way.

"Just checking security," I announced, on the off chance that one of them might speak English. "That's the dining room, right?" I marched toward a pair of double doors and pushed through without waiting for an answer.

There were maybe forty people in the dining room, sitting in clusters at round, white-clothed tables. Breakfast was ending and a few of them were up and starting to mingle. Richardson wasn't in sight. But the mayor of the city was there, and the president of the County Board, and Sam Drake, all of them sitting at a table with Harriet and Jerry Wakefield.

I leaned over next to Harriet's ear. "I need you—now," I whispered. Wakefield made a move like he was going to stand up, and I leaned on his shoulder—hard—and gently pinched a nerve in his neck. It hurt him, and he let out an angry hiss.

"It's all right, Jerry, please," Harriet murmured. Then, louder, she apologized to the rest of the table and walked with me to the side of the room, near the kitchen doors. By now, more people were on their feet circulating, so we didn't look as conspicuous as we might have.

Harriet was absolutely stunning. She had on a dress that was businesslike and beautiful at the same time, made out of some sort of linen-looking material the color of peaches—real ones, not the dyed kind that come out of a can. She was wearing a scent that made me want to brush my hand across her cheek.

She should have been furious at me for barging in at the worst possible moment, but the look in her eyes was alarm, not anger.

"What's going on?" she asked.

"When's the show start?"

She looked at her watch. "Probably just a few minutes. You need a shave; you look terrible."

"Where's Richardson?"

"I don't know. He was supposed to be here. But...something happened, at his office. That's probably—"

"That's part of it," I said. "There's more to come. Kevin's in danger. I need your help."

"Hey, Happy!" It was Drake, calling from across the room.

"Just a minute," she called back.

I held on to her arm to keep her with me. I told her I hadn't stayed out of it like she'd told me to. I told her about Kevin's sister, and Carl Hemming. I talked fast, and she listened to every word I said without interrupting. There might have been no one else in the room.

I was getting to the end. "And now they've got her, Kevin's mother—Celia, I mean. And another woman. Kevin's out there. He's got a briefcase full of ten thousand dollars he's supposed to pay them, now, right outside, as ransom."

"Ten thousand dollars? That's absurd. And why here? Why in front of all these people?"

"I don't know. But you're right. It doesn't make..."

And then, all the sudden, it *did* make sense.

"It's a setup," I said. "They'll give him something in exchange for the money. Drugs, probably cocaine, maybe heroin, I don't know. But right in front of all the cops, the media, you..."

She got it, too. Her eyes flashed with anger. "How could you let him do such a stupid thing?" she hissed. "He's my son! Why didn't you stop him?"

"I tried talking to him. But if you were in his shoes, would you have listened to me? And what if I locked him in a closet or something, and then his mother...I mean the only mother he..." I stopped. "Look. He's the one who opened the goddamn door for the men who grabbed Celia. He was sloppy drunk and—"

"Hey, Happy! Let's go! You're onstage!" It was Sam Drake. He was careful not to look at me as he took Harriet by the arm. He didn't seem pleased.

She stared back at me as she let herself be led across the room and out the door to the waiting cameras. I followed with the rest of the hangers-on. No one told me not to. No one was interested in anything other than getting close to the portable podium where the microphones were clustered and the cameras would be pointed. I stuck close to Harriet.

The cameras were lined up and ready, the reporters wedged in between and behind them. A row of portable lights suddenly burst on, making the shaded area in front of the building brighter than the sunlight beyond. Harriet was smiling and shaking nearby hands for the cameras. And she was trembling.

I looked for Patrick. He wasn't sitting where I'd left him. Then I spotted the old man, standing next to one of the cameras. He was grinning and looking right at me. I couldn't tell whether or not his brain was engaged.

Someone started to talk into one of the microphones, a preliminary speech about how the party was on the move. He didn't get far before he was interrupted by a rising volume of chanting from the marchers, a few of whom broke ranks and pressed forward now, waving their signs and shouting, "No more dead babies! No more dead babies!"

The cameras pivoted in their direction, just as they'd hoped. Uniformed police moved in and pushed them back into their oblong circle—not really much of a confrontation. The chanting dropped to a lower level again.

"There he is," Harriet whispered. She nodded slightly to the left, to where Kevin was marching with the protesters. He carried a sign in his left hand: NOT HAPPY WITH HAPPY! In his right hand was the leather case with the money. As he walked, he glanced around furtively, searching for his contact.

"Damn him!" she whispered. "Why must he be so stubborn?" Her voice shook and her eyes shone bright with tears.

With order restored, the cameras turned back to the podium. Sam Drake had the mike. "... few minutes, you'll hear from the one who'll make us *all* happy," he said, then paused for the obligatory chuckle from the cluster of payrollers around him, grinning, squeezing together to make sure they were on camera. "But first," he continued, "a few words from the mayor of this, the world's greatest city."

The group applauded enthusiastically as the mayor stepped to the microphone.

What he said I don't know. Because just then I saw the man Kevin was looking for. He came around the corner of the building, to our right, and stood alone in a grassy clearing out past the cameras, staring at Kevin, trying to get his attention without making himself obvious. He was dressed in white, with a green, gauzy net on his head, and held a yellow plastic shopping bag in his right hand.

I leaned toward Harriet's ear. "There," I whispered, "to your right. Kevin will spot him, too, in a minute."

Just then Kevin's back was to the man, but as he continued around in the slow circle, he was bound to catch sight of him. When he did, it wouldn't take long for him to make his way through the media people and the sparse crowd of joggers and dog walkers that was starting to gather.

"Damn him," Harriet repeated, staring at Kevin. "Damn him!"

Leaving Harriet's side, I pushed through the knot of people pressing around the mayor, heading toward the man with the shopping bag. The mayor's speech droned on at the edge of my mind. When I was free of the group I stopped. At least three plainclothes cops were within thirty feet of the man with the bag, and a couple of unmarked cars were inching their way closer.

I was running down a very short list of options when things started to happen around me.

What broke first into my consciousness was the mayor's voice. "Hey! Where the hell is Happy going?" He tried to say it softly, but it was the most sharply enunciated thing he'd said into the mike all morning. He caught himself then, and launched into more political talk, buying time, while voices murmured in confusion.

"... maybe sick or somethin'," someone said. I looked around for Harriet.

She'd broken loose from the group and was making her way toward Kevin. One of the TV crews picked her up on camera and started tracking her. She smiled sweetly and pointed back toward the struggling mayor, making hand gestures that said not to worry, she'd be right back. The cameraman obeyed her and swiveled back to the mayor.

I knew what she had in mind and didn't want everyone else to know. Waving my arms frantically at the old man, I hollered, "Now, Patrick! Now! Do something!"

So he did. Still grinning, he stepped into the open space in front of the podium, wiggled his rear end provocatively, and dropped his pants around his ankles. He wasn't wearing any shorts.

To say chaos reigned would be an understatement. TV cameras swung this way and that, not sure where to aim.

I turned my back on the man with the yellow shopping bag and went after Harriet. Beyond the media line, she picked up speed, straight at Kevin from behind. The marchers were confused, unaware yet that the enemy was in their midst. She slipped up behind Kevin, grabbed the leather case from under his arm, and kept right on going. Kevin didn't know what happened, and by the time he recovered I was holding his arm, keeping him from going after Harriet.

She'd broken up the scheme, and I expected her to march right back to the podium. She could have done it. She was the only one there with the nerve and the presence to have pulled everything back together.

But she never broke stride, continuing across the roadway, then the sidewalk, then the lawn. The mayor kept talking. The cameras swung this way and that. The man in the green hairnet had a confused look on his face. But when Harriet gave him the leather case he handed over the yellow shopping bag.

The two of them turned abruptly away from each other. As they did, plainclothes cops moved in from all sides, most with guns drawn.

Confusion continued for a long time then, much of it captured on videotape. When it was over, they took Harriet and the man in the hairnet away in handcuffs. For a while, no one noticed Kevin lying on the pavement. When they did, they called an ambulance.

Things still didn't quite make sense to me, but it was becoming clearer that the Lady had been right about the sort of person who might be behind all the killing, after all—and Harriet and Sam Drake and Rogelio Sanchez, too.

One thing was certain, though. The announcement that Happy Mallory was running for attorney general of Illinois was canceled.

FORTY-ONE

AT NINE O'CLOCK the following Monday morning, Corinne Macklin burst into Harriet's office. She stopped short, as surprised to see me as I was to see her. She'd put on a pound or two since I'd talked to her outside Judge Klapp's courtroom. Her face was less drawn, more relaxed. She was wearing a print dress, too, instead of a tailored suit. Good changes—to my sexist mind.

"Sit down, Corinne. If you'd rather Mr. Foley leave—"

"Oh no, that's fine, Miss Mallory." She sat in a client's chair and I dropped back onto the sofa.

We all looked at each other for a while, until Corinne said, "You asked to see me, Miss Mallory?" I thought she blushed a little.

"It's about the Krackauer case. I'm sure you know I'm leaving the firm. But I'm telling whoever takes over the case that you should continue assisting." Harriet smiled—drug charges pending, law license under threat, political hopes down the toilet—but she still smiled. "Your work, Corinne, has been really quite impressive."

This time Corinne blushed for sure. "Thank you," she said. "But...I'm leaving the firm too."

Harriet was clearly surprised. "Surely, Corinne, not because..."

"Oh no. I've been thinking about it for several weeks. I'm not sure exactly what I'm going to do. But I...I've signed up for some dance and voice lessons." She paused. "I suppose you think that's foolish."

When she glanced my way, I gave her a wink and a proud grin. I couldn't help it.

"... not foolish at all, Corinne," Harriet was saying. "You should do what you like to do. And whatever it is, I know you'll do well." She looked at her watch. "Of course, you have to be in front of Judge Klapp in fifteen minutes, to get a continuance in Krackauer. Then, who knows?" She smiled again.

Corinne was on her feet and out of there before I could tell if she was blushing again.

"Nice work," I said to Harriet.

Her face sagged, visibly, from fatigue. "There's just...just so much to absorb."

She was right about that.

To begin with, at about the time Patrick Cunningham had been mooning the TV cameras, Celia and Edna, some twelve miles to the south, were with the desk sergeant at the First District, trying to describe the man who'd left them bound and blindfolded in a nearby alley that morning.

Less happily, sometime late that same night Cleveland Richardson ran his office elevator to the basement and then, up on the second floor, opened the ornate, wrought-iron door and stepped out into the empty shaft. He fell about ten feet, and his secretary found him hanging there Friday morning. The suicide note was clearly genuine, even if it explained nothing.

"There's more, though," I said. "Take a look at this."

A few minutes later, Harriet was pacing again. In her hand was the slip of computer paper I'd gotten from the court clerk:

*PCtrSb MDSuQu/Brf/Arg/Dn PG/FG NPrCv MD1410/Dn
Pr18Mo J Mallory*

She could translate the abbreviated summary as well as I could. "Alex Boyd," she said, waving the flimsy paper thoughtfully, as though the ink were still wet. "I do remember. Possession of a controlled substance. The usual motion by the defendant to suppress the evidence—cocaine it was—and to quash the arrest..." Her voice trailed off.

"There were written briefs in addition to oral argument on the motion—not that frequent in Drug Court, right?"

"That's right. Lou Aquino was Boyd's lawyer and I wondered where the kid got the money. I never liked Aquino—an arrogant bastard. He was stunned when I denied the motion and upheld the search and the arrest. I admit, it was a close call." Harriet's admitting it was a "close call" meant most judges would have thrown the case out.

"Then," I said, "with the State able to use its evidence, Boyd's only choice was to plead guilty. You found him guilty on the plea and, with no prior convictions, you could have given him Section 1410 probation. If he stays out of trouble the whole time, he gets the charge wiped out. No conviction on his record. A perfect solution for a first-time offender, law school grad, bright future."

"Yes, I could have done that. But...well, I didn't like Section 1410. Besides, I wanted to send a message—Happy Mallory was tough on drugs."

So, on a questionable case, she'd denied the motion for 1410 probation and hung a straight probation of eighteen months and a felony conviction around Alex Boyd's neck. No jail time, though, so she probably went to bed that night wondering if she'd gotten soft on crime.

I didn't say what I was thinking. But I explained how, six months later, when he couldn't get certified for the Illinois Bar, Boyd jumped off the Franklin Street bridge. And how his leap left him paralyzed from the neck down. I told her how it chilled my blood, and I hadn't wanted to go and see him for myself.

"Cleveland Richardson used to go see him, though—twice a week, every week." I told her that, and then explained the first part of my theory.

She sat behind her desk and stared at me for a long time. "You're saying the plan to strip Kevin of everyone he cared about, leave him out of his mind and absolutely alone in the world, and then lock him away with a cocaine conviction—that the whole thing wasn't really aimed at Kevin at all?"

"Exactly," I said. "Kevin's destruction was important only if you were there, watching it all unfold."

"Insane."

"But carefully planned. The opening move was to remind you of the son you thought you'd forgotten. You're curious first, then worried. Naturally, you want to identify him."

"So I hire you."

"That was probably a surprise. You could have moved in a more...conventional way. Anyway, once you knew who Kevin was, you'd think about him, and eventually...well...come to love him." Harriet stood up and went to the windows, her back to me, but I kept talking. "Only then, after you had a son you loved, would that son's suffering and anguish cause you the pain that was desired."

"My God," she said, her voice shaking.

"The destruction of Judge Mallory's son—'dashed to pieces,' the note said—just as, in the killer's eyes, Judge Mallory destroyed Alex Boyd."

"Alex Boyd. My God...you mean he was Cleveland Richardson's son?"

"I think so."

"Then...what happened drove Richardson insane. He blamed me and..." Her shoulders slumped uncharacteristically. "And now Richardson's dead. It's over."

"It's not over."

She swung around. "What do you mean? Celia and that other woman were let go that morning, apparently even before the press conference. What—"

"Celia was let go because of a shortage of manpower to keep her, and because there was no sense killing her just then. She could be killed anytime, or be used again, especially if something went wrong with the drug bust—which it did."

"But it was Richardson's plan."

"I thought so too. But was it? Don't forget he was with you, at meetings, all day and until nearly midnight the night everything happened."

"Of course. But he had all the money in the world. All those people were hired. They just had to follow his instructions."

"It still doesn't work. Richardson couldn't have guessed all that would happen that afternoon and evening. Besides, he had so many interests—his law practice, politics, investments. He was running all the time just to keep up with everything—and succeeding. This scheme...it wasn't just insane, it was the plan of someone who had no other life beyond that boy."

Harriet stalked around her office, not agreeing, not saying anything.

"Someone else," I continued, "someone whose life was otherwise empty, someone who'd had endless hours to spend nurturing hatred into insane revenge."

Harriet leaned over her desk, straightening stacks of papers absently. "The human mind is capable of anything," she said. "Why couldn't Richardson carry on a hectic but basically normal life and still live another life? Why isn't that possible?"

"Maybe it is," I said, "but we don't have to decide what's possible." I stood up and looked out the window. In the distance, a small plane circled above Meigs Field, like a fly looking to land on a postage stamp. "Because," I said, "I know it wasn't Richardson's scheme."

She twisted sharply and stared at me, eyes opened wide. "What are you talking about?"

"Does that Ms. Pennington of yours know shorthand?"

"Yes, but—"

"Ask her to come in. I want to dictate something." When she hesitated, I said, "Please."

R. Pennington came in, her dictation pad in one hand, a handbag over her shoulder, and the usual haughty look on her face. "Yes, Miss Mallory?"

"Sit down, please," Harriet said. "I...Mr. Foley wants to dictate."

"Certainly, Miss Mallory." She settled into a client's chair, taking a tissue from her handbag and dabbing politely at her nose. "I've a bit of a cold." She stuffed the tissue back in her bag, and came out this time with a pen.

"I'm not used to dictation," I said. "Stop me if I go too fast."

The look on her face said my getting ahead of her was an unlikely possibility. "Just let me know when to start a new paragraph," she said. "The punctuation I'll take care of."

"It's a letter. To Deputy Chief Wendell Curtin, Lake County Sheriff's office. Dear Deputy Chief. Uh...paragraph. Regarding the Masterson and Caseliewicz investigations, it has been suggested that these were random incidents. However, they were not random but part of a premeditated scheme that included the murder of a certain Carl Hemming in Chicago, attempts on the lives of several other persons, and possibly the shooting death of Noreen Cunningham in Palos Heights. I have reason to believe that Cleveland Richardson was involved. Unfortunately, his suicide may prevent us from learning the true extent of that involvement. Paragraph."

Harriet hadn't moved since I started to dictate. I'd never seen her stand so still before. She was beautiful, her face and figure profiled against the bright blue sky beyond the windows.

Ms. Pennington broke the spell with a stifled sneeze. She pulled a tissue from her handbag and blew her nose softly. "Excuse me," she said. "Go ahead."

"It is clear, however, that the author of the scheme was not Richardson, but rather someone with a surprising ability to influence him," I continued. "I believe Richardson fathered a child out of wedlock, a son whom he never publicly acknowledged. Several years ago this son, Alex Boyd, attempted suicide and the incident left him a quadruplegic. Seeing him fully conscious, but locked up inside the prison of his body, turned frustration into rage in someone very close to Alex, someone who kept a daily watch beside him. As time passed, a plan evolved—a savage plan of revenge and retribution against the one held responsible for Boyd's condition. Paragraph.

"The plan included taking a job, but not for the money. Richardson provided plenty of money because this person knew he was Alex Boyd's father, and was blackmailing him. No, the reason for the job was to position this person in a particular place, to put her in a place very close to Happy—"

R. Pennington sneezed again. "Excuse me," she said, reaching into her handbag.

I moved toward her. "No, Rebecca," I said. "Don't move."

She froze for an instant, her right hand in the handbag, then slowly raised her head—and found herself staring into the barrel of my Beretta, two feet from her face.

Harriet stepped forward. "What—"

I waved her back. "Rebecca, please, take your hand from your purse, empty. Otherwise, it's all over."

She didn't move, only stared at me, her eyes unblinking and cold with something more primitive than mere hatred.

"Get out of here, Harriet," I said. "She'll kill you if she can."

Harriet broke then for the door, and something flashed in Rebecca's eyes. My left palm hit the side of her head—hard—simultaneously with her hand coming out of the handbag with a small automatic. She flew sideways, toppling her chair. The sharp discharge of her gun and the slam of the office door echoed back and forth against each other.

FORTY-TWO

THE ACRID SMELL of burnt powder stung my nostrils, and bits of acoustical tile fluttered down from where the bullet had torn through the ceiling.

Gathered into a crouch on the floor, Rebecca Pennington stared up and across the room at me, her lips curled back in a snarl like a cornered, rabid dog. All the facade of civilization had dropped away, leaving only naked canine madness. She still had the gun in her hand.

"You were that 'Rebecca' on Richardson's answering machine," I said. "It was your voice. And every time they picked up on where I was, it was after a visit or a call to Harriet. I kept thinking it must be Jerry."

She shook her head mournfully from side to side. "I could have killed the bitch long ago." Her voice was hardly more than a rasping whisper. "But death is so quick, so easy. I wanted her to know her son, to love him and then watch him crack apart...watch him turn into something less than human. She would suffer as I suffered."

"Set the gun down, Rebecca."

"You're so stupid," she said. "Absolutely wrong." Her lips curved into a smile that came out as a sneer, showing who it was that had become something less than human. "Richardson wasn't Alex's father at all. Alex was my baby brother. I was eight years older. Mama got wild then, almost never home. I'm the one who raised Alex. Such a beautiful boy. I loved him and he loved me. We were...very close. When I got my job at Richardson's office I got him to hire Alex as a file clerk. Alex was only sixteen. I wanted him where I could watch out for him. I didn't know about Richardson."

"Know about him?"

"Know he was a queer...a fag. He...he took my Alex away from me. Alex couldn't help it. He was so young. But he promised when he got out of law school he'd break from Richardson. Start his own practice and I'd work for him. Then that bitch Happy Mallory, she ruined everything. After Alex's...accident, I made a solemn vow I'd get even. I had proof about Richardson. Dirty little notes and...and Polaroid pictures. Richardson said he'd pay for Alex's care, but I made him give me money too—lots of money—and I put it all away. I sat with Alex every day and read the Bible to him. I still went part-time to the office, too. I wouldn't work, though. Just sat and read files, especially the juicy ones with doctors' and psychiatrists' reports. Meantime, I prayed to God for revenge on the bitch.''

"Rebecca," I said gently, "please..."

She peered at me, wide-eyed, but droned on. "Then the miracle came. I read the investigator's report about that disgusting Judas-priest. How he was adopted...how his birth mother was Happy Mallory, the bitch herself. God put that file in front of me, and God gave me a plan. Richardson wanted to drop the case, but I made him stay in it. God told me how to use the money. I paid the bitch's secretary to leave town and recommend me. I found out Richardson knew people...you know...mobsters. And I found out you can buy them...buy anyone, policemen even...people who'll do anything. So I did. I broke that drunk, faggot priest. He didn't go to jail for cocaine like I planned. But I broke him all the same. He's nothing, no backbone, not like my darling...my Alex."

She was swaying wildly now from side to side, waving the gun, losing control.

"The gun, Rebecca. Lay it down. If you don't I'll have to kill you."

She stopped suddenly, and studied the automatic in her hand, as though she hadn't noticed it before. Then she twisted her wrist, turning the gun barrel in the direction of her mouth, slowly.

Far too slowly.

I thought I could feel the breaking of each of dozens of bones in her hand through the leather of my shoe as my foot made contact and sent her gun flying loose. It crashed against the side of Harriet's desk and clattered to the floor.

Rebecca stared at her shattered hand and began to moan softly.

I picked up the gun and dropped it in my pocket. "I'll get help for you, Rebecca," I said soothingly, backing away from her, reaching behind me for the doorknob. "You don't have to worry. You'll get help. You'll be fine." In my heart I meant the words. In my mind I knew they were a lie.

No matter. She paid no attention. She slid backward on her haunches until she had her back against the wall, knees bent, left arm wrapped around her legs, pulling them into her, hugging herself against all the bad, bad things that were to come. Rocking slightly side to side, her voice came in a soft, singsong chant. "My Alex. My Alex. You never even knew about my plan. Why tell you? Ruined already, ruined forever. I'm so sorry, poor Alex, darling Alex. Not dead now, worse than dead, wishing dead...wishing dead...wishing..."

I couldn't face her and tell her more lies, and I stepped outside and closed the office door on her chanting.

A crowd had gathered at the end of the hall, hanging back in fear of what might burst through the door. Harriet pushed her way through and came toward me.

"The police are on their way. Where..." She stopped. "You shouldn't have left her alone," she said, reaching past me for the door. "She'll hurt herself."

"No," I said, stepping sideways to cut her off. "I have her gun. She'll be OK." I called down the hall, "It's all right, everyone. Go on back to work. No one's hurt."

"No! You don't understand!" Harriet cried, pushing at me, her voice high, strident. "Rebecca knows I've—"

The sound of another gunshot exploded from behind the office door.

Gasps and stifled cries from the end of the hall, as though drifting in from a long distance on the wind. And after that a long, sad silence, and a hopeless pain that gripped and squeezed my gut and cursed me, damning me for not being willing to stay in there and lie to Rebecca.

Harriet leaned against me, her body trembling, her face pressed into my chest. I could barely make out her whispered words. "In my desk. Rebecca would have known. I didn't want it, but Jerry...He was afraid for me. He got me a pistol..."

FORTY-THREE

MID-JULY. Hot and dry and dusty again, but too early in the day for the air-conditioning. We were on our way in the Lincoln Town Car to visit Kevin at the Wayfarer, a rehabilitation center in the Ozarks. Not talking much, taking our time, keeping to Least Heat Moon's "blue highways."

"What will happen to her?"

It was our second day. I was driving, and the Lady's question came out of nowhere.

"What will happen to Happy Mallory?" the Lady repeated. She spoke slowly and deliberately. She had picked up that habit much more quickly than I had. Most of the time, it didn't matter anyway.

"Harriet?" I said. "She'll do fine. Wakefield's standing by her. I guess there's always been more there than I wanted to admit. That setup...the drug deal...they were watching the guy with the coke. No one told them who the buyer would be. No one saw where she got the money, either, and she won't say. But she's still got connections. The whole thing stinks, and the U.S. attorney's got his own future to think of. She'll work it out."

"And what will she do then?"

"Who knows? Maybe fight to keep her law license, but I'm not sure how interested she is in that. Politically she's dead, and I don't think she cares. I mean, it's not that she's depressed. She wants to get all this behind her, go on to something else. She's still herself, you know? Aggressive, high-strung—but different now, somehow."

"She has a son now."

"Yes. And Kevin doesn't know yet, apparently, even now. You think she'll finally tell him?"

"Yes, if he doesn't come to it himself, when his thinking clears up. But if no one else does, Celia will."

That surprised me. "I think you're wrong there, Helene."

She ignored me, so I tried another subject. "Phyllis Drzedzedevic—and Mark too—they want to set the record straight. I sent them to Renata Carroway. Phyllis might break the confidentiality agreement—or threaten to, and cut a deal with Jack Butterfield. Then he'll go after Richardson's estate for a million dollars for the archdiocese. Renata won't do anything, though, till Kevin's better—and she can work out all the conflict-of-interest angles.''

The Lady didn't seem interested in that, either.

A while later she said, "I wonder if Kevin will remain a priest when he finishes at The Wayfarer—if he finishes.''

"He'll finish," I said.

"I hope so."

"And he'll stay a priest, too. He likes that stuff."

"Maybe. But I think of my women. It's so very, very difficult to change. And then, when one does begin to change, so *much* changes.''

Later, after lunch, the Lady took her turn at the wheel. She loves it. She drives like a panther stalking the jungle. With her I feel perfectly safe, which is rare for me when I'm not the one driving.

I was staring out the window, half dozing, half counting the hours till supper. Cass and I had made a deal. I'd call her every evening. There was still a lot to say, and I needed the practice.

"Poor Mr. Richardson," Helene said suddenly.

I jumped. "Sorry, Helene. I don't buy that one. Poor Pamela Masterson. Poor Carl Hemming...Casey...Kevin...his sister...Celia..." Poor *me,* for that matter, I thought. "But not poor Cleveland Richardson. No one made him tie that rope around his neck.''

"Yes," she said, not really agreeing. "But I mean all that suffering. All those years. So foolish. Then, finally, so like Alex, and so like poor Rebecca." She was silent for a moment. "We all do the best we can, I suppose."

"I don't—"

"Oh look!" she shouted. "The mileage! My car's going to turn a hundred and fifty thousand miles!"

Looking around the car's interior, I said, "Helene, it's amazing. This car looks new, inside and out." And it did.

"It's the only car I've ever owned, and I love it," she said.

"When you love a thing and take care of it, it can last a long, long time."

As the five and the four zeroes got ready to roll into place, we watched—all of us, the Lady and I...and even Casey.

Casey was having trouble hearing, and he was drawn and thin and so weak that he slept most of the time. Just then, though, he was alert and awake. He struggled to lean forward from the back-seat. The tubes down his throat all those weeks had done something to his vocal cords. Talking was difficult. He grunted. "Damn," he managed to croak, "'at's 'mazin'."

We all watched as the four zeroes rolled into place beside the five. The first three settled in—but not the final zero. That one didn't settle in, but slipped right on by, slowly giving way to another mile to come.

Nothing stops. The wheel turns.

A NEW YORK STATE OF CRIME

MICHAEL JAHN
DORIAN YEAGER
BARBARA PAUL

Three Tales of Murder Most Manhattan

MURDER ON FIFTH AVENUE by Michael Jahn

A killer is stalking the elegant stores on Fifth Avenue in a wave of murder that puts Captain Bill Donovan on the most perplexing case of his career.

LIBATION BY DEATH by Dorian Yeager

Vic Bowering is back, looking for an acting job, but she lands another mystery when she's hired as a bartender after the regular loses the gig to his own untimely death.

CLEAN SWEEP by Barbara Paul

This original short story spotlights Marian Larch's companion, Curt Holland. His effective—if not always exactly legal—computer investigation firm and team of brilliant hackers uncover a sweepstakes scam that's murder for the unlucky winners.

Available August 1999 at your favorite retail outlet.

Look us up on-line at: http://www.worldwidemystery.com   WNY317

DEATH AT THE TABLE

JANET LAURENCE

A CULINARY MYSTERY

The table is set, the wine is breathing and the television viewers are invited to delight in Darina Lisle's next episode of her top-rated food series, *Table for Four*. Death isn't on the menu until Darina's charming costar, Australian wine expert Bruce Bennett, drops dead on camera.

Has one of the other guests poisoned the brash Aussie? Darina starts from scratch, and unless she unmasks a killer before the plot thickens, she might become the final ingredient in a recipe for how to create the perfect murder.

Available July 1999 at your favorite retail outlet.

SOUR GRAPES

NATASHA COOPER

A WILLOW KING MYSTERY

Now a full-time mother and bestselling writer, Willow King is content to leave crime solving to her police chief husband. But she can't resist a case involving Andrew Lutterworth, accused of a fatal hit-and-run that landed him in prison for manslaughter.

But what could motivate a man to admit to a crime he did not commit and willingly go to jail because of it? The truth behind the puzzle is as dark and perplexing as the human psyche.

Available August 1999 at your favorite retail outlet.

Detective Jackie Kaminsky returns in her
toughest case yet when murder strikes too
close to home...

Fourth Horseman

Spokane detective Jackie Kaminsky finds her
instincts as both a cop and mother are put to
the test when she unearths the bodies of a
murdered woman and her baby buried behind
her new house. As a cop, she suspects this
peaceful neighborhood is hiding sinister
secrets. As a mother, she fears for her own
baby's safety...because a murderer may be
about to strike again.

MARGOT DALTON

"Detective Jackie Kaminsky leads a cast of
finely drawn characters..."
—*Publishers Weekly*

MIRA

On sale mid-July 1999 wherever paperbacks are sold.